BLACKSHROUD

BLACKSHROUD

by J. M. Campbell

Bluemoose

Copyright © J. M. Campbell 2026

First published in 2026 by
Bluemoose Books Ltd
25 Sackville Street
Hebden Bridge
West Yorkshire
HX7 7DJ

www.bluemoosebooks.com

British Library Cataloguing-in-Publication data
A catalogue record for this book is available from the British Library

ISBN: 978-1-915693-40-2

Printed and bound in the UK by Short Run Press

Chapter 1

The first death I can remember was when I was eight years old. My father sat me down after breakfast and told me a lady was coming to kill my grandfather.

"A blackshroud," my brother Francis explained twenty minutes later. "Blackshrouds kill people. *Everyone* knows that."

"I didn't!"

"Well of course *you* didn't. You're a girl. You don't know anything."

We were in the garden, and Francis had been idly swinging from the rope tied to the big horse chestnut. He dropped to the ground and cleared his throat rather grandly to announce an imminent lecture. I sat down on an upturned pot to listen.

"When a man reaches a certain age," he announced in a voice dropped a tone or two below its natural pitch, "his body and mind start to disintegrate. His memory falters, his faculties cloud, his senses diminish. He becomes odorous, and experiences great pains, and parts of his body begin to fall off."

"No part of Grandpapa has ever fallen off!" But the rest of the description fit all too well. By that time my grandfather didn't hear very well, and he forgot surprising things, and he did have a certain smell.

"Don't interrupt. At some point, a man may discover he's had quite enough of that sort of thing, and is actually looking forward to getting on with it and being dead. So he decides to hurry the business along a bit, and calls for a blackshroud. And the blackshroud... well, perhaps I'd best not tell you the grisly details."

"Why not?"

"Because it's really very grisly, and you'd start to cry."

"I would *not* start to cry," I insisted, even though I'd already had a cry when Father told me about Grandpapa.

"You *would* start to cry. As soon as I told you about the knives."

"...Knives?"

"Knives. You'll see, when she comes. She'll have a black leather bag, all full of knives. There'll be different-shaped knives for men and women, and little knives for children, and some extra heavy knives for really tough-skinned old people." He moved close to whisper conspiratorially, dropping out of his lecturing voice. "They say that when old Mrs Stanton died the blackshroud had to use a billhook."

"She's going to kill Grandpapa... with a knife?"

"How else is she going to get all the blood out, silly? First she'll take Grandfather upstairs and send us all away, so we can't hear the screams. Then she'll hang him upside-down from the ceiling."

"Why would she do that?"

"So that all the blood pours out when she cuts his throat, of course." He mimed the action. "It goes *everywhere*. Billy down the lane said it took three weeks to clean the room where his mother died."

"You're *lying!* You *always* lie! I don't believe *anything!*"

I had ample reason to be distrusting. Just days before, he'd told me that if I ran fast enough over a muddy patch I wouldn't get wet feet, which got me into tremendous trouble when I tried it out. And before that, he'd told me very solemnly and convincingly that our father was bald because an owl had stolen his hair. I'd refused to step outside without my bonnet for a week. But then he'd also spun me a colourful tale about where babies come from that I hadn't believed for one moment, until Grandpapa confirmed it was true, in most details at least.

So when the blackshroud arrived I was more than a little mortified to see her carrying a black leather bag.

She was a tall woman, thin and angular but very straight-backed. Her dress was black and steel grey, with the pleats ironed down into razor edges. It made a silken swish as she stepped into the hall and delivered a short, sharp curtsey to each member of the family in turn.

She was shown into the parlour, where my mother had earlier whipped the sheets off the furniture, set a fire in the hearth and laid out the best china. While the blackshroud shook my grandfather's hand I hid slightly behind my mother's skirts, keeping a close eye on the bag in case any knives spilled out.

"It's time, Caroline," my father said. "Go say goodbye to your grandfather." And he pushed me forwards with a firm hand between my shoulders.

"Caroline, my dear," Grandpapa said in a croaky voice, wrapping his trembling hands around my own. "Don't cry. It's alright." He managed to give me a weak smile. "Be a good girl for your mother and father." He tried to lean forwards to whisper in my ear but didn't quite make it, collapsing back in his chair with a groan. I moved my ear to his mouth instead. "And be a little devil for me."

"I will. I'll miss you, Grandpapa."

I did miss him. I still miss him. My grandfather's story is best described as a sequence of daring escapes. His first was when he ran off to join the Navy as a boy. He was aboard Nelson's fleet in the Mediterranean in '98, the year of the Battle of the Nile. He wasn't part of that famous victory, however, since just days beforehand he'd jumped ship for the Egyptian coast, having grown tired of the discipline of naval life. From then on he meandered all across Europe, making strategic retreats from one country after another as Napoleon's wars spread like plague over the continent, only coming back to England after the bloody business had finally run its course. He continued to be a restless wanderer until my grandmother – one of many fleeting women in his life – turned up one morning to dump a newborn baby girl into his arms before making an escape of her own.

Mother never talked about him after his death; I think she was embarrassed. I only know his story through the wild, lurid, sometimes self-contradictory tales he liked to relate to Francis and me by the fireside, whenever our parents were safely out of earshot.

He wasn't such an inspiring figure in his last months. He didn't get out of bed very often, and when he did he could only limp around slowly, letting out a soft curse every time his left foot touched the floor. On the day of his death Father had to carry him up the stairs, with the rest of us following behind. He demanded to be put down on the upstairs landing, to make his final walk on his own two feet. And he did, slowly and with oaths that grew more descriptive with each left step until Mother had to clap her hands over my ears. Then the blackshroud closed the door with herself, my grandfather and her black leather bag on one side of it and the rest of us on the other.

"Come along, Caroline," my father said, leading me back down to the parlour. "Let's give your grandfather some privacy."

There was a terrible quietness while we waited. Mother babbled something about damsons while wringing a handkerchief. Father sat stiffly reading a newspaper. Francis tried to look manly and indifferent like Father but couldn't stop a tear rolling down his cheek. And all the while I was thinking of the blackshroud's bag of knives, and Grandpapa hanging by his feet from the ceiling. At last I could take it no longer and decided to see for myself.

"Caroline!" My father barked as I reached the door. "Just where do you think you're going?"

"I need the privy," I lied.

"*Now?*" He sighed. "If you must. But be quick."

He stood in the doorway and watched me as I walked through the kitchen, out the back door and into the privy.

4

And as soon as the door was closed behind me I had the little window open and wriggled out into the garden, safely out of view of the house.

Next was the scary bit. Up the woodpile onto the sloping slates of the privy roof, then along the flat top of the wall that separated our garden from the Roberts' next door. From there I could ease open the sash of our bedroom, all while careful not to tear or dirty my best petticoat. Francis used this route frequently when he went out to meet the milkman's daughter at night, and he'd taught me the trick of it to buy my silence on the issue.

My heart was pounding as I crept to my grandfather's door, my feet carefully avoiding the creakiest floorboards. I turned the handle slowly and pushed it open just a crack.

He wasn't hanging upside-down from the ceiling. He lay on the bed, his eyes closed as though sleeping, and the blackshroud sat on a chair holding his hand. There was no blood and no knives, just an empty glass on the bedside table with a silver teaspoon. A smothering stillness filled the room. I couldn't tell if Grandpapa was still living or already dead.

The blackshroud's eyes snapped round to stab into mine. For a moment I was terrified she might pull out a knife after all. But instead, her face lost its sharp edge and she beckoned me in with a crook of her fingers.

I didn't move a muscle. Part of me was drawn towards that bedside like a moth towards a flame, but another part of me was equally repelled. The latter instinct won the day. I turned and fled.

Half an hour later she came downstairs and told us, "He went with a smile on his face."

Later, I became troubled by that line. I'd seen my grandfather on his deathbed, and he hadn't been smiling. Writing now after half a lifetime as a blackshroud myself, I can say with some authority that people almost never die with a smile. My own preferred line for the relatives has always been, "He died very peacefully," which has the benefit of usually being true. But that too seems inappropriate in the case of my grandfather, who never did anything peacefully if he could help it.

Perhaps, "He escaped one last time," would have fit him best.

Chapter 2

At the age of twenty I grew frustrated with life in my parents' house in Wetherby, and decided to make myself a career. I took a sheet of paper and wrote down all the professions I could think of that were open to a woman and started crossing them off one by one.

First went the ones that were just plain silly. I knew full well that I couldn't be a castle designer or a highwaywoman, and scolded myself for putting such nonsense on the list in the first place.

Next came everything that I thought beneath me. No factory work, no laundering, no whoring, no floor-scrubbing and certainly no going into service.

After that was a more painful category to eliminate: professions that were above me. I'd had a modest education, mostly reading, writing and needlework – and remembering how much I disliked needlework I scratched "seamstress" off the list too – but I had neither the background nor natural talent to be an artist, musician, philosopher or the like.

Other options could be ruled out for financial reasons. It's not that my parents were poor, but they'd spent nearly every penny they had putting Francis through his fancy law school down in London, leaving nothing for my own betterment. That ruled out another raft of careers (shopkeeper, landlord...) that demanded a certain amount of capital.

Some careers were just too dull to contemplate. Clerk, book-keeper and the like were dutifully removed from the list.

Anything involving children was firmly out. I had no patience at all for children. Life as a schoolteacher, nanny or governess would have been as trying for me as it would have been for my charges.

Looking over the list, there were only two things left on it. One was "nurse". Being a nurse sounded like terribly difficult, messy work. I crossed it out.

The last entry was "blackshroud". I laughed out loud, crossed it out three times over, crumpled up the list and threw it into the fireplace.

My parents had their own idea of what I should do with my life.

"A woman should marry young," Mother told me. "The younger she is, the better she can please her husband and the better her chances of bearing healthy children. You'll soon find there's nothing more rewarding than devoted married life."

She didn't stop at just advice, and began to arrange visits from a whole series of modestly but comfortably-situated bachelors. These specimens always inexplicably arrived in what seemed the exact same brown chequered waistcoat with scarlet cravat. They always bowed and declared they were "charmed" to meet me, and they all had an uncanny tendency to turn any conversation onto the subject of "prospects".

This was entertaining at first, but it soon became an annoyance. I wasn't opposed to marriage *per se*, but I was quite set that if I were to marry, it was to be in my own good time and certainly not to anyone dangled in front of me by my mother. So these suitors needed to be put off.

The simplest way was to convince Mother they weren't up to my high standards. The first one, I said, was the most terrible bore, and she was forced to concede it was true. He wasn't invited back. The next one was uncouth; the one after grotesquely fat. Another managed to neatly scupper himself by trying to steal a silver salt cellar in a clumsy sleight of hand. He claimed when accosted that he was setting up a conjuring trick to impress us with later, which may or may not have been true, but either way he was safely out of the running.

The real problem came when William Johns arrived at our door. He was not fat, nor a thief, nor uncouth. He could perhaps be described as a bore, but not to an extent to disqualify him in Mother's eyes. I tried quite hard to find sufficient fault to have him fall out of favour, and failed. I did not, in fact, even particularly dislike him. I simply did not want to marry him. It was time for desperate measures. If he could not be dismissed, he must be dissuaded. I treated William Johns to a long, dry discourse on the merits and demerits of different types of ribbon, but he nodded along amiably and treated me to an even drier discourse on different grades of string. I told him a tall tale about some fairy people who lived in the garden and only I could see, which he found "enchanting". I recounted one of Grandpapa's most colourful tales and he laughed along with it. I explained that I had a taste for the fine and expensive things in life and that I expected a husband to indulge his wife – didn't he agree? – and he did. By God, I even expounded on the importance of abstinence in marriage, but the man just would not be put off. Quite the reverse: everything I said seemed to further enamour him.

There seemed to be only one way out. I was going to have to choose a career after all.

I found my escape in one of Father's papers.

"The General Infirmary in Leeds are looking for new nurses," I told Mother.

"Nursing?" She worried a handkerchief between her fingers. "That's old maid's work, isn't it?"

"Nonsense. It's very respectable these days. And besides, don't you think it'd be a fine thing to save someone's life?"

They wanted letters of reference, which I provided. I took care to copy out the one from my old schoolmistress in a close imitation of her handwriting, substituting the word "diligent" for the original's "mouthy". They lapped up my application, and in a surprisingly short time I found myself walking uncertainly through the echoing corridors of the Infirmary in an almost spotless new uniform. It was a plain but not unbecoming black dress with a white apron tied around the waist, and an absurd little white lace cap perched on my head. I say *almost* spotless, because somehow on the short journey down from my dormitory I'd already managed to get a big greasy stain down the apron. I tried to cover it surreptitiously with a hand as I introduced myself to Nurse Haines, the sister in charge of Ward Nine, who sat perched in a rocking chair at the head of the room.

"Listen carefully, because I don't want to have to say any of this more than once," she told me. "I expect you to work hard, work fast, and work thoroughly. When I tell you to do something, you say, 'Yes, Sister.' When a doctor tells you to do something, you say, 'Yes, Doctor.' Is that understood?"

"But what if—"

"This is where you say, 'Yes, Sister.'"

"Yes, Sister."

"That's better. Furthermore, I expect you to be polite and professional when speaking with the patients, doctors or other nurses, which you should do *only* when necessary. And I expect you to keep yourself and everywhere you work perfectly, pristinely clean. Is that understood?"

"Yes, Sister."

"Good. Then take these sheets and get yourself down to the laundry. Ask someone to show you how we wash things *properly*. And while you're down there clean that apron, it's shameful."

"Yes, Sister."

These were the days just after Miss Nightingale had persuaded everybody that nursing needed to be a trained profession, but just before dedicated nursing schools began to appear around the country. New probationers like me were placed straight onto the wards and expected to learn while we worked. I spent most of my time on Ward Nine, under the exacting watch of

Nurse Haines. From her rocking chair she could see every bed, every patient and every nurse. I learned to keep a careful ear on the steady creak of that chair. If the sound stopped, it meant she was on her feet and coming for someone; usually for me.

"Nurse Summers! You call this a dressing? Just *look* at this! Come back here and do it properly!"

"Nurse Summers! When I say attend, you attend *instantly!*"

"Nurse Summers! Why is this soup so hot? Are you trying to scald the patient?"

"Nurse Summers! The leech should be on the patient, not on the floor!"

"Nurse Summers! Your apron is dirty *again!*"

It did make me strive to improve, if only to demonstrate that I wasn't quite so incompetent as she seemed to believe. I'll never forget the time she came to look over a simple dressing I'd applied, peering and prodding at it suspiciously from all angles, and the only thing she could find to say was a short disgruntled "Hm." I couldn't quite suppress a grin and she immediately chastised me for unprofessional conduct.

When the long day's work was done, we nurses were penned up safely inside the Infirmary. We were expected to live like nuns, being chaste, abstinent and generally dull.

There were four of us probationers squeezed into one awkward little roof space. We took turns to steal a bottle of medicinal brandy to share between us, until clumsy Clara got caught in the act and very nearly dismissed. The gossip ran quite freely, unchecked by any barriers of discretion, decency or truthfulness. There was also a long-standing competition to see who could tell the best rude story, in which I felt I had a commanding lead until shy, giggling Susan came out with a tale that would have made my grandfather blush.

"So the vicar's daughter quickly hides the goat under her skirts as she hears her father enter the church, and the bishop with him too…"

I was sitting between two beds pretending to be busy at something while I retold Susan's tale to an eager audience. In one bed lay Mr Watkins the baker's assistant and in the other Mr Ross the brewer. Both were listening in rapt attention, leaning over towards me to hear the words, which I had to speak quietly so that Mr Trent – a godly and humourless man in the bed beyond Mr Watkins' – didn't overhear.

"Nurse Summers!" a voice cut across the ward. "Attend!"

With a silent apology to my audience I stood up and bustled over to attend Nurse Haines. "Yes, Sister?"

She was standing by the bed of Mr Sancton, a severely fat old man who'd been wont to flirt quite inappropriately with me, but could now barely breathe in laboured gasps. She glared at me.

"What were you up to over there?"

"Changing Mr Ross' bedpan, Sister."

"You finished that five minutes ago! I'll tell you what you were doing, Nurse Summers, you were nattering. You're constantly nattering. I swear you do half as much work as any other nurse in this hospital because you spend so much time nattering."

"Yes, Sister."

"We're moving Mr Sancton here to Ward Eleven."

"Ward... Eleven, Sister?"

"Don't pretend to be deaf, Nurse Summers. Find the blackshroud and let her know."

"Yes, Sister."

"And no nattering on the way!"

"Yes, Sister."

Ward Eleven wasn't a real ward. It was a small, one-bed room that was always laid with fresh flowers. One door led out into the corridor and another – well concealed in the panelling – connected to the mortuary. Patients went in one door and left by the other. I'd been aware for a while that the General Infirmary, like many large hospitals, employed its own dedicated blackshroud. I knew she went by the somewhat contradictory name of Blackshroud White. But, despite having been there for over three months already by that point, I hadn't yet encountered her. A few enquiries directed me towards an unremarkable door in an obscure corner of the building. Only when I looked closely did I see her name and title written in unobtrusive lettering across the top. I knocked warily.

"Come in."

I'd always imagined blackshrouds to be elegant yet severe, in dress, face and manner alike, probably because that was a good description of our local practitioner in Wetherby. But Blackshroud White was a long way from either elegance or severity. She was white-haired and elderly with a wisp of a body haunting a big puffy old dress, as though she'd shrunk considerably in the many years since it was new. The dress had probably once been black but now it was grey, and patched up with an oddment of scraps. The silver brooch marking her trade – a dove astride a dagger – was almost hidden in the folds of fabric.

She gave me a cautious smile as I entered. "Delightful to see you, Nurse... ah..."

"Summers, ma'am." I bobbed a curtsey. "I'm to tell you a patient's waiting on Ward Eleven."

"Oh." Her smile faded. "And there was me holding a small, foolish candle of hope that you might have come for a spot of conversation. Perhaps even for a slice of cake and a cup of tea."

"No, ma'am."

"Ah well. So who's the poor soul today?"

"Mr Sancton, from Ward Nine."

"Oh, that is a shame. When I talked with him on Tuesday there still seemed a chance he might pull through."

"I'm afraid not, ma'am. He keeps on getting worse."

"I really am very sorry to hear it. You'd best come in."

The room, I realised as I stepped inside, wasn't just a room but a small suite of rooms, with a narrow doorway leading to what looked like a bedroom.

"You live here, ma'am?"

"I certainly do. I have to be on call at all hours of day and night, you see. Imagine you were dying in pain in the small hours. Would you care to be told to linger until I came into work in the morning?"

"I'd rather not imagine that if it's all the same, ma'am."

"Ha! Good to hear it. It's fiercely unhealthy to spend too much time thinking about death. A danger of my profession, I'm afraid. Anyway, if a patient ever needs me – even just to talk to me – do go ahead and rap on my door until I appear, no matter the hour."

I glanced around her chambers. They had an unruly, well-lived-in look. Most of the hospital had a brutal tidiness with scrubbed-clean surfaces, but here was a haven for clutter and dust. The walls were crowded with paintings, the shelves overloaded with books and knick-knacks and the chairs so piled with heavily-tasselled cushions that it was challenging to find space to sit on them. Blackshroud White unhurriedly filled a kettle and placed it on the stove.

"Tea?"

"No thank you, ma'am."

But she fished out two mismatched and chipped cups anyway, arranging them on a tray with equally mismatched saucers and a shiny brown teapot.

"Um... you do remember why I'm here, don't you, ma'am?"

She gave me a sharp look, but not without a hint of amusement behind it. "I haven't lost my marbles yet, if that's what you're thinking. But there's always time for a cup of tea."

I nodded, unconvinced, and sat down gingerly on the edge of a cushion-heaped seat. I watched as she dumped some leaves into the pot, humming a tune under her breath that I couldn't quite make out.

"Ma'am?"

"Yes, my dear, what is it?"

There was a question I was bursting to ask, but curiosity was at war with propriety in my head. Curiosity won a temporary victory, and I blurted it out.

"How many people have you killed?"

To my relief she seemed completely unfazed by the question.

"None."

"*None?*"

"None. I've never killed a single soul. But I've helped over a thousand to die."

"There's a difference?"

"All the difference in the world. Say if I smothered you right now with a cushion. That would be killing you."

I inched slightly away from her.

"But if you *wanted* to die and asked me to make it happen, that would be helping you to die. In one case I'm giving you agency over your own life. In the other I'm taking it away."

"I wish to state quite clearly then that I *don't* want to die, thank you very much."

She chuckled. "Oh, please, no need to worry about that! I don't help anyone unless they make it very, *very* clear that's their true desire. If I were to begin killing off everyone I met simply because they looked a little fraught and tired... well, I think I'd be the Infirmary's only surviving member of staff before the month was out."

"Are you saying I look fraught and tired?"

"Of course you do, dear, you're a nurse."

She gave me a long look. Her pale blue eyes were strangely penetrating, making me feel somehow naked. Instead of meeting them I cast my gaze around her little home. "You must get rather lonely living here on your own."

"Yes. I do. But not so lonely as you might think. I get to meet all manner of interesting people. Fleetingly."

"You should come up to Ward Nine some time. I'm always happy to talk. Nurse Haines says it's my greatest failing."

She shook her head. "It's best I don't. A blackshroud wandering the wards tends to make patients nervous. But why don't you visit me, instead? Say, a cup of tea and some pleasant conversation on a Sunday afternoon? I'd appreciate the company, and I imagine you'd appreciate the break. I'll tell Nurse Haines you're helping me with my paperwork, or some such contrivance. Ah, there's the kettle."

She lifted the whistling kettle off the stove and filled the teapot. Then she completed her tea tray with a pot of sugar and a spoon. Then a second pot of sugar next to the first, with another spoon. I frowned in confusion.

"What's that for?"

"This one's sugar. I like a nice big spoonful in my tea."

"Then what's the other one?"

"Not sugar. That's for Mr Sancton's tea."

"Ah."

"Would you mind carrying this?" She handed me the tray.

"Yes, ma'am." I looked down at the ill-assorted service with its two pots of white crystalline powder. "You... you will remember which is which, won't you?"

"I've never mixed them up yet, or I wouldn't be here."

"But don't you thing it's tempting fate to keep the sugar and the... the not-sugar next to each other like that?"

She gave me a thoughtful look. "Let me ask you something. What do you imagine my greatest fear might be?"

"Um... death?"

"No. That's nothing to be afraid of, and I've seen enough of it to know."

"What then?"

"Senility of the mind. Degenerating into a gibbering halfwit, or an empty shell. The very thought brings me out in cold shivers."

"You don't seem to be losing your wits yet, ma'am."

"No. But those who travel that path don't always realise until they're too far down it. I've seen brilliant people slide

16

into imbecility, quite oblivious. It happened to my mother, and to her mother. I'm *not* letting it happen to me."

"So the sugar...?"

"As long as I have my full wits about me, there's really no chance at all I'll mistake the sugar for the draught. They look quite different to a trained eye, you know. But if my mind starts to fray, then... well, it's bound to happen sooner or later. Then it's a nice cup of tea and a nap I never wake up from. Not a bad way to go, all things considered."

I carried the tea tray down the corridor with Blackshroud White behind me. The Infirmary's corridors were full, as usual, with hurried, harried men and women, but she drifted along as slowly as a leaf sliding in the breeze. When we reached Ward Eleven I knocked on the door.

Clara was in attendance, sat beside Mr Sancton's rounded bulk, looking deeply uncomfortable. Her eyes widened as she saw me enter. "Caroline? Are you promoted to tea duty now?" And then, seeing who was behind me, immediately dropped into a curtsey. "Ma'am."

Blackshroud White ignored Clara and went straight to Mr Sancton's side with a wide smile on her face, taking his big clammy hand in her ethereal one. "Edward! Lovely to see you again, although I'd so hoped I wouldn't."

"I'm glad... you're... here," he wheezed, apparently with some effort.

She made a couple of gestures with her free hand, out of Mr Sancton's sight, that I should leave the tray on the side table and that Clara and I should then make ourselves scarce. I did, and we did.

Mr Sancton never returned to Ward Nine.

I visited Blackshroud White that Sunday, and the Sunday after that, and almost every Sunday for the next few months. It quickly became a time I looked forward to. She'd welcome me with a big, open smile and would ask to hear all the gossip from the wards. She always gave me cake and tea, although I was careful to avoid the sugar.

I found out a lot about her. I found out she'd been married until her husband had died six years ago. I found out she'd never had any children, which was a source of grief to her. I found out she'd been in private practice most of her life, but had taken this job in the Infirmary in her old age as it didn't involve travelling.

"You must have some stories? All those people you've killed... sorry, helped die. Shocking deathbed confessions, funny last words, that sort of thing?"

"Quite shocking, yes. And some extremely funny stories too."

"Do share."

"I never shall. Anything you tell a blackshroud is in confidence. *Absolute* confidence. Like doctors or priests, and entirely unlike nurses."

Still, she did have an uncomfortable knack of letting any conversation meander inevitably towards the topic of death. "I'm sorry dear, I didn't mean to be so dreary. Terrible thing; I've spent so long dealing with life and death I've quite lost the knack of idle chatter."

But I got idle chatter enough every night with Clara, Tabitha and Susan that it was quite refreshing to hear her frank, knowledgeable discourse on life's weightier topics. She had a way of talking that was more like thinking aloud than conversation, and I would fall silent and let her speak. Often she'd turn to stare out the window and carry on talking with her back to me. Sometimes there would be pauses, long pauses, while she worked something over in her mind. Sometimes the pauses would grow so long that I started to wonder if she'd quite forgotten I was there at all, and felt obliged to clear my throat. But she never had forgotten. Or if she had, she never let on.

* * *

Autumn passed into winter. The General Infirmary was built on the most modern principles to control contagion: the wards were spacious, well isolated, and with ample light and ventilation from high windows along both sides. As a result, they were absolutely freezing by November. We were kept busier than ever distributing extra blankets and hot water bottles, and Nurse Haines scolded me severely when I dared to wear a coat over my uniform.

In truth, I was becoming a little disheartened with my prospects in nursing. I didn't excel in any practical skills. My medical learning wasn't coming easily, and lagged behind that of my peers. The one area in which I'd made major strides was the art – under the weight of Nurse Haines' constant reprimands – of self-organisation and discipline. I'd learned how to work hard, and how to be exactly where I was supposed to be exactly when I was supposed to be there. I'd learned a habit of tidiness and cleanliness which has never quite left me. In short, I'd learned to really be – as my forged reference letter claimed – diligent. However, I remained decidedly mouthy.

I loved talking to the patients. All sorts of people came to our ward for all sorts of reasons. They had so many stories, and most were more than happy to tell them. A bit of chit-chat, a joke or two, sometimes a spot of light flirting, did wonders for their morale.

Nurse Haines had a different philosophy of nursing. She told me off over, and over, and over again, for "nattering". She claimed I had the lowest productivity of any nurse in the hospital, which probably wasn't far from being true. Coupled with my decidedly mediocre skills and knowledge, I started to worry I could be facing dismissal if I didn't improve soon.

I even started to wonder if that would be such a bad thing. Six months in and I felt six years older, with a growing weariness I couldn't shift. I may have loved the people in the hospital – Nurse Haines not included – but I didn't much love the work. The routine was an exhausting one. We got only a couple of short hours off duty each day, and I usually tried to spend those outside the walls of the hospital, exploring the streets of my adopted home.

Leeds was a noisy, dirty, stinking, fascinating town. Frowning, florid edifices jostling for street space with tottering old townhouses. Brightly-lit rows of shops selling every imaginable variety of useful and useless object. Monstrous clanging mills belching out heat and smoke from towering chimneys. The organised chaos of hissing, screeching steel in the busy railway stations and goods yards.

As time went on these wonders became commonplace, and I developed a distaste for the bustle and miasmic air of the town centre. My explorations turned outwards rather than inwards. It was on one of these outward excursions on a crisp December day, while enjoying the fresher air and open space up on the Woodhouse moor, when I heard my name called from behind me.

"Miss Summers!"

I turned, and recognised the brown-waistcoated, red-cravatted figure of William Johns closing in on me.

"Mr Johns."

He bowed. "Charmed. Absolutely charmed to run into you again."

"What are you doing here, Mr Johns?"

"Going up in the world. I've got myself a new position, right here in Leeds. You'll find my prospects are quite improved since we last met."

After the minimum of conversation that politeness demanded I made my quite honest excuse that I needed to get back to the Infirmary. But from that day forwards, even though the places of my wanderings were deliberately erratic, they frequently led me into encounters with William Johns.

"God guides us towards each other, Miss Summers," was his only explanation.

The situation had been continuing for some two months before he got down on one knee – in front of the town hall of all places, after pouncing out from behind a stone lion – and asked me to be his wife. I said I'd consider it, and asked him to give me a week.

"Are you going to say yes?" Billy Chaplin asked me the next day as I sat at his bedside. "He's a right lucky man if you do. I'd ask you meself, if I had any prospects."

Billy was certainly a man without prospects. He'd been brought in two days before with his legs badly mangled by machinery. The doctors had tried their best, but his wounds had turned bad. In the end they'd only had three options to offer him: amputation of both legs; a slow, painful death; or an appointment with the blackshroud. Billy had made his choice, and now we waited together in Ward Eleven for Blackshroud White to appear with her tea tray.

"I might say yes. I think I ought to. I *quite* like Mr Johns. I'd have to stop nursing if I were married, of course, but I don't really mind that. I can't think of any really sensible reasons to say no."

"What about daft reasons then?"

"Oh, I've got plenty of those. Here, look at the state of these bandages, they're a disgrace. Wouldn't you like some fresh ones?"

"No point now, is there?"

"No *sensible* point, perhaps. But wouldn't you prefer to face this with nice clean bandages on than soiled ones?"

"Go on then. Make me right handsome."

"Oh, you don't need me for that, Billy."

I set to work.

"Caroline?"

"Mmm?"

"When the blackshroud comes, will you... will you stay with me? While she... while I die?"

I gave him my best attempt at a smile. "Sorry. I can't. I would, truly, but I can't. There's strict rules about that. Only you and her can be in the room. I am sorry."

"Alright." He closed his eyes for a moment and took a deep breath. "I'm just... I'm fucking scared."

"Course you are." I finished removing one horrid old bandage and started winding a fresh one. I didn't change the dressing underneath, which would have caused him pain without purpose. "But you don't need me, a big brave man like you. And Blackshroud White is lovely."

"Lovely?"

"You'll see. The loveliest person in the whole world. Kind and gentle as you like. I'd be scared too in your place, Billy, anyone would, but I'd be a lot less scared if I knew it was her who was coming." I heard the door open behind me. "See, here she—" I looked over my shoulder and the sentence caught in my throat. "*You're* not Blackshroud White."

"Bloody observant of you."

In the doorway stood a large woman. Not large as in tall, large as in fat. And that fat was mercilessly squeezed into a dress of frilly black lace as tight as butcher's twine. Many fat people take on a soft, round, friendly appearance, but this woman's fat gave her face all the friendliness of a diseased and swollen limb, with greasy dark hair tied back as tight as a tourniquet and an expression like she'd just swallowed a spoonful of bitter medicine.

"Blackshroud Cartwright." She jabbed a thumb in my direction then towards the door. "Out."

"But... what happened to Blackshroud White?"

"Didn't you hear me, nurse? I said *out*."

"Didn't *you* hear *me*? I said *what happened to Blackshroud White?*"

She looked at me like she was considering amputating my head with her bare hands. "She's laid up in Ward Two. Now *get out*."

"Ward Two? But... what's wrong with her? Is she alright?"

"She's not in need of my services yet, if that's what you're worried about. Now what in Heaven's name are you still doing in this room, girl?"

"I'm not leaving until I've finished changing Mr Chaplin's bandages."

"Changing his bandages? *Changing his bandages?* Are you *completely* thick, girl? You do know why I'm here and why he's here, don't you?"

"Yes but—"

"Then what exactly do you think is to be achieved by changing his bandages?"

I struggled to control my temper enough to give a civil answer, but Billy saved me from having to.

"I asked her to, ma'am."

She looked at him as though he were a squashed frog.

"If you're so precious about your legs, Mr Chaplin, perhaps you shouldn't've tried feeding them into a flax-spinning machine, or whatever mechanical contrivance it was that did this."

I tied the end of the bandage rather too tightly, and felt Billy wince. "Right. That's *it*. Blackshroud, I'd like a word with you outside."

"After." She unclasped her black leather bag and began unloading the tools of her trade onto the side table: a glass, a spoon, a small vial of white powder...

"*Now.*"

She stopped unpacking, stared at me, made a little snorting sound and stepped out with me into the corridor. "There'd better be a bloody good reason for this, girl."

I took a deep breath. "In there," I said, pointing to Ward Eleven, "is an unfortunate young man who is about to die. A *terrified* young man. *Your* job," I pointed a finger at her brooch, "is to smile, to try and soothe him, and to help him die in as kind a way as possible."

"Are you trying to tell me how to do my job?"

"Seeing as how you appear to have *no idea* how to do your job, yes I am! Or even better, perhaps you should call by Ward Two and talk to Blackshroud White. She could teach you a thing or two about it."

She let out a sort of whistling grunting sound that might have been a laugh. "Think on this, girl. There's a man in that room who'd already be slipping off into his last sleep right now if you hadn't been flapping about and getting in my way. Instead, he's still in pain and still suffering. Because of *you*. Now are you going to let me do my job or aren't you?"

I couldn't find an argument to that, so I resorted to abuse. "You arrogant, small-minded, bat-tongued—"

"NURSE SUMMERS!" Nurse Haines' voice rang through the corridor, freezing me before I could reach the word *hag*. "What... on *Earth*... do you think you're about?"

Blackshroud Cartwright gave her a civil nod. "Sister. I'd appreciate it if you'd remind your staff of their place." And she disappeared into Ward Eleven with a heavy slam of the door, leaving me alone with Nurse Haines.

"Nurse Summers." Her voice was granite. "I don't have time to deal with you right now. You will go to my office and you will wait there until I get back. Do you understand?"

"Yes, Sister."

But I didn't go to her office. I went straight to Ward Two, where I found that Blackshroud White had already been discharged. After a short search I found her. The Infirmary's central courtyard was roofed over in glass, forming a pleasant winter garden in which patients might rest and recuperate. She was sitting there resting and recuperating, looking pale and thin amongst the full green bushes and colourful flowers, while a light February rain plinkered over the panes above.

"Blackshroud White!" I sat down beside her. "What happened?"

"Oh, Caroline my dear, there's no need for worry. I simply had something of a funny turn. One of the many delights of being old. The doctors promise me I'll be back on my feet by tomorrow. I've got someone covering my duties."

"I know. I met her."

"There's no need to pull such a sour face."

"She's abominable."

"She's not."

"She is. She's not fit to call herself a blackshroud. I told her to come talk to you, that she might learn something."

Her eyes widened. "You said that? To Esther?" And she laughed, so loud that it drowned out the rain on the roof. "Oh my dear, she learned *everything* from me. I trained her, you see. She always was a most troublesome apprentice, but I assure you she's perfectly capable."

"Oh." I wrung the corner of my apron between my fingers. "I think I'm about to be dismissed."

"Ah-ha! That's excellent news!"

"No it's not!"

"But it is! You see, I was about to ask you if you wanted to be my next apprentice, and now you have no reason whatsoever to say no."

I blinked. "A blackshroud? *Me?*"

"Well you do seem to have a strong opinion of how it should be done."

"But—"

"I don't need an answer right now. Give me one when you come round on Sunday. But first let me give you three good reasons why you should consider it.

"One. It's *respectable*. I think that's important to you. You wouldn't have to say 'Yes, Sister' to anyone, or even 'Yes, Doctor'.

"Two. It's helping people. I think that's important to you too. It's not helping people in the way you'd *like* to be able to. But it is helping people in the only way they can be helped when nothing else is left.

25

"Three. It's a better job than nursing. Much better pay, and for considerably less work. It isn't an easy job mentally, mind, but it is an easy job physically. If you're even half as lazy as I am, you'll appreciate the value of that.

"Four—"

"You said *three* reasons."

"*Four.* It only takes twelve months to qualify, compared to... is it two years these days, to call yourself a trained nurse? It's a very much simpler job, you see. A nurse needs to know hundreds of treatments, while a blackshroud only needs one."

"But *I* can't be a blackshroud!"

"Of course you can. I've been sizing you up for months, and I think you can be an exceptional one."

"But I don't *want* to kill anyone!"

"Good. You'd make the worst sort of blackshroud if you did."

"But—"

"Don't answer now. On Sunday. Have a good think."

I had a good think. Then, when I was still undecided, I had another. I kept returning to that day my grandfather died, peering in through his bedroom door, and the blackshroud beckoning me towards them. Did I make the same choice again and run away as fast as my legs could carry me? Or did I dare step inside the darkened room and face death in the eyes?

I stayed up late that night, watching the ghostly disk of the moon drift in and out of sight behind wispy clouds, while Clara snored roundly behind me. And I made my decision.

Nurse Haines had a long shout at me in the morning, and sent a report up to the directors. I didn't wait to be dismissed but handed in my notice with immediate effect. And on Sunday I reported to Blackshroud White.

"Your new apprentice," I announced myself with an elaborate curtsey.

"Caroline! This calls for a celebration! Sit down, have a nice big slice of lemon cake. I'll make us some tea."

I was in a giddy mood as I devoured not one nor two but three slices of lemon cake. I couldn't stop my toes from tapping on the carpet, nor keep my tongue from doing what it does best, even through greedy mouthfuls of cake.

"And Tabitha said – this is really good tea by the way – Tabitha said, she said, 'You? A Blackshroud? What are you going to do, talk them to death?' And then Clara, it's positively scandalous what *she* said, she said... wait, Blackshroud, are you alright?"

She sat quiet, her face pale, looking down at her emptied mug.

"No, dear. I... I'm sorry. I thought I had more time."

"But what is it? What's wrong?"

"There was no sugar in this tea."

"But I saw you put a whole spoonful of—" I felt like I'd just swallowed a brick. "Oh no, you didn't..."

"Yes. I'm afraid so."

I jumped to my feet, almost knocking the little table over. "Wait here. I'm getting help."

"No, dear. It's too late for that. Please stay."

"But—"

"I only have a minute or so. I'm sorry about the circumstances, but I do just have time to teach you one important lesson. The only one you really need to know."

I sat down beside her, feeling as though ice ran through my veins. I could see her blinking hard, as though fighting off sleep. "What is it?"

"Hold the patient's hand. Be calm. Be reassuring. That's all it is."

I held her hand between both of mine. That much I could do. But calmness seemed impossible; my hands shook badly. I couldn't say if she found my presence in any way reassuring.

"Caroline... Caroline, promise me something." Her words were slurred now as the fingers of endless sleep pulled her downwards.

"What? Anything."

She mumbled, barely audible. "Eat that cake up. Won't keep."

And then her eyes fluttered closed, and never opened again.

I stayed with her for a while, I couldn't say how long, my cheeks wet with tears as I listened to the soft whisper of her breath. Eventually that whisper fell silent, and Blackshroud White was dead.

There was an inquest. I was interrogated. Fortunately, her habit of testing herself by leaving the sugar next to the draught was widely known, so my story was readily believed. The coroner's only concern seemed to be whether to record her death as Suicide or as Death by Misadventure, a knotty decision of which I never heard the outcome.

The funeral was a modest one. It was sad to see how few people attended. A representative from the General Infirmary stood up and said a few rather formal and generic words. There was a long empty pause after he sat down, and it seemed that was going to be that. But then Blackshroud Cartwright got to her feet.

"She was a bloody wilful, stupid woman, and she died in a bloody wilful, stupid way." The congregation shifted uneasily in their chairs. Someone coughed. "But she was a bloody good blackshroud."

She sat down with an audible thump.

After the service she appeared in front of me.

"I hear she took you on as apprentice."

"That's right."

She looked me up and down. "She really *must* have been losing her wits."

I glared. "I do *not* have to stand here and—"

"Still want to be a blackshroud?"

"...Yes."

"My shop, Monday morning at eight. Be punctual."

On my way home I chanced into William Johns. It had been well over a week since he'd asked for my hand, and he was eager for an answer. Before I gave him one, I told him that I'd just become apprenticed to a blackshroud. A look of panic crossed his face. When I told him I was flattered by his offer but didn't really want to marry him, he looked more relieved than I'd ever seen a man look before.

Chapter 3

Dearest Caroline,

Extremely excited to hear of your new career; also, slightly terrified. You well know how often I tend to lapse into legal blather at dinner, and just in case you find it similarly difficult to refrain from bringing your professional skills into inappropriate social settings, I shall recommend to Mother to seat you next to one of our more expendable relatives at family gatherings from now on.

It occurs that you must have been a truly abominable nurse if the end result of it all is that you've discovered a talent for killing people. I suppose the survival rate at the hospital shall improve dramatically in your absence?

Yours,

Francis

P. S. I have a couple of colleagues I would dearly love to see retire to an early grave. Do you offer a family discount?

Along with the letter were two small but weighty packages in brown paper, one cigar-shaped and one rectangular. I opened the cigar-shaped one first. It was a pocket-sized whetstone. A label tied around it read, "For your many knives."

"Francis, *really.*"

The other package contained a book neatly bound in black leather. The title read *A Modern Guide to Practical Blackshroudery*. I flicked it open to a random page.

> *A blackshroud is a mountain. Fortitude is her bedrock; compassion her lofty summit. Her virtue stands tall and unassailable; unyielding against the winds of compromise.*

My new mistress was, I reflected, heading towards the *size* of a small mountain, if nothing else. I leafed a few pages forwards.

> *A blackshroud's premises are known as her surgery; never her "office" and certainly nothing as vulgar as her "shop". Indeed, she must take great pains to avoid any appearance of vulgarity. Her surgery should be sited in a respectable and salubrious neighbourhood, not close to any tavern, tea shop, theatre nor other establishment of low repute or frivolous nature, nor to any noxious or noisome industry. Proximity to a church is desirable; proximity to an undertaker or cemetery is not, despite the obvious convenience. Ideally the surgery should also be well removed from the principal thoroughfares, allowing an atmosphere of peaceful seclusion.*

Blackshroud Cartwright's surgery was certainly well removed from the principal thoroughfare. The thoroughfare in question was Briggate, one of the most principal in all of Yorkshire. But its plate glass and gilt facades were curiously riddled with doors and passageways, leading into shady labyrinths of little yards and lanes. Tenterhook Yard was not untypical of its kind: a crumbling brick crevice dimly lit by a narrow strip of sky three stories above. The smell of stale beer wafted strongly from *The Tenterhook*, the old coaching inn that ran along one side of it and gave it its name.

Her doorway was immediately to the right of the inn, and it looked so unpromising and unlikely that I'd walked straight past several times in search of it before I finally spotted the sign reading "E. Cartwright, Blackshroud" in faded, spidery letters. It didn't help that on that first morning there was a drunkard slumped there, slumbering noisily, his shoulders against the peeling black-painted door and his legs straight out across the cobbles. The yard was so narrow that his boots almost touched the wall opposite.

Another man was bent over him, busily engaged in rummaging through his pockets. He looked around as I hovered nearby.

"Problem, Miss?"

"Um, I was looking for the blackshroud."

"Ah! Apologies." He manhandled the drunkard out of the doorway, propped him – still snoring contentedly – against the adjacent wall, and began to strip him of his coat.

I knocked. I waited. There was no response.

"She'll be away, Miss," the man said helpfully, having finished with the drunkard. "Best try at the inn."

The landlord of *The Tenterhook* – Mr Battersby – was a small man with a large walrus moustache that wobbled hypnotically as he talked. "She'll be out on her business," he informed me across the bar. "Spends a lot of time out on her business, she does."

"Might you guess when she'll return?"

He shrugged and blew through his moustache, making it ripple. "Care to leave a message?" He pointed to an iron spike at one end of the bar with a couple of notes impaled on it.

"No thanks. I'll wait." I parked myself on a stool and drummed my fingers on the bar as I glanced around. The inn had a particularly thick tobacco haze, so the figures in the farthest corners seemed blurred and indistinct. The nearer, clearer figures directed inquisitive frowns in my direction between puffs of smoke, no doubt wondering what business a young lady had loitering unaccompanied in such a place. I frowned right back at them and stayed where I was.

"Drink to drown your sorrows?" Mr Battersby asked.

"What makes you think I have sorrows?"

"You're waiting for the blackshroud. Course you've got sorrows. Beg your pardon for prying, but is it on your own account, or another's?"

"I suppose it's on my own account."

"Well I'm deep sorry to hear that, I'm sure. Go on, love, order a drink. It helps."

I narrowed my eyes. "You must get a fair bit of custom out of being next to the blackshroud."

"There's few folks as ready to drink as folks facing death."

I found myself wondering if the proximity was beneficial in the other direction too: if *The Tenterhook*'s more mournful drunks sometimes found a more permanent answer to their sorrows at the next door down.

"Well, I'm not facing death. I'm Blackshroud Cartwright's new apprentice."

"Goodness gracious and gravy!" It was difficult to read his expression through his moustache. "Another one!"

"Another one?"

But the conversation ended abruptly as a large shadow loomed behind me.

"Messages, Battersby?"

"Three." He pulled the two scraps of paper from the spike. "One from a Mrs Clefton, says you did for her husband last week."

"She wanting to follow him, or is she after a refund?"

"Neither. She was proper welled up, wanted to talk about his final moments with you. Help come to terms, she said."

"Pff. What does she think I am, her nursemaid? If she comes back, tell her to stop being such a drip. Next?"

Mr Battersby looked uncertainly at the other note. "There was a Mr Rogers, wanted to know if you did dogs..."

She gave him a look to indicate very clearly that she did not do dogs.

"...I told him you probably didn't."

"And the last message?"

"This girl arrived, says she's your new apprentice."

I bobbed my best curtsey. "Ma'am."

She looked at me for the first time since entering, with the expression of someone discovering a loaf of bread left in a cupboard three weeks before and now quite gone to mould.

"Well what are you doing loitering in this cheap den of sin?" she asked, making Mr Battersby's moustache twitch. "Since it seems I don't have any patients at the moment, I might as well show you around my shop, I suppose."

There wasn't a lot to show me around. The black-painted door led straight onto a steep creaky staircase, connecting to a set of chambers. It was something of a warren up there, with a lot of narrow corridors and very little in the way of rooms at the end of them. "This is where I work, this is where I live, this is where I sleep, and this is where you sleep," was the entirety of the tour as she jabbed her thumb towards four doorways.

There was no room for dispensing the draught. Some surgeries do have a room for that, but Blackshroud Cartwright offered home visits only. "Let *them* have corpses littering up the place because I certainly don't want any," she explained. The room she'd pointed at as she said "this is where I work" was her parlour.

A Modern Guide to Practical Blackshroudery had a passage on parlours:

> *The parlour should present an appearance*
> *much like that of the blackshroud herself: clean*

and well dressed but without frills or excessive
ornament, in neutral colours, and with a calm
and professional personality. Artwork should
be limited to landscape or still life, with no
portraiture or religious imagery. Furnishing
should include several comfortable chairs and a
small tea table.

Blackshroud Cartwright's parlour contained only two chairs, neither of which was comfortable. One was a threadbare old upholstered thing that somehow managed to look mismatched with itself. The other was a long-suffering three-legged stool tucked under a desk in the corner. This was where she sat to execute her paperwork, burying the expired documents somewhere in an ominous, creaking pile of books, ledgers and dusty leather folders.

The very worst thing about the room was the picture on the wall. It was a small portrait of Jesus on the cross, in an old-fashioned style with a black background. The artist had managed to give Him an accusing look, as though He were trying to tell you that His situation was somehow entirely your own fault. His resentful eyes followed me around, and if I turned the other way I could almost feel His gaze prickling my back.

Perhaps thankfully, she very rarely received clients in her parlour. More often, anyone knocking on the door got to arrange their business in extremely brief terms over the threshold, or – on days when she felt disinclined to make the arduous journey downstairs to answer the door – shouted up to where she leant out of an upstairs window.

The *Modern Guide* had a lot to say about conversation. In fact, it seemed to suggest that talking to people was the larger part of the job. For example:

Whilst the terminal service is the blackshroud's
principal function, it is by no means her

*principal expenditure of time. She must expect
to be called to record a natural death, and to
help the bereaved with the legal and practical
particulars ensuing. She must interview every
prospective patient and have their consent
witnessed. She must dispense spiritual
and moral comfort to those whose death is
approaching, whether by her own hand or the
hand of God, as well as sound advice on closing
their financial and legal affairs. Sometimes she
must act simply as a convenient pair of ears for
those who have none other for their quandaries
of grief and mortality. Whatever the occasion,
her principal skill is to deal with all these clients
in a manner professional but sympathetic,
presenting whatever wisdom she has with infinite
patience and without inappropriate display of
emotion.*

A man arrived at Tenterhook Yard about a week into my apprenticeship, hoping to talk to Blackshroud Cartwright about life
and death and the meaning of his existence. He had the bad
luck to find her in a shouting-through-the-window sort of a
mood, and she bellowed down something like, "do you imagine
I don't have better things to do than listen to your maudlin
moaning? It's a simple enough question: do you want to die or
don't you? If *you* don't know, how in Hell's name do you expect
me to know?" She slammed the window. Then she had me go
out and chase him down for a shilling as a "consultation fee".

Most of my duties were more mundane. When she was out
on calls I was to wait in and take messages. I wasn't to make
small talk, wasn't to negotiate, wasn't to answer any questions,
just take down their details and send them on their way. I
had become, in short, a replacement for the iron spike on the
bar of *The Tenterhook*, sparing the teetotal blackshroud the

embarrassment of sending her clients into what she described as "the Devil's taphouse".

Despite this opinion of her neighbours, she seemed to have no issue with having our every meal prepared in *The Tenterhook*'s kitchens, brought up by Mrs Battersby three times daily on a tray. Mrs Battersby was a thin spectre of a woman who regarded Blackshroud Cartwright with nervous awe. Whenever she caught me alone she'd subject me to a eulogy on what a great lady she was, and how lucky I was to have her as a mistress. These speeches became more than a little tiring after a while and I began to avoid Mrs Battersby whenever possible.

Actually, Mrs Battersby's meals were one of the few things that *did* make me feel lucky in my situation. She was worthy of a far better class of establishment. There was luscious roast meat dripping in gravy; roast potatoes with just a slightly crunchy crust; creamy shellfish stews; heavenly bread and butter pudding with just the right amount of marmalade; Victoria sponge so light and fluffy it seemed in danger of floating away. Blackshroud Cartwright received these divine offerings with no more thanks than a grunt, and stuffed them down her gullet with the same pleasureless industry as a starving man might apply to a pot of flavourless gruel.

Otherwise, life in Tenterhook Yard was less than satisfactory. Beyond room and board I was paid only one and sixpence a week, a paltry sum that made even my probationer nurse's salary seem extravagant. And when I wasn't taking messages she expected me to keep her home severely clean, scrubbing grease, dust and cobwebs from a building that seemed to exude all three at a scarcely credible rate. The worst time, though, was Sundays, when the blackshroud would allow no work to be done. My own room being barely large enough to contain a narrow bed, and the parlour being too unsettling, I was forced to share my Sundays with her in the living room. She sat deeply buried in a chair by the fire, slowly reading and rereading a small pile of novels with a frown of disapproval and an occasional tut.

One Sunday night, feeling especially useless and frustrated, I blurted out, "*When* are you going to start training me, ma'am?"

She peered at me over the top of her least favourite and most read book, *Wuthering Heights*. "I already have."

"No, you haven't!" I got to my feet and started pacing, earning me a new look of reproach. "All I've done is take your messages, clean your rooms and sit about endlessly!"

"Those are all important skills for a blackshroud."

"What, even sitting doing nothing?"

She turned a page. "*Especially* sitting doing nothing. And by the look of it, you need a lot more practice."

"Well I've had quite enough of it and then some. I've been here almost two months now. Will you *please* teach me something?"

She sighed, and put down the book. "Very well. I'm going to tell you the single most important thing you need to know. Are you listening carefully?"

I sat back down and nodded eagerly.

"Always collect your fee *before* killing your patient. It's bloody hard to collect it after."

"What? *That's* it? That's your best advice?"

"Well if you didn't want to hear it, I don't know why you bothered asking." She picked up her novel again and opened it with a snap.

In the end, the first death I attended during my apprenticeship was nothing whatsoever to do with Blackshroud Cartwright. It was that of my Awful Aunt Adeline.

Awful Aunt Adeline had married above herself, and had spent her life looking down on our side of the family with a sneer. Her house in Harrogate was three times the size of ours, and on the day of her passing there was a steady queue of cabs and carriages dropping off ladies and gentlemen in ostentatious mourning dress. I slipped inside and slunk through the crowds until I found a friendly face: Francis, up from London for the occasion.

"Caroline!" We embraced warmly. "Thank God you're here. I was afraid if I had to talk with one more of these nobs I might turn into one myself."

"Good thing you've got your penniless ill-bred sister to talk to, then."

"Rather! *And* you dress like a scarecrow to match. Are you really still wearing that ragged old thing?"

"I refer you back to the word 'penniless' in my last reply."

"I just thought now you were a blackshroud—"

"Blackshroud's apprentice."

"—that you'd look a bit more... you know..."

"I don't know, what?"

"Like her, perhaps?" He gestured over his shoulder.

I looked. Across the room from us, Awful Aunt Adeline sat crumpled in her wheelchair at the centre of a circle of wellwishers; a thin, grey, mildewed figure, glaring out at the world with sour contempt even at her last. But the wellwishers weren't looking so much at her as at the woman standing behind her, with one hand resting possessively on the handle of the wheelchair, and a most enormous crinoline skirt marking out a wide circle of the room as her indisputable personal territory. She wore long strings of black onyx and Whitby jet looped around her neck and wrists. Whenever she tossed her head back to laugh at some remark – which she did often – the jewellery glittered and tinkled as though it were laughing along. It wasn't until I spotted the dove-and-dagger brooch hiding amongst the jangling loops that I realised who she must be.

"Blackshroud Ambrose," Francis supplied. "I hear she costs a fortune."

"I'll bet. Only the best for Aunt Adeline."

"Uncle Oscar hired her. Didn't want to skimp. Got to make sure she ends up nicely dead and stays that way. I hear he's already got the tombstone: a big heavy slab of granite, to keep her safely in the grave once she's in it."

"Sssh!" I glanced around nervously. "Don't talk about her like that, on today of all days. What if someone hears?"

"Piffle! Everyone's thinking the same thing. This isn't mourning we're here for, it's a bloody big party. Oh, everyone will *say* the right things, what a shame it is and all that, but we all know that we're here to say good riddance. Look, here comes Uncle Oscar now, watch carefully."

"Francis," said Oscar in a leaden voice, "Caroline. Thank you for coming."

"It's a sad day," said Francis, shaking his hand. "A sad day indeed." And he flashed him a wink.

"I barely know how I'll manage without her," Oscar replied sombrely, and then winked back before mingling away into the crowd.

"You're unbelievable," I told Francis.

"I thought you'd have the measure of these fancy passing away parties by now. Aren't they your bread and butter these days?"

"Not really. Blackshroud Cartwright never takes me with her. And I don't think this is her clientele, anyway."

"But… things are going well, I hope, little sister?"

"No. They're not. She's awful. As awful as Awful Aunt Adeline. Well… maybe that's going a bit far, but she's still *quite* awful. And she hasn't taught me a damn thing. Everything I've learned I've learned from that book you sent me. To be honest, I'm thinking of quitting."

"Again? You only quit nursing a few months ago. Is this going to be a pattern with you? Seeing how many different careers you can jump into and then walk away from?"

"I don't *want* to quit, I just… I can't see another way. She's hopeless at her job, and she's not even *trying* to train me."

"I learnt some of my most valuable lessons from my worst teachers. Their mistakes saved me from having to make too many of my own."

"Well, perhaps..."

"Hey, I've spotted someone you just *have* to meet..."

He led me by the hand and presented me to a well-dressed young lady of my own age.

"Caroline, let me introduce Miss Selina Abbott, apprentice to Blackshroud Ambrose. Miss Abbot, let me introduce my sister Caroline Summers, apprentice to Blackshroud... umm, what was it again?"

"Cartwright."

"Cartwright?" said Selina, sucking on a finger with a puzzled frown. "I don't think I know her." She looked like a miniature version of her mistress, complete with ballooning crinoline and an embryonic loop of black jewellery growing around her neck. The terrifying thought came to me that I might myself turn into a miniature version of Blackshroud Cartwright. I looked round to Francis for reassurance but he'd vanished.

"So how long have you been apprenticed?" I asked.

"Eighteen months now."

"Doesn't it normally take just twelve?"

"Yes, but Blackshroud Ambrose believes that two years is a more suitable time to train an apprentice. There's simply too much to learn in just one. There's the medical knowledge, the legal knowledge, the business knowledge, not to mention all the fine points of ethics and deportment. And one simply must know ever so much about religion and philosophy to be able to really talk to clients about death. Don't you agree?

"I'm three months in and I feel I've barely scratched the surface," I said, choosing my words carefully.

"My mistress always tells me that clients should be taken on a spiritual journey, to put their soul at peace before they die. Does yours say anything like that?"

"I've heard her say it's a long and difficult road." She'd been complaining about making a trip out to Morley town.

41

"Oh, it's *so* nice to meet another apprentice! You must have come a distance; I've been introduced to all the blackshrouds of note in the West Riding, and I don't remember a Cartwright."

"She's based in Leeds. Tenterhook Yard. Esther Cartwright."

Her eyes widened. "You can't mean... not *Bloody* Esther?!"

"Why... why do you call her that?"

"Oh, Blackshroud Ambrose told me all about *her*. She says she's a disgrace to the profession. Bloody Esther will kill anyone for two shillings, she said, no questions asked. Is it true?"

"No!" I almost shouted, my cheeks flushing.

It wasn't true, at least not literally. Her standard service was six shillings, plus travel; she also had a "deluxe" service priced at twelve shillings, which she described when pressed as, "Same as the standard service, only for those who looks to afford it." She claimed to be the cheapest in Leeds, which I believed, as it seemed the only way to explain how she got so many customers.

The "no questions asked" part, however, rang rather true, and I mumbled an excuse to Selina and went to hide in the crowd before she could ask me anything else. As soon as Awful Aunt Adeline had been seen out of this world, I stayed only for the minimum time that propriety demanded before giving my last condolences to an inappropriately happy-looking Uncle Oscar and slipping away quietly. I could hear the real party just getting going behind me as I left.

When I arrived back on Briggate I had a chance encounter with Mr Battersby.

"You still here, Miss?" he said, catching my arm.

"For now."

"Look Miss," he said, dropping into a confidential whisper, glancing around furtively. "I shouldn't say anything, but you seem a smart girl, I thought you'd've figured it by now."

"Figured what?"

"The blackshroud's had a lot of apprentices, and most don't last as long as you have."

"What are you trying to say?"

"I just don't like to see a young lady being taken advantage of, that's all."

"Spit it out, Mr Battersby."

He took another glance around and leaned in to whisper, his moustache tickling my ear. "The blackshroud... only keeps apprentices... because she finds them cheaper than servants." And before I could blink he was hurrying off down the road, moving so much faster than his usual gait that he almost broke into a trot.

I was still digesting this intelligence when I turned into Tenterhook Yard to find Blackshroud Cartwright arguing across her doorstep with a tatty wisp of a girl.

"But two shillings's all I've got..."

"The fee's six shillings, girl."

"Please. He's in such a state you won't believe. We can't hardly stand listening to the screams no more."

"Six. Shillings."

"Do you want me to go down on my knees and beg?" She dropped to her knees, landing in a puddle with a sad splash. "Here I am. Look! Look at me. Begging. *Please*, ma'am."

"Try begging out on Briggate. You might just be able to raise the six shillings."

Fire flashed in the girl's eyes, and for a moment she looked as though she might punch her, but she quenched her pride. "I might manage two and sixpence..."

The blackshroud sighed. "Look, girl, every dose of the draught costs me *three* and sixpence. How am I supposed to make money if I dish it out for two and sixpence? Now can you cough up six shillings or not?"

"No, but out of the goodness of—"

"Do you think I'm a bloody charity?" And she closed the door firmly. The girl knelt staring at the black-painted wood for a few seconds before getting to her feet, her ragged skirt wet and stained. She added an angry gobbet of spit to the puddle on the cobbles before marching out towards the main road. I tried to give her a sympathetic look, but she shoved past me with a swipe of the elbow without giving me a glance.

Her anger was contagious, and by the time I opened the door I was fuming. Mr Battersby was right. I'd wasted too much time here already. And I'd had quite enough of Bloody Esther.

"Ma'am?" I called up the stairs.

"That you, girl?"

I ascended and found her in her bedroom, packing her black leather bag. "I wish to resign my apprenticeship."

"Can't. Not yet."

"And why not, exactly?"

"Because I might need you on this job." She clipped her bag shut. "You can resign after."

"What job? Where are you going?"

"Didn't you see that little sniveller on the way in? I'm going to be a bloody charity, yet a-bloody-gain." She thumped down the stairs.

"You mean... you're going to help her? Even though she can't pay?"

She threw open the door, but then – seeing I wasn't following – closed it more gently and walked back upstairs.

"Look, girl, I'm no monster. A man's in pain, and where else is she going to go? If she can't afford me, she can't afford no-one."

"But you were horrible! You slammed the door in her face!"

"Well I had to know she was *really* desperate, and not just taking advantage of my kind heart. I don't give out the free service willy-nilly."

"What's the free service?"

"Same as the standard service, only for those who can't afford it. Now are you coming or not?"

"I'm coming."

"Good, then you can carry this." She threw the bag at me. I caught it, staggering under its surprisingly heavy weight.

It was a short walk up Lady Lane to Quarry Hill. The address led us into a narrow court off the main road, and I hesitated before entering. It had an ill look and an iller smell; the kind of place that made Tenterhook Yard look like a genteel neighbourhood in comparison.

"What the devil's the problem, girl?"

"Sorry. It's just that this is the kind of place my father always warned me never to go."

"A blackshroud belongs everywhere, and you'd better learn that."

"Alright. Lead on, ma'am."

She made to march in, but then paused and turned back to me.

"Word to the wise, girl. This is our patient's home, so show a little respect. No comments, no wrinkling your dainty little nose, no staring at what isn't right. Act like you haven't even noticed it's a cesspit."

"*You're* worried about *my* manners?"

But it was hard. The temptation to put my hand over my nose, when stepping over unspeakable pools overflowing from the communal privy in the courtyard, was overpowering. The rooms themselves – a damp, cold, cramped, ill-built cellar – were barely any more pleasant, with sagging ceilings, mouldy walls and a pool on the floor of what I dearly hoped was water. A rat fled into a crack in the wall as we entered.

The girl met us with a crying child in her arms, although she barely looked old enough to have one. She'd clearly been crying herself, but she wiped her eyes dry with her sleeve, leaving a dirty smudge over her cheek. "I'd given up hope on you. Here." She rummaged down to the bottom of a small purse. "Two and sixpence. I'll get you the rest somehow, I will, but—"

"Stop whining, girl. Keep your shillings. Where's your father?"

She showed us into the only other room, which contained a single bed and a second mattress laid straight on the floor. A man lay on the bed. My nurse's eye quickly told me the man was dying, and had been dying for quite some time.

Esther knelt down by him at once. "Can you hear me?"

The man groaned wordlessly.

"I said *can you hear me?*" She shook his shoulder and he shuddered but didn't open his eyes. "Do you want the draught or not?" More groans.

I knew, at this point, that we had a problem. The man was as clearly in need of her services as anyone I could imagine, but to be able to perform her work legally, she needed his explicit and witnessed consent. And he was too far gone to be able to give it. To quote the *Modern Guide* again:

> *If written or verbal consent cannot be obtained and witnessed, and the patient has made no provision in advance, then the blackshroud has but one course of action. The patient's fate must be left to Providence.*

She asked him again. And then again, shouting in his ear and shaking him. There were gasps and wails, but no words.

"Right." She clipped open her bag and pulled out an ink pot and pen. A large, ornate but battered green-bound volume followed, which she spread out on the least filthy part of the floor and flipped open to the first blank page. She scratched in a few details and scrawled her signature across one of three lines beneath. "This says I've heard verbal consent. It needs two witnesses to sign that they heard it too." And she held the pen out to the two of us.

The girl took it straight away and signed with an X. The blackshroud wrote her name and address beside it, then she handed the pen to me. I knelt down before the book and paused with the pen in my hand. I looked at the man, lying shaking on his deathbed. I looked into the eyes of his daughter and granddaughter. I looked at Blackshroud Cartwright, who stared at me darkly, as though daring me not to sign.

I signed. She snatched the pen from me and ushered us from the room.

I tried to find something reassuring to say to the girl, but for once I found myself short of words. So we sat in silence, except for the babbling of the child and the sounds of distress from the next room. After a few minutes those sounds fell quiet. The girl sat looking at the floor, apparently absorbed in the slow shuffle of her feet. The terrible atmosphere of that room reminded me strongly of that time as a child, sat waiting while my grandfather died. I couldn't quite stand it.

"I'll wait outside," I whispered.

The smell out in the courtyard was as bad as ever, but right at that moment it could hardly have seemed fresher, and I took a deep breath.

A man approached me. He was thick-set and dirty, with a face like a mallet. I took a nervous step back.

"You lost, sweetheart?" he growled in a coarse accent, his breath reeking of old beer.

I shook my head, backing up until my shoulders were against the bricks. "No. Not lost. I'm here with the blackshroud."

"What, Esther?" He glanced at the windows of the dying man's rooms.

I nodded.

"Poor old John." He peeled his cap off his head and held it in both hands. I let out the breath I'd been holding. "He's been bad for a long while, he has, but she'll have him at peace soon."

"She's with him now."

"Course she is. She's an angel, our Esther. Saw to my Emma when she was at her end, and she looked right peaceful after."

A window opened, and an angular pox-marked woman leaned out. "That our Esther down there?"

"Aye."

"It were Esther who brung peace to my poor Samuel. The typhus were eating the last of him and no-one else would go near. Bless her soul."

More folk appeared. More stories about lost loved ones, and how Blackshroud Cartwright – invariably referred to only as "our Esther" – had swooped in to make their passing a merciful one. All of them spoke in the same hushed, reverent undertone. And all of them fell silent at the exact same moment when the blackshroud appeared in the doorway behind me.

"Done. Come along, girl."

The people parted for us, hats in hands, bowing their heads as we passed, with respectful mumbles of "Blackshroud" or "ma'am" all round. She acknowledged them with a nod and a grunt before stepping out onto the road, with me trailing in her mountainous shadow.

"Still want to resign?" she asked half-way back to Tenterhook Yard.

"No, ma'am. I think I'll stay around, if you'll have me."

"Good. Then I'd better start making a blackshroud of you, now I know you're serious. Mr Battersby'll be disappointed."

"How so?"

"Big bet on with his wife. He said you'd be gone before Whitsuntide. She said you wouldn't."

"Huh."

"But try to pretend you're still wavering. Mrs Battersby's food has been far above her usual on account of the whole business, and I wouldn't want it reverting just yet."

"Good thinking, ma'am."

"And for goodness' sake, girl, call me Esther."

"Thank you... Esther."

Chapter 4

The ancient symbol of blackshroudery is a dove perched on a dagger. The dove is symbolic; it represents that we come in peace. Or that we *bring* peace. Or maybe it represents freedom. Something in that direction. I've never been quite certain.

The meaning of the dagger is more literal. Traditionally, blackshrouds used them to perform their work. Patients were bled to death, or sometimes stabbed through the heart; an effective means of dispatch, if far from painless, not to mention messy. But the medieval blackshroud was free to employ even more gruesome means if it took her fancy to do so. There are records of patients – or perhaps "victims" is a more suitable word here – being suffocated, drowned, decapitated, hanged and even burned to death, with one blackshroud in Portsmouth becoming famous for taking her clients out with a quite literal bang, thanks to liberal quantities of gunpowder.

After the Worshipful Society of Blackshrouds was formed in 1612 they gradually started to crack down on this sort of silliness, until only the dagger and certain lethal draughts were permitted. *The* draught as we know it today was an eighteenth century invention, and its recipe remains a fiercely guarded secret. It was more reliable, easier to prepare and caused a much more peaceful death than competing concoctions, and by the time the Society finally outlawed use of the dagger in 1828 the blade had already fallen well out of favour.

I still remember the day Esther introduced me to the draught. She had a small steel safe next to her bed, and unlocking it she pulled out one of several stoppered blue glass bottles, which she handed to me with reverent care. A large skull and crossbones on the front label gave a clearer indication of its contents than words ever could. It felt cold and heavy in my hands, which to my surprise I found were shaking slightly. Removing the stopper, the bottle was full of innocuous-looking white powder. I put my nose to the neck and took a sniff. A sweet, slightly cloying smell, but not very strong.

Esther showed me what to do with it. How to dispense from the big bottle into small vials without spilling a single speck. How to weigh out the precise dose with a tiny set of scales that measured in delicate grains instead of big coarse ounces. How to dissolve the powder in a glass of water and stir until every trace of sediment had disappeared. Then she poured a small splash into a second glass and slid it to me across the table.

"Here. Drink it."

"Ha! Not a chance."

"You need to know what it tastes like."

"Oh God, you're serious."

"When have I been anything but, girl?"

"But won't it... you know, *kill me?*"

"A tiny dose like that? I doubt it'd kill a squirrel."

I looked at the glass sceptically.

"A blackshroud can't be afraid of her tools, girl! I take a sip from every new batch, just to make sure it's right, and no harm done yet."

"But—"

"Stop shilly-shallying and get it down you!"

I raised an eyebrow. "Is that what you say to your patients? 'Stop shilly-shallying and get it down you'?"

"What I say to my patients, girl, is none of your concern."

But it *was* a matter of great curiosity. I had a theory that when Esther was alone with them for the final act, she let her brusque facade drop a little. That her approach was closer to her old mistress' advice of "hold the patient's hand; be calm; be reassuring" than she'd have me believe.

There was no way of knowing for sure. One of the strictest and most arcane rules of our strict and arcane profession was

50

what's known as the sanctity clause: that a patient's death is a sacred and private moment between them, their blackshroud and God. Nobody else could be in the room. *Nobody.* Not a sibling, not a child, not a parent, not a spouse, not a doctor, not a priest, and not an apprentice either. It was frustrating for me, as it meant I had no opportunity to learn the central business of my occupation by observation. Although Esther had eventually begun taking me with her on many of her calls, I was invariably left outside with the relatives when the door closed.

"Are you going to bloody well drink it or are you going to sit there staring at it?"

I raised the glass to my lips and took a very, very small sip. It had a strong, queer taste. Something like aniseed, but at the same time definitely not aniseed.

"Well?"

"It doesn't taste like I'd imagined."

"And how'd you imagine it'd taste?"

"Like poison."

"We'd have a bloody hard time getting folks to drink it if it tasted like poison. Bet you've never tasted the likes of it before, have you?"

"I can't quite place it. It tastes... different."

"That's the whole point. Nothing tastes like the draught except the draught. The pure draught's tasteless, but they make it taste like that so you can't slip it in things without folks noticing. Remember that taste, girl, and if you ever taste it again, spit, unless you're lying on your deathbed and you're looking for it."

I pondered the draught for a while in silence, swirling it around the bottom of the glass, trying and failing to see anything to visually mark it from ordinary water.

"Blackshroud White drank a whole mug of tea laced with the draught," I said.

"What's your point?"

"She must have tasted what it was from the first sip. But she drank the whole mug."

"No blackshroud can take the draught by mistake."

"But she did."

"No she didn't. Look, girl, Martha was a sad, lonely old woman who'd had enough of this world and wanted to be with her husband in the next. She may have been too much a coward to pour herself a draught and get it over with, but she wasn't going to refuse it when chance put it to her lips."

"I suppose you knew her better than I did."

She sniffed. "Yes. I did."

I thought about Blackshroud White for a while. Then I thought about Esther.

"Do all blackshrouds end up sad and lonely?"

"What? No. Of course not! Where'd you get such a daft notion? Just look at me, do I look sad and lonely to you?"

I hesitated a moment too long, and she put her hands on her hips.

"Don't even *think* about saying what you're thinking of saying, girl, if you plan on spending one more night under this roof."

"Just promise me you won't have an 'accident' too? I don't want to have to find *another* mistress."

She let out one of her rare laughs, like an asthmatic pig wedged in a steam engine. "Don't you worry about me, girl. I'll take the draught when I can't stand on my own two feet and not one day before. And that day's coming no time soon. I've got legs like an elephant's."

It would probably be uncharitable for me to make too close a comparison between Esther's legs and those of an elephant, but in terms purely of strength the comparison was perhaps justified. She walked everywhere. Typically a blackshroud has a horse and carriage, but Esther had a great fear of horses and refused to have anything to do with them, or even to get into any conveyance attached to one. "Demons on four legs," she told me once as we walked past some particularly placid beasts tethered to a lamppost, munching on hay from their nosebags. "You never know what they're thinking. If you'd seen some of the ruined people I've seen, trampled under horses' hooves, you'd know never to turn your back on one."

And so she walked. Rain, snow or howling gale, she walked. Even if the patient was miles and miles out of town, she walked. And she walked fast. You wouldn't think it to look at her, with her great sedentary weight, but once she got going she built up some impressive momentum. She hurtled through the streets, expecting pedestrians, carts and even tram cars to respect her self-declared right of way, as negotiable as that of a careering grand piano. Many were the angry shouts of "Oi! Who do you think you—" which transformed magically into a meek "ma'am" and a tip of the hat when they spotted the dove-and-dagger pinned to the front of her bosom like a Valkyrie's breastplate.

It was always a strain to match her pace, especially since her heavy black bag was invariably weighing on my shoulders rather than her own. If I fell behind she'd shout, "Keep up!" and walk even faster. If I kept up she'd quiz me on road names.

Esther felt that a blackshroud should immediately know an address when given one, without having to ask for directions. I'd be assaulted by a random fire of questions such as where I might find Spencerley Street, or if I could name – in order – all the rows of back-to-backs off Kirkstall Road from Angel Street to Ventnor Street. In time I became quite proficient at this, and I reflected that if the apprenticeship didn't work out then I'd have a fine novelty career lined up as Leeds' first female cabbie.

Occasionally she'd quiz me on dosages instead.

"Him?" she asked, pointing at a portly gentleman wrapped in a thick coat and muffler despite the mild weather.

"Fifty grains?" I hazarded.

"You've just wasted five grains. He may be fat as a prize bullock, but he's none too tall. What about her?" She pointed to a young girl perched on a low wall, swinging her legs and singing a rhyme to herself, looking about as in need of a blackshroud as a sparrow is of a panther.

"Eighteen should do."

"Probably. But I'd use twenty-two, just to be sure. How much would you use for me?"

I made a point of looking her up and down critically. "I think you might take the whole bottle, Esther."

She stopped and scowled at me. "Less of that bloody cheek, girl!" she said, but I caught a slight twitch of a smile she didn't quite manage to hide.

One day in November, I was following Esther and I noticed she was unusually quiet. Her eyes had drooped to the paving stones, her feet moving at such a reduced pace that I could keep up with a fast walk instead of a jog. We were heading up Armley Road which ran right alongside the railway. I knew something was very wrong when an express train screamed past us, letting out a vast cloud of smoke and an exuberant whistle, and elicited no complaint from Esther about infernal noisy contraptions, nor a single comment on why anyone needed to be anywhere in such a rush anyway.

"Where are we going?"

"Ugly business. Very ugly business."

"You said blackshrouding's *always* an ugly business."

"Not as ugly as this."

I didn't realise our destination until we were almost in its shadow. Leeds Borough Gaol. Its gateway loomed over us, a crenellated fortress of blackened stone, heavy ironwork barring its windows, looking more like a medieval stronghold than a modern institution. Esther, straightening herself, marched up to the towering wooden doors and rapped on them. A small hatch slid open, and she announced herself abruptly. The hatch closed again.

I knew she had business at the gaol, time to time. Prisoners facing longer stays sometimes opted for a dose of the draught instead of seeing it through. Esther called these cases "gaolbreaks". But gaolbreaks had never appeared to trouble her before, and she was most certainly troubled on that day. And I could only think of one thing that might have got her so ruffled.

"*Please* tell me we're not here to—"

"*I* am. You're not."

"But... an *execution?*" I said the word in a whisper. "And you *agreed* to that?"

"Pays bloody well."

"Please don't pretend you lack a conscience. I do know better."

"I can look after my own conscience perfectly well without *you* pecking at it, girl." She looked at me for a moment, then her eyes turned rigidly back to the door. "I don't *want* to be doing this. But you don't get to say no. When you become a blackshroud, they make you put your hand on a bible and swear all sorts of things. One of them's to perform hangings if they ask for it."

"I... I didn't know that." I swallowed down my hot temper, only to find a cold dread rising in its place. "So one day I might have to..."

She snorted. "Doubt it. They always ask *me.*"

"Why you?"

"Because this sort of work ruins a reputation. And I've got none to ruin."

The oversized door creaked open slightly. The governor stepped out – a well-groomed and well-dressed man of middling years – and greeted Esther with a stiff bow. He invited her in, and she stepped over the threshold.

"Not you," she said as I made to follow. "Unless..." She narrowed her eyes. "The sanctity clause doesn't apply here. An execution has to be witnessed. Do you *want* to watch?"

"No! No I certainly do *not* want to watch."

"Good. If you'd said yes to that you'd've been looking for a new position tomorrow." She stepped inside, but turned back

55

to me just before the door closed. "Don't wait on me; this'll be a slow business."

But I didn't head back straight away. I sat down on a nearby wall and took a few moments to let my thoughts run. I tried to imagine the scene that would unfold inside. There'd be a small crowd lining the walls. The governor, the chaplain, the surgeon, a couple of guards, perhaps a visiting judge, all watching hungrily to see justice done. It wasn't a blackshroud's job to tie the knot, nor to calculate the right length of rope for a clean kill, nor to bind the man and put the noose around his neck. All Esther was there to do was pull the lever. A simple job, perhaps, if she could avoid looking him in the eye.

At first the prisoner in my imagination was a burly, tattooed brute, more animal than man, snarling and straining at his bonds, even foaming a little at the mouth in his fury. But then a different mental picture formed: a young, scrawny figure, barely adult, weeping and quivering as his end drew near. Or maybe – somehow even more tragically – an ordinary, unremarkable-looking man, who'd stand in dignified silence with his eyes closed, accepting the inevitability of his fate without resistance.

I was still deep in this morbid reverie when a sharply suited individual approached me.

"Excuse me, ma'am, but are you here for the execution?" he asked.

"I... in a way?"

He introduced himself as a reporter from the *Leeds Mercury*. "You must be keen."

"Must I?"

"Well, it's not scheduled until noon."

It couldn't have gone ten yet. "It doesn't hurt to get here early."

"Exactly right. I don't suppose the blackshroud has arrived yet?"

"No," I lied, "but I'm sure she'll be here soon."

And then others started appearing, and I came to understand why Esther had chosen to arrive so far ahead of time. There were reporters from other newspapers. And ordinary people too, who seemed to have no business there at all except to hover around hungrily like flies attracted by the scent of death. By half eleven there was quite a swarm of them building around the prison gates, and some enterprising street vendors had even set up stalls to sell them baked potatoes and treacle tarts. There was a giddy buzz of gala-day gaiety in the air that repulsed me. Even the weather was inappropriate: it was a bright autumn day, with cool sunshine and the sweet song of a robin wafting through the air. Dark clouds and the caw of crows would have suited the occasion better.

I've heard people talk – sometimes admonishingly, sometimes wistfully – of hangings of old, when they were public events, and huge crowds would turn up to cheer as some unfortunate soul twitched and gasped on the end of a short rope. This group of enthusiasts felt like the aimless ghost of those jeering crowds, drawn to haunt the scene out of habit or primal instinct, even though the prison gates would remain firmly closed. It's easy to criticise, but in truth I must acknowledge that I myself lingered that day for almost two hours, for no really good reason. I told myself it was just curiosity that was keeping me there, and that was true to an extent. But at the same time, I think a little of their morbid eagerness had infected my spirit. I may not approve, but... I do understand.

I probably would have stayed there right until the bells struck noon, if it hadn't been for Jacob Arthington.

Jacob stepped out of the gaol doors not twenty minutes before midday, causing a small kerfuffle of excitement that quickly died away when they realised he had nothing whatsoever to do with the execution. He was simply dressed, with a bag slung over one shoulder. When he'd walked ten yards clear of the crowd he let the bag fall onto the cobbles with a clunk, swayed, and then fell to his knees.

I was by him in a trice. "Mister? Are you ill? Are you hurt? I'm a nurse," I said, deciding that – while not *quite* true – it sounded much more reassuring than, "I'm a would-be blackshroud".

He looked up at me with pink eyes and shining cheeks. And the purest, most undiluted expression of joy I've ever seen on the face of a human being.

"I ain't ill, I'm just... I've just taken me first steps as a free man in six long months."

I gave him my warmest nurse's smile. "Well, let's get you back on your feet to take a few more steps," and held out a hand.

He grasped my hand, pulled himself upright, threw his arms around my shoulders and pulled me into a full-blooded kiss.

I was so astonished that I stood limp and unresisting for a good few seconds under the onslaught of his chapped lips and hot breath. By the time I recovered my wits to protest he was already being pulled bodily away from me by the man from the *Mercury*.

"Animal!" shouted the reporter, pushing him so roughly he fell over.

"Scandalous," agreed his rival from the *Yorkshire Post*. "The moral condition of the criminal classes really is below contempt. What the gaol is doing letting men like *that* out into the street is unimaginable." He punctuated his point by kicking Jacob's bag towards him, sending several of his meagre possessions clattering over the cobbles.

Jacob scrambled to retrieve his effects and made a hasty retreat, a couple of thrown stones striking his shoulders as he went. As for myself, I was swooped upon by some female vultures, who smothered me with questions about the state of my nerves after my ordeal, and was there no gentleman to escort me home? I could see reporters prowling the edge of the conversation, waiting to pounce on me as soon as I escaped.

I'll say this for Jacob's unwanted kiss: it shocked me out of the strange spell I'd been under, and I now wanted nothing more than to be away. As soon as the reporters were distracted by more enticing prey – some dignitary arrived to witness the execution – I made my excuses to the women and ran for it.

Just round the corner I was accosted by an unwelcome voice.

"Miss! *Miss!* Wait!"

I scowled at Jacob without slowing my pace. "I don't want to talk to you, thank you."

He scurried to keep up. "I just want to say I'm sorry, Miss. I can't believe I did that. It's not the sort of thing I do, Miss. It's not the sort of man I am."

I stopped and whirled on him. "But you *did* do it. You took advantage of me. It was humiliating."

"I know, Miss, I know." He took his cap off and wrung it between his hands. "I'm sorry, Miss. I really am. I weren't meself."

"Who were you then? Did the Devil possess you?"

"It felt like it, Miss, it did." He looked up at the sky, a haunted look in his eyes. "It were awful in there. Joyless place. Cold stone walls and iron. Then, when I stepped outside, everything seemed blessed. The clouds above, even the weeds by the road, they were all so beautiful I had to weep." His eyes turned down from the heavens, and met mine. "And then there you were, all smiling, and you would've looked beautiful on any day. It were like a spell were over me, and even I were surprised at what happened. And I'm real sorry, Miss, I am. Can't say it enough."

I was reminded of something Esther once told me; one of her more surprisingly human bits of advice. She'd said that in extreme moments, people said and did extreme things, and I should pay them little heed. So I decided to forgive Jacob his transgression. Besides, the man looked genuinely mortified about the whole business.

He hadn't any intentions in pursuing me beyond an apology, but I persuaded him to take me for a spot of lunch. Well, I say a spot, but Jacob ate a *lot* of lunch. Plateful after plateful disappeared. It was only a working man's cookshop, and the fare basic indeed – badly fried fish, served with dry bread and greasy butter – but from the look of bliss on his face you might have thought it was finest turbot in lobster sauce.

"Didn't they feed you in there?"

"Barely."

"What were you in for, anyway? You're not a murderer or something, are you?"

"Nah, Miss. Larceny." I subtly moved my hand to check my purse was still in its proper place. I can't have been subtle enough, because he said, "No need to worry about that, Miss. I'm a reformed character, me. Never want to wind up back in there again. Never."

I was curious about what life behind bars was like, but he seemed reluctant to discuss it. It was just about the only topic he was quiet on, however. He opened up on every other with the true abandon of a man making up for six months of silence and solitude.

"Trees! Have you ever really looked at trees?"

"No?"

"Me neither. I never knew how much I'd miss 'em till I were inside. They were always just, sort of, there. And now I'm out, and I'm seeing trees again, and it's like I'm seeing 'em for the first time. I mean, look at that one." He gestured out the window to a thin and sickly thing, with a few shrivelled autumn leaves still clinging to its sooty branches. "Have you ever seen anything so perfect? Wonder what it's like to climb a tree? I never have. Not even when I were a boy. Bet it's like nothing else, being inside a tree."

"Is this what you're going to do with your freedom? Climb trees?"

"Oh no. I've got bigger plans than that. I want to go to sea. I want to see the world. All of it! I want to see jungles, and pyramids, and polar bears. Wouldn't that be something?"

"But you haven't been to sea before?"

"Never even *seen* the sea before."

He was serious. He had just enough money for a one-way ticket to Hull, a journey he was set on making that very afternoon. I walked with him to New Station to see him off. There on the platform he said his goodbyes leaning out of his compartment window.

"And, Miss Summers? Really am very sorry about, um, you know. The kiss."

"I've already forgiven you for that, Mr Arthington." And, my devilish streak surfacing, I added, "But now that I like you, I wouldn't object if you did it again."

We kissed through the window until the train pulled us apart with a whistle and a forward lurch. I stood waving on the platform, hoping the sea would treat Jacob better than the land had.

I never thought I'd see him again. I was quite wrong about that, but that's a story for later.

It seems remarkable to me now, but all this business with Jacob had completely driven the execution out of my mind. It wasn't until a couple of hours later, contentedly whistling while I leaned half out of the parlour window to wash the latest grime from the glass, that I spotted Esther storming into the yard like a black cloud and happened to wonder where she'd been. Then the whole matter intruded back into my consciousness as unwelcome as Jacob's first kiss, and much harder to shake off.

I ran down to open the door. "Welcome back."

She grunted and pushed past without looking at me. I followed her upstairs.

"Did you—"

"It's done."

"You were a long time."

"Bureaucracy. The killing was mercifully quick."

She sat down at the table with a heavy thump that threatened to shatter the chair legs, and I hovered nearby.

"So... what did he do?" I said.

"What?"

"The man you hung. What did he do?"

"God be thanked I've no idea, girl."

"But don't you want to know? It must have been something terrible."

"I don't want to know in case it *wasn't* something terrible."

"But it *must* have been. They wouldn't sentence a man to death unless he'd done something really evil, would they?"

She shot me a withering look, then snorted. "If you want to do something useful, girl, stop spouting idiocies and open up that cupboard there. Green bottle, right at the back left. You'll have to rummage for it."

I pulled out – to my surprise – a bottle of brandy.

"Esther, what do you want with this? You don't drink."

"I drink after an execution, girl. Now bring me a glass."

With some reluctance, I fetched her the smallest glass I could find.

"That's my girl." She unscrewed the lid and poured out a generous slosh. "Did you ever ask Martha how many people she'd killed?"

"Yes. She said she never had. Only helped people to die."

"Well by her counting I've killed four now." She raised the glass to her lips and emptied it in one gulp, with a grimace. She poured another. "Be gone, girl. I'd be alone with my thoughts."

I did as she asked and retired to my room. But, alarmed by her behaviour, as I went I discreetly removed her black leather bag containing the tools of her trade. After a few moments' thought I also pocketed the key to the safe from where she kept it under her pillow. I worried at the time that I was being excessively paranoid. Later in life I learned that suicide is sadly common amongst blackshrouds. A combination, I think, of the sometimes harrowing nature of our work and too-ready access to the draught in a moment of weakness.

I stayed perched on my bed well into the evening, one eye on the passageway, but Esther never emerged from the living room. Eventually I heard snoring, and I crept in to find her slumped unconscious with her forehead on the table, the brandy bottle standing completely empty beside her. I lifted her head to place a cushion underneath, then went to bed.

The next day, Esther went out and bought a new bottle of brandy. I was worried when I saw it, but she didn't seem inclined to drink it right away; it went straight to the back of the cupboard, where it stayed for the rest of my apprenticeship.

When I finally qualified, I had to lay my hand on a bible and swear – with heavy heart – to perform my duty as executioner should I be asked. For over a decade I lived with the fear that such a request would come. I'm thankful to say it never did. In '88, a change in the law meant that private blackshrouds could no longer be obliged to kill in the name of Justice instead of Mercy, and I felt I could breathe a little easier from that day forth.

As for Esther, she never talked about the execution again. I don't know for sure whether or not the count on her conscience ever rose higher than four. But I do remember the last time I ever visited Tenterhook Yard, after Esther's death some two dozen years later. I was helping to clear the old place out, and at the back of a cupboard I discovered a bottle of brandy, its upper slopes fouled by a thick layer of dust and grease. I'm almost certain it was the very same bottle I'd seen her bring home in '74. It was unopened.

Chapter 5

My twelve month apprenticeship didn't automatically make me a blackshroud. I first had to be approved by the Worshipful Society.

"A formality," Esther dismissed it without lifting her eyes from her newspaper. "Nobody ever actually *fails*."

"But what happens? Is there a test?"

"Of course there's a test."

"What sort of a test?"

Instead of answering she peered closer at the paper and grunted. "Listen to this. 'We sadly report the death of Mr Samuel Baker, former alderman of the borough...' etcetera etcetera... 'died peacefully at his home in Roundhay on Wednesday following a long illness, put to rest by Blackshroud Shepherd.' Shepherd! She's getting a bit above herself isn't she, knocking off aldermen?"

Like many in the trade, Esther had the bad habit of using the local obituaries columns as a way of keeping score. But I wasn't willing to be distracted today, not a mere week before my appointment with the Society.

"Never mind that. What sort of test?"

"Nothing you can't handle. And they ask a few questions."

"What kind of questions?"

"Oh I don't *believe* it, look at this! 'We regret to announce the death of Mrs Amelia Michaels of Sheepscar...' then the usual wearisome drivel... 'finally brought peace by Blackshroud Weston on Tuesday.' And after *I* did for her husband, six years back! Whatever happened to family loyalty? Perfidious old hag."

"Esther! *What kind* of questions?"

"Just the usual asinine claptrap to make sure you can string a sentence together. You'll do fine. Oh, God be damned, will you look at *this!* 'Jane Ellen King of Harehills.' She was one of *mine!* And is there a mention of my name? No! There is not!"

"Good service is its own reward." She gave me a Look, so I quickly hurried on. "Could you give me an example of a question they might ask?"

"Oh, I don't know, some vague nonsense like... let's see... what is being a blackshroud all about?"

"Being a blackshroud is about..." I gave it a few moments' thought... "giving people a good death."

Esther gave me another Look over the top of the paper, then folded it and closed her eyes wearily. "A *good death?* Good grief, girl, have I taught you *nothing?* Go fetch me a glass of water, I can feel one of my headaches coming on."

I fetched her some water, which she promptly set down on the table without drinking and forgot about.

"What was wrong with my answer? It is about giving people a good death, isn't it?"

"Please stop using that idiotic pair of words. There's no such thing as a 'good death'. Death's a bloody awful thing. A tragedy. There's nothing good about it whatsoever, no matter how many flowers and pretty words you pile around it. If some folks welcome it, it's only because living's become an even worse option, like how you might welcome a potful of piss if your clothes were on fire."

"Alright, so how would *you* answer the question?"

"Easy. Being a blackshroud's about showing folks a shortcut to Hell."

The next day, as Esther led me into another narrow passage just a few down from Tenterhook Yard, the colourful phrase came strongly to mind.

"Is this that shortcut to Hell you were talking about?"

The smell hit me even before we reached it. An archway, with the carved head of a bull protruding from the keystone, and blood trickling down the gutter. A sheep, wild-eyed with terror, was being manhandled forcefully through, pinned between two men with their hands on one horn each. To my dismay Esther turned in through the archway herself, and I followed barely less reluctantly than the sheep.

What lay beyond the arch may not have been Hell in the literal sense, but if such a place exists then I can't imagine it being much worse. Frightened animals bleated and shrieked in tight pens. Beyond, a room of blood and hooks and flashing knives, where men in red-brown aprons that may once have been white hacked and sliced at grisly hanging carcasses. And the smell. The smell made me hold my sleeve to my nose and fight the urge to vomit.

I hung back while Esther approached one of the men. A long conversation I didn't catch, and she handed over a few coins.

"Esther," I asked when she returned, "what on Earth are we doing in this God-forsaken place?"

"You wanted to know what test you'd face at the Society."

"Yes...?"

"This sort of test." And she handed me a knife.

"What?"

"This," she said, leading me to a mire-mesh pen where a single squealing sow was confined, "is Edith. Edith is a pig."

"I can *see* that."

She opened the gate, shoved me quickly inside, and slammed it. "Kill the pig."

"*What?* I'm not killing a pig!"

"How can you kill a person if you can't kill a pig!"

"But the pig isn't asking to die!"

"Look at where the pig is, girl. It's not likely to retire to a nice mud wallow in the country."

"But why—"

"The Society will ask you to kill a pig. That's the test. It's to see if you've the stomach for the job. If you hesitate, or botch it, they'll fail you."

"But... with a *knife?*"

"Centuries old tradition."

"I don't know how to kill a pig with a knife!"

"It's not surgery, girl. Grab Edith between your legs, pull her head up with one hand and cut her throat with the other."

I looked at the pig, who cowered in the far corner of the pen in mortal terror, as though she'd understood every word of our conversation. I was barely less afraid of Edith than Edith was of me. The knife in my hand was very large and very sharp.

"Damn it, Esther, why'd you have to give it a name?"

"Your patients will also have names."

I moved towards the pig. She squealed and pelted round to the opposite corner, fast as a greased sausage.

There was a whoop of laughter. Looking out of the pen, I noticed I'd attracted an audience: half the red-overalled men in the slaughterhouse had stopped work to come watch the spectacle, shouting deeply unhelpful things like, "Don't be so ham-fisted, love!" and, "She's making a pig's ear of it!"

I looked at Edith again, who stared back at me through her too-human eyes. Abruptly I realised I couldn't – no, *wouldn't* – kill her. I tucked the knife into the waistband of my dress and opened the pen gate.

"I'm not doing it." I heard the pig grunting just behind my ankles, snuffling cautiously towards the open gate. I should have darted through and slammed it shut quick. Instead, I took a small step out of her way and held it open.

Edith bolted out like a streak of pink lightning.

Instantly, that dreadful place blossomed into beautiful chaos. Two of the men moved to block the pig, but they got in each other's way and it eluded them. Esther leapt on top of it, but it squirmed out of her grip and left her sprawled on her hands and knees in the dirt. I rushed to help her to her feet.

"You'll bring that pig back," shouted the overseer as the pig fled through the archway, "or you'll pay for it."

"Damn it, girl, look what you've gone and done!" Esther hurried off after the pig, and I hurried off after Esther.

She pursued it out through the yard and – to my horror and delight – right out onto Briggate. It weaved through a crowd of squealing parasol-wielding ladies, ran into the road – narrowly avoiding a tramcar, whose horse shied up in alarm – and upset an overladen manservant, scattering armfuls of fancy boxes across the cobbles.

Esther took a deep breath and hollered, *"Stop that pig!"* When no-one seemed inclined to do so, she blasphemed loudly, hitched up her skirts, and sprinted off after it herself.

It was hard to decide which of them caused the more turmoil as one thumped down the street after the other. I found myself joined at the lane end by several of the slaughterhouse hands, all laughing and cheering at the progress of Edith and Esther. We followed a little to keep them in sight as they barrelled straight across the busy junction with Boar Lane, under the railway bridge, and finally disappeared around the corner onto – rather appropriately – Swinegate.

The entertainment was over. The zig-zag scar of chaos they'd cut down Briggate began to heal. The overseer ushered the slaughterhouse men back to work in good spirits, and I drifted with more uncertainty back to Tenterhook Yard.

It was an hour before Esther returned, rising up the staircase like some dreadful sea monster emerging from the ocean waves. She puffed and billowed, her skin shining with sweat and her dress streaked with mud. Strands of hair had worked loose from her tight bun and hung limply down from her head like seaweed. She stopped rigid when she caught sight of me and fixed me with a wordless glower.

"Good afternoon, Esther. Did you enjoy your pig hunting expedition?" Her left eye twitched. "Can I make you a cup of tea? You look like you could use one." She made a faint growling sound deep in her throat. "I'll take that as a yes. Did you find dear Edith?"

She raised a hand, pointing at me with one shaking finger. "You," she said in a voice like a breaking storm, "owe me a pig."

Esther didn't talk to me very much over the next few days, and I worried in silence about the coming examination. Refusing to kill Esther's practice pig had carried very little consequence, but if I refused to kill the Society's pig then I'd be giving up on my career. There was nothing for it: I'd just have to grit my teeth and do it. But my thoughts and nightmares alike were haunted by entreating pig eyes, and knives, and squeals, and squirting hot blood.

I was fretting harder than ever when I finally arrived in London, stepping onto the platform at King's Cross to find Francis waiting for me. He carried a large box and a wide grin.

"Caroline!" he called, embracing me warmly. "Welcome to the Metropolis."

"Good Lord, Francis. What is that thing on your head?"

"This, little sister, is a top hat."

"Are you wearing it to look taller, or to make your head look bigger?"

"A little of both. But mostly because I've realised that one of the best ways to get anywhere in life is to look like you're already there."

"Ah, so you're dressing like a nob because you intend to become one?"

"Not exactly, but I do intend to become fabulously rich."

"Much progress on that so far?"

"Not much. I spent half my riches on this hat."

"And the other half?"

He patted the box under his arm. "On a present for my little sister."

"Ooh! Gimme!"

"Such ladylike grace," he said as he handed it over.

I threw it open. Inside was a dress, which I frowned at as I unfolded. It wasn't my sort of thing at all. It was muted and dreary – matronly, even – with no colours beyond black and dark grey. It was obviously a high-quality garment, but it had a total lack of frills, decoration or other ornament. The sort of dress worn by a lady who never smiled.

"I asked Mother for your measurements, then added a bit for how much you've fattened out over the last couple of years. Looking at you now, I'm worrying I didn't add enough."

"It's... um..."

"It should make you look like a no-nonsense middle-aged blackshroud."

"I'd've preferred something to make me look like a young, glamorous blackshroud, I must admit."

"No-one wants youth and glamour in a blackshroud. You're altogether too young and full of nonsense by half. Wear this for your interview tomorrow and hopefully they won't notice."

"You're right. It's perfect. Thank you so much! I shall change into it immediately."

"A lady stripping down in the middle of a busy railway terminus is frowned upon here in the capital, my dear provincial little sister. Perhaps I should see you to your accommodation?"

He led me down to an unpleasantly crowded, unpleasantly smoky underground railway for a ride to Moorgate Street station. We emerged into the heaving thoroughfares of the City of London.

"Francis?" I said some minutes later as we dodged through a mad hurly-burly of men and horses clattering in every conceivable direction.

"I know. You're going to say how terribly grand it all is compared to dreary old Yorkshire, aren't you?"

I *had* been going to say something of the sort, but decided not to give him the satisfaction of guessing me. "No. I was going to remind you of your school days. How you used to hide your sandwiches under your hat to try and stop the other children from finding and pinching them."

"Ah, you think I'm growing above myself and need reminding of my humble roots?"

"No, I was just wondering how much food you could hide under *that* hat. I'm imagining a whole roast chicken and all the trimmings."

"My little sister is hungry?"

"Your little sister is ravenous."

"Well I'm sorry to disappoint, but these days my hat hides nothing but air and hair. However, I do know an acceptable yet marvellously affordable restaurant."

Francis dined me, and wined me, and provided such good cheerful company all evening that I quite forgot to worry about the next day's examination. In fact it barely entered my head at all, until the morning dawned and I found myself standing in front of the stark grandeur of Blackshrouds' Hall in my dreary new dress.

"I'd tell you to knock them dead," Francis said as we embraced farewell, "but it seems a little too appropriate."

The inside of the hall also seemed a little too appropriate. Its architect had clearly been inspired to give the space the feel of a mausoleum, and nobody had had the good sense to stop him. Polished but muted granite columns framed a series of wreathed stone urns around the walls. Daylight pierced that space in only a few mournful beams. Even the door handles were unfortunately reminiscent of coffin handles. As I approached the reception desk, which looked like nothing so much as a sarcophagus, I found my voice automatically dropping into a respectful whisper.

I was shown into a small anteroom where another candidate already waited. She was none other than Selina Abbott,

Blackshroud Ambrose's apprentice from my aunt Adeline's passing.

"Miss Summers! Or may I call you Caroline?" And then, without waiting for an answer, "it's so good to meet you again, Caroline! It warms my heart to see your simple, honest face in this dark metropolis."

I opened my mouth to protest that I wasn't at all "simple", but she hadn't finished yet.

"I *must* apologise for my manners last time we met. I was ever so rude about your mistress, wasn't I?"

"Think nothing of it. I've said much worse."

"I mean, I do understand there's a need for people like you and her. We can't *all* have the quality patients."

I opened my mouth again, but didn't find the words to fill it.

"I *do* hope we can be the best of friends," she said, holding out a hand with a disarming smile. I took it, warily. She beamed at me.

"I'm surprised you're not qualified already. Weren't you eighteen months into an apprenticeship when we first met? And that was a year ago."

She looked suddenly uncomfortable. "Well... to be honest, this isn't my first attempt to qualify."

"It isn't?"

"No. The Society is *very* selective. It's not unusual to fail the first time around." She reached over to pat my hand. "Don't you give up if you don't make it. It's quite alright if it takes *you* three, or four, even five tries."

I pulled my hand away sharply. "So you've done this before? You know what happens?"

"Oh yes. There's an interview, and then a practical test. There'll be three on the panel, but only one of them matters."

"How so?"

"I'll show you."

She opened the door and beckoned me out. It was a long, straight corridor, and at one end a portrait of the queen glowered down it, bearing – I couldn't help but notice – a passing resemblance to Esther. Looking the other way, a portrait of another lady glowered right back, as though trapped in a staring match from which neither would flinch. She had a thin angular face, pursed lips, and eyes as grey and hard as millstone grit.

"That," said Selina, "is Blackshroud Rokeby. They say that no blackshroud in England for the last thirty years has been allowed to practise without her say-so. The other two panel members are window dressing. She's the one you need to impress."

We returned to the anteroom.

"So what happened last time?" I asked. "Didn't you impress her?"

"Oh, I'm *sure* I impressed in the interview. But I lost my nerve a little on the practical."

"Ah yes. The pig."

"What do you—" but she never finished the sentence, as at that moment the door opened and Selina was called in.

"Good luck," she said as we embraced farewell. "I'm *so* sorry you have to go after me. I intend to dazzle, and I'm afraid I might cast you in quite a poor shadow afterwards."

"Good luck, Selina," I said through gritted teeth.

Then I had an hour to wait and worry and damn Esther several times over for calling it a "formality" before I was called in myself. The interview took place in a small, dark-timbered hall that looked like it belonged to an older part of the building. Blackshroud Rokeby sat perched straight-backed and severe on a dais behind a carved oaken screen, peering down at me with the same slightly contemptuous expression I'd already seen in her portrait. I thought there was a slightly pained look, too, in her face that hadn't been captured in the painting, but that might just have been the after-effect of an hour's conversation with Selina Abbott.

On her left and right were sat two white-haired ladies on slightly lower seats, introduced as Blackshrouds Smith and Smyth, although I was unclear which was which.

"Name?" asked one of the two.

"Caroline Summers."

"And the name of your mistress?"

"Esther Cartwright of Leeds."

At this point Smith (or possibly Smyth) blinked twice and leaned over to whisper in Rokeby's ear, just loud enough that I could hear, *"Bloody Esther."*

"Ah." Rokeby's lips pursed a little tighter. *"Her."*

And with that unpromising start, the interview began. The one I had – correctly or incorrectly – mentally labelled Smyth did most of the talking, while Smith took notes. Rokeby sat without speaking, studying me as though I were an interesting microbe caught under a microscope.

There were three tiers of questions. The first was about who I was, my background and motivation, to make sure I was the respectable sort of person they were looking for. I answered these honestly, and even got some nods of approval from Smith and Smyth when I described my training in the General Infirmary, although Rokeby never indicated the slightest approval of anything. The second tier was about my blackshroud's education, to make sure I'd had one. I answered most of these questions more creatively, trying to make Esther sound like the very model of a mistress and educator. Rokeby stared down at me with what I imagined to be dark amusement, as though she knew every mistruth for exactly what it was.

The final tier concerned the delicate tangle of laws surrounding our profession. Here I stumbled badly. It wasn't that I didn't understand the subject, although I probably didn't understand it quite as well as I should have done. But both Esther and the *Modern Guide* had taught it in plain English, and the interview wrong-footed me with unfamiliar words and Latin phrases. More than once I found myself gaping like a goldfish before babbling incoherently around the subject, watching Rokeby's brows furrow deeper and deeper.

Finally, when Smyth had wrapped up her questioning, Rokeby added one question of her own.

"How, Miss Summers, would you best summarise the role of a blackshroud as you see it?"

I hesitated, seriously considering for a moment whether I should parrot Esther's line about "showing folks a shortcut to Hell". I thought better.

"A blackshroud's role is to give people a good death."

Smith and Smyth nodded in agreement, but Rokeby looked almost as disgusted as Esther had been, so I frantically appended, "Or at least, as good a death as possible. Because no death is good, but death *is* inevitable, and some deaths are much worse than others. And the death a blackshroud offers is better than most."

She eyed me stonily. "You should work on your answer to that question. Bear in mind that your duty is not merely to act as a practitioner of our profession, but as a defender."

"I'm sorry. I wasn't aware that it needed defending."

"It *always* needs defending. Those who have benefited from it cannot speak on its behalf, so it falls upon us." She looked left and right, to check if Smith or Smyth had further questions. They didn't. "Very well. That concludes the interview. We shall now proceed to the practical."

My heart thudded, but I pulled myself up straight and affected calmness. I felt that after that interview, I was going to have to make an impression in the practical to retain any chance of passing. "I'm ready," I said. "Hand me a knife and show me to the pig."

Rokeby raised an eyebrow. "The *what?*"

"The pig," I repeated, a little less certainly. "The one I have to kill."

There was an uncomfortable silence. "We do *not* kill pigs."

"You... don't do that any more?"

"We have *never* done that."

I looked from face to face and all three were looking down with the same odd expression, as though trying to decide if I were making some poor attempt at humour or if I were just an honest imbecile. I felt myself shrink under their combined gaze, while a small part of my brain was already planning just what unpleasant things I was going to do to Esther Cartwright when I got back home.

Rokeby shook her head as though to shake my nonsense out of it, and stood up. "For the practical test, you shall kill *me*. Your tools shall not be a knife, but those typical of our profession." She stepped down and gestured to a side table, where was laid out – I'd previously failed to notice – a set of scales, a glass, a spoon, and a small bottle of white powder. She sat down rigidly on a high-backed wooden chair beside the table. "Pretend I am your patient. Begin."

I eyed the bottle suspiciously. "Is that really—"

"No, of *course* it's not."

"Right. Alright." I glanced at the bottle, at Rokeby in her chair, and at the other two ladies watching over at us, and wondered where to begin.

"So, Blackshroud Rokeby," I said, taking a seat. "Why do you want to die?"

She stared at me stonily. "The function of a blackshroud is to terminate their patients, not to engage them in idle chatter."

"With respect, that's completely incorrect."

There was a tense silence, while Rokeby stared at me inscrutably. She nodded slightly, and I let out the breath I'd been holding.

"Good," she said. "You do know *something*, at least."

"So could you please explain why you wish to die?"

"Certainly not."

"No?"

"No."

"Then I'm afraid I can't help you." I pushed my chair back and stood up. Smith and Smyth – who'd been making notes – both stopped writing abruptly.

Rokeby remained seated. "There is nothing in the laws of England or the rules of this Society that requires a patient to explain themselves, Miss Summers."

"Actually, there is."

"Then may I recommend that you read our rules more carefully?"

"I have. They tell me I have a moral duty to ensure you've fully considered the consequences, and the alternatives. I can hardly do so if you don't offer your reasons. So I'm afraid I must insist."

She closed her eyes and nursed her temples, a gesture reminiscent of Esther when one of her headaches was coming on."Very well. If only to allow this test to reach a conclusion before I die of natural causes, I'll provide an explanation."

I sat back down.

"I'm suffering from an ailment, a sort of rot slowly consuming me from the inside out. It is incurable, and will surely fell me within the next few years, if not the next few months. It already causes me great pain, and I wish to avoid the greater pain to come, and the indignity of a slow wasting."

"Thank you. I'm sorry to hear about your condition. May I remark that you don't look to be ill, or in pain."

"Showing pain is for infants and the feeble-minded."

I disagreed, but chose not to argue the point. "Let's talk about your situation. Are there people around you to nurse you in your sickness?"

We talked back and forwards, exploring her prospects for living. I refused to let the conversation end until she satisfied me that she understood those prospects, yet was still resolved to die.

"If you're ready, shall we proceed?"

"I was ready ten minutes ago."

I stood up and addressed Smith and Smyth. "I'm afraid I must ask you two ladies to leave the room."

"*What?*" snapped Rokeby.

"Only the blackshroud and her patient may be present in the room during the terminal service."

"Smith and Smyth are your assessment panel, Miss Summers. How are they supposed to assess you if they aren't even present?"

"I can see the inconvenience, but I must insist. The sanctity clause is inviolable."

"For Heaven's sake, this is ridiculous."

I dug my heels in, and Rokeby yielded with a sigh, gesturing to the other two ladies to make themselves scarce. They shuffled out in confused silence.

"*Now* will you finally give me the draught?"

"Patience. There's a little paperwork to fill out first."

She looked visibly disappointed; I think she'd been looking forward to laying into me for neglecting the paperwork. No papers or pen had been laid out on the table, presumably to encourage me to forget, but she reluctantly pointed out one of the standard books of forms, an ink pot and a pen concealed inside a small cabinet. She did get a small smirk of triumph when I had to recall Smith and Smyth from their premature dismissal, to witness her signature.

When we were alone again, she said, "You remind me of your mistress. She was obstinate too. Only candidate I ever had who demanded an upfront fee."

"But you passed her."

"Obstinacy is a virtue in a blackshroud."

"So you'll pass me?"

"First let's see if you can make up a dose of the draught without bumbling it."

I prepared the dosage (thirty-five grains) without bumbling, and sat beside her with the glass in my hand.

"There's no rush to drink this," I said, slipping back into the fiction of blackshroud and patient. "You can still change your mind, even now. And if there's anything you want to talk about, we can do that, for as long as you need before—"

"Let's just get on with it, shall we?" And she snatched the glass from me, raised it to her lips, tipped it back and drained it dry.

I tried to hold her hand but she whipped it away from me in annoyance, so I settled for sitting there in respectful silence. I maintained my quiet presence while she did a very good impression of slipping into a final sleep. As the minutes ticked by, I started to wonder at what point the test ended. I understood that part of a blackshroud's job was to be still and quiet at the end, and not to impose herself on her patient's final moments. I waited until enough time had passed that any real patient would certainly have been unconscious. And then I waited some more. Growing impatient, I ventured to whisper, "Blackshroud?"

She didn't respond. Realising she'd genuinely fallen asleep, I shook her shoulder gently. "Blackshroud?"

No response. A horrible suspicion opened up beneath me, and I dipped one finger into the dregs in her glass. I touched the wet finger to my tongue, and then spat at the familiar taste.

"Oh, bugger."

An hour later, I found myself in front of a panel formed of Smith, Smyth and various others of the Society, for the second time in my short career forced to explain my role in the unexpected death of a blackshroud. It became clear that Rokeby had switched the harmless salt usually used to test applicants with the real draught while preparing the room between Selina's interview and my own. The jar of salt was found locked inside her own personal office, so there seemed little doubt of that. However, nobody seemed to understand *why*. She'd left no note to explain herself, and had told nobody of her intentions. Personally, I think that the reason she gave me – that she had some terminal disease eating away at her – was likely to be true. Probably her doctor could have confirmed this; however, whatever enquiries were made in the matter after that day, I never heard the result of them.

In some ways, Rokeby's death was quite unremarkable. It had been properly consented, and witnessed by two eminent members of the Society, no less. The only legal irregularity was that the draught had been administered by someone who was *not* yet a qualified blackshroud. But that irregularity was quite enough to warrant a coroner's inquest of some magnitude. Although the Society seemed certain that an inquest would attach no blame to anyone, they were still very keen to avoid the whole business; or, more to the point, to avoid the inevitable scandal whipped up in the newspapers.

A simple solution was found. I was immediately sworn in as a blackshroud. The date on my certificate reads May 12th, 1875, and there's absolutely nothing to indicate that it was granted two hours *after* Rokeby's death on that same date, rather than two hours *before*. Then they ushered me out the door, making it very clear that I should keep the precise timings to myself if I knew what was good for me.

I stood on the steps outside Blackshroud's Hall, with my rolled certificate in one hand and my new dove-and-dagger brooch in the other, trying to blink away a dizzying sense of unreality. I was still feeling numb the next afternoon when my train pulled into Central Station, and the familiar foulness of the Leeds air brought me somewhat back to my senses.

To my surprise, I found Father waiting for me on the platform.

"Francis sent a telegram," he explained. "May I offer my congratulations." We shook hands, stiffly, as though I were a new and uncertain acquaintance instead of his own daughter.

80

It turned out he'd deposited Mother in a moderately expensive restaurant nearby, to which he now escorted me, lapsing into uncomfortable silence on the way after a couple of attempts at small talk floundered badly.

"It's not just your mother," he whispered as we entered. "I thought it best we invite..." and instead of speaking the name he just gestured with a quick flash of his hand, over to the corner where – to my horror – Esther was sitting with Mother.

I say *with* her, but in fact they were stretching the limit of how far two people could sit apart while still be said to share the same table. Esther had lurked her chair right back into the corner, where she sat looking suspiciously at the laced and jacketed diners, as out of place as a dripping sandwich on a tray of fancy cakes. Mother – frilled and bustled up in her very best dress – was perched on the edge of her seat, itself pulled well away from the opposite side of the table, so that she could almost be mistaken for being part of the party at the next table instead of her own.

"Miriam," Father said to Mother as he sat down beside her. He nodded at Esther. "Blackshroud."

"Did they fail you, then?" Esther asked as I took my seat half-way between them.

"No thanks to you, Esther, but no, they didn't."

"*Caroline!*" Father interjected. "That's no way to speak to your mistress."

"Then why aren't you wearing your brooch?" Esther asked me, carefully ignoring him.

I slid the shining silver dove and dagger out of my purse. It felt cold and alien in my fingers.

Father cleared his throat. "I'm sure there's a better time and a place for that."

"Bollocks." Esther jabbed a thumb at her own brooch, proudly perched on her bosom as always. "A blackshroud wears her brooch at any time and place. Unless you're ashamed of your calling?"

I pinned it to my dress, just above my left breast, looking defiantly at Father as I did so. The effect was rather spoiled by my pinning it on upside-down, but that was soon rectified.

The meal progressed exquisitely slowly. The conversation made several valiant efforts to establish itself, but inevitably ran into intractable obstacles before it could really begin.

Father stared at Esther stuffing a whole Yorkshire pudding into her mouth with her hand and then licking the gravy off her fingers, an act she would have scolded me for severely if I'd tried such a thing in Tenterhook Yard. "Caroline," he said, "I must admit that I've had some misgivings abut your choice of career. But please promise me that if you must be a blackshroud, you'll be a *respectable* sort of blackshroud?"

Esther's hands landed on the table with a bang that made the china shake. "What other sort is there, Summers?"

At this point Mother showed a sudden vocal interest in the salt cellar – wasn't it a fine piece? – which defused the situation nicely, and we returned to a safely stony silence.

"So," said Esther at last, "is that old hag Rokeby still terrorising candidates?"

"She... was," I said, choosing my tense carefully.

"*Was?* What's that supposed to mean?"

"I helped her die."

She guffawed, showering small fragments of her meal across the table. "Everyone who's earned her dove in the last thirty years has finished off Rokeby. The woman who *actually* does for her one day will go down in legend."

"That's what I'm trying to say. I did *actually* do for her. I gave her the draught."

"For Christ's sake, girl, is there pudding between your ears? That's just sugar or something. She's bloody good at pretending to die, she's done it so many times. Sometimes she lies real still for a real long time, so the candidate starts to think she's actually snuffed it and gets themselves in a panic. Then she sits up right as rain and tells them off for losing their calm. Tried to pull that on me. I gave her a prod and she yelped like a seal."

"But she wasn't pretending. She was really, really, dead."

"Caroline," said Father, "what have we told you about telling tall tales?"

"Lying's an important skill for a blackshroud," said Esther. "Rokeby herself told me that. But save it for the patients."

"None of you believe me, do you?" I stood up, pushing my chair back. "Fine. Wait here. I'll prove it."

I rushed outside and quickly found what I'd been looking for: a boy selling the latest London paper. I bought a copy and returned to the restaurant, clearing the crockery into a compact pile to let me spread it out on the table.

"Obituaries." I scanned the listings, hoping the writers had been as fast off the mark as they usually were. "Here!" I jabbed triumphantly with a finger. "'We regret to announce the death of Blackshroud Angelina Rokeby, aged 74, yesterday in the City of London.' I *told* you so!"

"Good God, she really is dead." Esther snatched the paper and squinted at it. "'One of the most distinguished and respected of English blackshrouds,' and most hated, too, but they didn't write *that*, 'she served as chief examiner to the Worshipful Society from 1846 until her death, and is widely credited with increasing standards of professionalism within that worthy company, and helping to maintain its good reputation.' What nonsense."

"Skip to the end!" I snapped. "What does it say about *me?*"

"Here we are. 'Rokeby passed away peacefully yesterday afternoon at Blackshroud's Hall, after examining two final candidates that very day. The blackshroud who attended her passing wishes to remain anonymous, but the Worshipful Society has confirmed she was one of her many former candidates.'"

"'*Wishes to remain anonymous*'?"

Esther's lips warped into something resembling a smile. "Someone once told me that good service is its own reward."

"Hell with that."

"*Caroline!*" Father snapped. "Language!"

Esther pushed her chair back with a screech and rose to her feet. "Thank you for the meal, Mr Summers, Mrs Summers. Bloody generous of you. Girl, congratulations, although I never had the least doubt you *would* pass. I mean, they passed *me*, they were hardly going to fail *you*."

"Thanks, Esther."

"Here. I've got something for you." She pulled an item out of her pocket and plonked it unceremoniously on the table. I picked it up. It was a silver lady's pocket watch, already wound and ticking. I opened the cover to find the letters "C. S." engraved on the inside in florid script.

"I..." I looked up at her and didn't know what to say. After fifteen months of her loudly begrudging every halfpenny she'd had to spend on me, the last thing I'd expected from her was a gift, much less such a generous one.

"It's not a toy," she said. "It's for recording time of death."

"It's beautiful." I stood up and embraced her, making her grunt in displeasure. "Thank you, Esther."

She extracted herself from my arms, and then she completely spoiled the moment by saying, "Only thing is, if you run into the family of Catherine Seabrook who I did for last month in Holbeck, I'd keep that watch out of sight."

My hand tightened around the watch. "*What?*"

My father got to his feet. "Are you trying to say, Blackshroud, that you *stole* this watch from a dead woman?"

"I'm sure I'm not trying to say nothing." She gave a stiff wobble of a curtsey. "Sir. Ladies." And with that she headed for the door. Just as she was about to disappear into the street she called out over her shoulder so that everyone in the restaurant could hear, "And, girl? You still owe me a pig."

Father stood blinking and gaping for a few seconds. "What a repugnant woman."

At that moment, I found it hard to disagree.

Later, as I sat with my parents on an evening train back to Wetherby, Father said, "Really, I feel we should buy you something ourselves, to celebrate your success. Something more appropriate than a pilfered pocket watch."

"I'm never averse to presents. What did you have in mind?"

"Why don't you tell us what you'd most like? Whatever it is, we'll buy it for you."

"Well, there is one thing..."

"Anything."

"Like Blackshroud Cartwright said, I do owe her a pig."

Father blinked at me. "A *pig?*"

"Yes, a pig. Fat pink thing with trotters."

"I know what a pig is. I'd assumed that was some grotesque attempt at humour."

"No."

"You seriously expect me to buy that woman a pig?"

"As a gift to me. You *did* say anything."

Father and Mother exchanged looks. "Well..."

"Thank you, Father. I *do* appreciate it. Just deliver it to her surgery in Tenterhook Yard. Perhaps tie a ribbon around its neck, to make it pretty."

My parents allowed the rest of the journey to pass in a dazed silence, while I sat happily imagining the scene when my Father turned up at Esther's door to hand over a pig. It was wonderfully difficult to decide which of them would enjoy the moment the least.

Sadly, I never got to witness this occasion first-hand. I accompanied Father next time he came to Leeds, but left him to negotiate the pig's purchase while I went down to Holbeck to call on the widower of Catherine Seabrook.

"Miss... Summers, was it?" He squinted down at my brooch. "Blackshroud Summers, sorry?"

"I'm sorry to intrude at this time, Mr Seabrook. How are you?"

"Not too well, since you ask." He shrugged. "But, a bit better each week. I miss my Catherine wretchedly, but I'm glad she's at peace. Won't you come in?"

"No, I shan't bother you any longer than necessary. I just came round because Blackshroud Cartwright discovered an item in her bag that doesn't belong to her, which she thinks she may have accidentally removed from your house while she was tending to Catherine. She's aghast at the incident, and has sent me round to return the object and to offer her most sincere apologies." I offered him the pocket watch. "I believe this belonged to your wife."

He took it and looked at it carefully. He flipped it over, opened it, closed it, then handed it back.

"I've never seen this before."

"You haven't?"

"No. I can see why you thought it was Catherine's, what with her initials in it. But my Catherine never had anything like that."

"Are you sure?"

"Sure as we're standing here. Heck, I can't afford a thing like that. It's a right nice piece, that, and it looks brand new."

"Thank you for your honesty, Mr Seabrook. I'm sorry again for troubling you."

"No trouble, ma'am. I hope you find the owner."

I stood for a few moments in the street, gazing at the silver watch and its inscription.

"Damn it, Esther," I said to nobody in particular.

Chapter 6

During my apprenticeship, I'd hazily imagined that once qualified I'd instantly start practising. Instead, I went to live with my parents in Wetherby for three frustrating months.

The problem was, as usual, money. Money to rent premises, money to hire an assistant, money to buy the safe in which the draught must be stored. I didn't have any money. And my parents, who might just have scraped it together, were unwilling to fund a career which they'd much rather I gave up to pursue a respectable marriage.

I was unpleasantly reminded of the days before I'd first left home, only things seemed even more stifling now I'd tasted the wider world. The exhausting discipline of the Infirmary and the frustrations of Tenterhook Yard both began to look like lost golden years. For all my complaints about Nurse Haines, and then about Esther, at least neither had treated me like an incapable child. Slowly, inevitably, to my own disgust, I found myself acting like one too, to fit the part my parents had written for me.

I had to do *something*. And when Mother started discussing the merits of various boring but available local bachelors over lunch, I realised that something had to be done *quickly*. I found my escape in the very same place I had last time: in an advert in the newspaper.

"The Leeds Board of Guardians is looking for a blackshroud."

Mother, who'd been pouring tea, spilt a few drops over the table. "The Board of Guardians? You are *not* working in..." she dropped into a whisper to finish the sentence, as though afraid the neighbours might overhear... "the *workhouse*."

"It's not just the workhouse. It's the infirmary too."

"The *workhouse* infirmary, Caroline, the *workhouse* infirmary!" She sat down, as though the strain of saying the word *workhouse* three times within a minute had stretched her to breaking point.

"It's worth considering. Something to get me on my feet. They're offering a decent salary, as well as room and board."

"Room and board... you don't mean you'd be *living* in the... in the..." Her face turned doily white.

I think Mother had imagined me sleeping and eating amongst the paupers, but of course she was quite mistaken. My room on the second floor was small, but it was private. It had the same strong scent of carbolic soap as the rest of the building, and the same feeling of well-scrubbed austerity; the only decoration was an embroidered panel on one wall, reading, "FAITH ~ HOPE ~ CHARITY". I didn't see a single inmate on my first night until a woman arrived at my door with a silver tray. The tray bore steaming meat, potatoes and gravy on blue and white china. The woman was a thin, bent creature in a blue and white petticoat.

"Why, thank you," I said. "Care to tarry a while? I'm new here, and I'd love someone to fill me in on the workings of this place."

She didn't care to tarry. She thrust the tray into my hands as though feeding a man-eating tiger, and beat a hasty retreat.

The master called on me the next morning after breakfast. He was a tall man who loomed in the small room, his shoulders neatly hiding the "FAITH ~ HOPE ~ CHARITY" panel from sight.

"I trust your accommodation is satisfactory?"

"Perfectly."

"Good. Here's your schedule for today." He handed me a slip of paper. It contained half a dozen names, with room numbers.

"What's this?"

"Your patients."

"*Six* of them? Already?"

"A backlog built up while we waited your arrival."

"A *backlog?* If people were in distress, shouldn't a private blackshroud have been called in immediately?"

He sniffed. "Their condition was not sufficiently urgent to justify the expenditure."

"With greatest respect, sir, questions of expenditure should surely be secondary?"

He was a dark-eyed, heavy-browed man, and he put both of those features to good use as he gave me a long, hard stare. "This is a public institution. Questions of expenditure are never secondary."

He left me to prepare. I laid out the tools of my new trade across my desk, and mentally ticked them off one by one as I placed them into my bag. A handsomely bound green book for recording consent. A smaller, black-bound book for recording deaths. A plain glass tumbler. A set of tiny silver measuring spoons. A flask of water. And, most importantly, a small blue vial containing a few doses of the draught.

I clipped my bag shut, adjusted my brooch and looked myself in the mirror. Blackshroud Summers looked back at me. At that moment the reality of my new profession hung heavy around my neck. My black book had nothing but crisp clean pages, but before the day was out it would have six deaths memorialised within. Six lives snuffed out. Six human beings turned into lifeless corpses at my own hand. Panic rose in my chest. This wasn't me. I wasn't the kind of person who could do that. Was I?

Below, a bell rang through the workhouse: the paupers were called to their morning labours. The rumble of shuffling footsteps and hushed voices drifted gently up from two stories below; the bang of doors and scrape of chairs as they filed into their day rooms like the groanings of some dusty old machine sputtering wearily into slow action.

I had my own labours to attend to. Picking up my bag and straightening my shoulders, I stepped out of the door.

The first name on my list was Anne Wilson. A poor working woman her whole life, she'd lost her husband and last two children in a single outbreak of cholera. Already of declining health, with no-one to support her, she'd had no choice but to resign herself to the mercy of the workhouse. After a couple of years of labour, her deteriorating condition led her to be struck off the "able-bodied" list and laid up in one of the invalid dormitories, to be fed, turned and toileted by the attendants on their rounds. And now she was passing beyond even their care, and needed mine.

She was a pitiful creature by the time I met her. Sores and ulcers covered her legs, and a nasty cough would make her face crease up in pain every time it came on. She'd asked to die an astonishing three weeks ago, since which she'd been lying there in obvious and increasing misery. Now I was come and she'd been moved to a private place for her last moments: a cramped storage room, with her bed wedged haphazardly into a narrow space between tall shelves of white linen. In her place, I'd have felt the right to be somewhat aggrieved at life. But Mrs Wilson accepted her end with the same good-natured resignation she'd borne all her burdens.

"Your hand's shaking," she said in a frail whisper as I prepared her last drink.

"Sorry." I perched myself on an upturned pail that was the best bedside seat I could engineer, the glass in my hand. "I'm just a little nervous. This is actually my first time doing this."

"Don't you fret now, love. It's my first time too, don't you know?" And she actually managed a reassuring smile.

God bless Mrs Wilson. I can only hope that when my own end comes I'll show a fraction of her courage and composure.

She drank, said a meek "thank you" and a small prayer, and quietly expired while I held her hand. Or perhaps she was holding mine. It seems absurd for a blackshroud to be comforted by their patient instead of the other way round, but there we were.

There was no time to rest and gather my thoughts. It was straight on to the next name on the list. And the next, and the next, and the next. And each of those names turned out to belong to a person, a person with their own history, their own treasured memories, their own sorrows, every bit as vital and human as Anne Wilson, or as Caroline Summers. And one after the other I got to know those people, listened to their lamentations, calmed their fears as best I could, and watched them die. Then they became once more nothing but a name: a timed and dated record in my black book; a crossed-out entry in the workhouse register.

It was late when I reported to attend the sixth and final name, and I was feeling shaky and thin. I admit to feeling the most intense relief when they told me he'd already passed away.

The next day was easier. There was no more backlog to clear. In fact, there was only one job for me the whole day: a woman had asked to record her advance consent, in case her condition deteriorated. She wasn't in the workhouse but in the new Union Infirmary next door. A nurse was tending her when I arrived on the ward, and I couldn't help but observe her work with a critical eye.

"Aren't you going to clean that, Nurse?"

"Yes ma'am, right away ma'am," she said instantly in a fluster, before turning around and looking at my brooch in some confusion. "Ma'am? But... if you think it best, ma'am?"

"Unless you want to do my job for me. What's your name?"

"Millicent Barden, ma'am." She bobbed a nervous curtsey and glanced around as though searching for rescue.

"And where did you train, Miss Barden?"

"Train, ma'am?" she said in a panicked squeak.

It was then that I noticed the familiar blue and white striped petticoat beneath her apron. "You're from the workhouse?"

She looked at her feet. "Yes, ma'am."

"But... why are you nursing this woman?"

She dropped to her knees. "Please, ma'am, don't say anything to the matron if I've done wrong. I'm only doing the work they set me, ma'am, and I'm trying me best, honest I am."

I looked around the hospital with a sharper eye after that, and noticed that Millicent wasn't the only nurse plucked from the workhouse. They *all* were.

"Yes of course we have inmate nurses," snapped the medical superintendent when I raised my concerns. "We also have inmate cleaners, inmate porters and inmate clerks. And if it were legal to have an inmate blackshroud, then by God, we'd have one of those as well."

I ate in a little space off the kitchen, rather than at the back of the dining hall with the other staff. It was my duty, the master had made clear, to keep out of sight as far as possible, so as not to spook the residents. I'd been glad when the chaplain, the Reverend John Gilder, volunteered to join me in my culinary exile, until his sermonising began to taint the taste of my food.

"This workhouse is an exemplary institution. Christian charity put into action. I'm immensely proud to serve here. I hope you will be too."

I stabbed a piece of meat pudding with more force than necessary. "From what I've seen of the state of your charges, you don't have much to be proud of."

"On the contrary. We give them things they never could have hoped for outside." He counted the paupers' blessings out on his fingers. "A regular diet. Sanitary lodgings. Medical care. A safe and well-ordered environment. Good honest work to keep away the Devil's idleness."

"Rather too much of the latter, I'd judge, and the bare minimum of the rest."

He jutted his chin out. "Say what you will, but I've seen Godless wretches walk into our doors, and walk out again with their heads held high."

But I remained unconvinced. I heard too much weeping from the dormitories at night. I should mention here, lest you get the wrong impression, that the master wasn't a cruel man. Nor did he tolerate cruelty amongst his staff. But he was a hard man, and his workhouse was a hard place. For some, too hard to bear.

Thomas McGough came to me in November.

"Why do you wish to die, Mr McGough? You don't look ill as far as I can see."

He was a greying middle-aged man with one bad leg, a wheezy cough and a squint. A picture of health by workhouse standards.

"A year I've been inside, and I want out."

"So does everyone here."

"You're the only way out I can see, ma'am."

"There are better ways out of here," I tried to explain. But he shook his head, having none of it. He was convinced beyond all entreaty that he was doomed to the workhouse until the day he died, and that being the case he'd rather the day came sooner than later.

It's one thing to give the draught to someone who's dying or in agony; it's quite another to give it to someone who's neither. I floundered for a way to change his mind.

"I don't think you need to die, Mr McGough."

"You reckon?" He shot me a black look.

"I think what you really need is a steady job and a roof of your own over your head."

"I wouldn't mind a knighthood neither."

"I'm just concerned that you're making a very serious mistake."

"I'm none too interested in your opinion, ma'am, I just want the draught."

"I'm not going to give it to you."

"Oh yeah?" He leapt to his feet, kicking the chair away violently. "And who are you to tell me I have to live?"

I got to my feet too. "I'm doing no such thing. I simply think you're making a hasty decision. I'd ask you to reflect on it for a while. For... let's say a week."

"A *week?*"

"One week. Go away and think it through."

Something snapped in Mr McGough, and he swung his fist. It slammed hard against the wall, leaving cracks in the plaster and blood on his knuckles.

"Do you imagine I haven't thought it through already?" he snarled, before turning on his heel and storming out the door.

His blow had knocked my "FAITH ~ HOPE ~ CHARITY" panel askew. I straightened it.

A week later, to my dismay, he was back, as determined as ever to see his miseries put to an end. Still unwilling to aid him in his suicide, I asked Thomas to wait for longer – a month this time – to try and find a less drastic solution to his problems. He didn't shout or even argue. He just regarded the floor with dead eyes, nodded, and left the room in silence.

As things turned out, I didn't have to wait a month for the next development. The very next day a chorus of screams disrupted my morning routine. I dropped my mirror with a clatter and hurried outside, my hair still in considerable disarray.

The main staircase was crowded with a long spiralling line of inmates from top to bottom, the men in dull green corduroy jackets and the women in blue striped petticoats. All were frozen in place, staring down over the banister, except for a couple of the women who were holding each other and weeping. I busied myself between two of the gawpers and looked down. There, on the tiles two floors below, a green corduroy-clad figure lay sprawled, a circle of scarlet blood expanding by his head.

I hurtled past the whispering paupers at frightening speed, taking the steps three at a time, but by the time I reached the bottom Millicent Barden was already bent over him. She looked up at the gathering crowd and announced, "He's alive!"

Thomas McGough moaned and tried to raise his head. His watery eyes met mine briefly, before scrunching shut in pain.

"I'm sorry," I said to him, pathetically.

The squeak of shoes on tile, and a sudden hush amongst the inmates, announced the approach of the master.

"What's going on here? Blackshroud?"

"Mr McGough fell, sir."

"Fell?"

"Jumped, I believe."

The master nudged Thomas with one polished black shoe, as though he were a dead dog in the street. Thomas groaned.

"Mr Stanley," he said to the porter, who'd just arrived at the scene. "Carry this man into the boardroom. Blackshroud, fetch your poison. Everyone else, proceed to the dining hall. *At once!*"

He clapped his hands twice, and the mass of paupers resumed their shuffle towards breakfast, the stream of them parting to pass either side of Thomas. Millicent lingered to remonstrate quietly in my ear.

"But ma'am... he needs to go to the infirmary!"

The bulky porter picked Thomas up none too gently, eliciting a whimper as he carried him away, leaving an irregular line of red drips across the tiles. I put a hand on Millicent's shoulder.

"He was *trying* to die, Miss Barden. It's best to help him, not frustrate him."

A few minutes later, and Thomas had recovered just enough to nod his consent in front of the master and the porter. A few minutes later still and he escaped the workhouse at last, on top of the boardroom table, with portraits of past and present luminaries of the Board of Guardians gazing down at him munificently from the walls.

After the body had been removed, the master pulled me back into the boardroom. "A word, Blackshroud."

He sat in silence for a few moments, regarding me from under his dark, furrowed brows. I found my eyes dropping to the table, where I noticed a small stain of red blood in the very centre that had been missed by the cleaner. The wood was so smooth and polished that I could clearly see the master's face reflected in it, and the position of the bloodstain made it look as though it were splashed across his forehead. I couldn't help but wonder if, from his perspective, it was splashed across my own.

"Could you explain to me why an inmate I've twice granted permission to speak to you felt the need to take matters into his own hands?"

My skin prickled uncomfortably. "Because on both occasions I asked him to give the matter more consideration, sir. I thought he could be persuaded to live."

"The Board didn't hire you to persuade people to live."

"Sir?"

"This institution spends enough money on inmates who *do* wish to keep breathing, without wasting it on inmates who don't."

"I'm not sure what you're suggesting, sir."

"I'm suggesting that next time an inmate asks for your help, you do what we pay you for and provide it, immediately and without fuss, and perhaps we can avoid future spectacles like this morning's."

That was the moment I decided it was time for me to get out of the workhouse.

"I want a loan to set myself up in private practice," I told a bank manager one cold day in December, with the first snow of the year pattering softly against the windows.

"Blackshrouding, hmm?" He leant back in his green leather chair and steepled his fingers. "Not a bad prospect. Steady demand. And there's certainly room for another blackshroud in Leeds. It's a big investment, though."

"Not so big. And I could start making repayments almost immediately."

He shook his head and tutted. "I'd need to assume you wouldn't turn a profit for the first year; maybe two."

"What? Why wouldn't I? People always need blackshrouds."

"Yes, but a blackshroud earns only in proportion to her reputation. It takes time to build one."

"I'll advertise."

"Miss Summers, may I speak frankly? I can see you have admirable ambition, but you appear to have a very limited understanding of your own trade."

"Excuse me, but I am a fully qualified—"

He cut me off with a hand. "I'm sure you're a very capable professional, but you also need to be a businesswoman. You're very young. Which, incidentally, is a problem in its own right. People prefer age and experience in a blackshroud."

I leant forwards in my seat, placing my palms on his desk. "I can *learn* to be a businesswoman. And time will give me age and experience eventually."

He touched his still-steepled fingers to his chin. "Perhaps. Let me understand where you're starting from. Where did you train?"

"Here in Leeds, with Blackshroud Cartwright."

"Bloody Esther?"

I nodded, feeling my chances of a loan slipping further away from me.

"That's not a good start. Do you have any practical experience, since you qualified?"

"Yes. I'm employed by the Leeds Board of Guardians, since September."

His fingers unsteepled at last. "You're the *workhouse* blackshroud?"

"That's right."

He straightened himself in his chair. "Then we cannot possibly offer you a loan. Far from building your reputation, it seems you've done enormous damage to it already."

I spent the next few weeks in a very low mood. There was a lot to do – a blackshroud is always busier in the winter – but even in that baleful place there wasn't always someone dying. I had a lot of time to myself, pacing my small room or just slouched in my chair, staring at the "FAITH ~ HOPE ~ CHARITY" panel and trying to make the words mean something.

The *Modern Guide to Practical Blackshroudery* was scarcely more helpful. It held every manner of advice on how to go about my job, but not a single sentence on how to cope with it. "A blackshroud is a mountain," it told me. Perhaps I just wasn't stony enough.

I often found myself thinking back to my nursing days, and the room in the eaves I'd shared with Clara, Tabitha and Susan. The gossip, the rude stories, the giggling, all of it. I would have given a lot to spend just one night in that attic room again. The pauper nurses at the Union Infirmary all curtseyed when they saw me and called me "ma'am". Any gossip or giggling stopped dead the moment I walked into the room. Even my fellow members of staff kept a polite distance. I could hardly blame them. No-one really wants to banter with someone whose business is death.

My solitude began to wear heavily on my spirit. I spent a lot of time staring out of my window. Too much. It had, quite unfortunately, a fine view over Burmantofts Cemetery. I could watch the funerals: big showy top-hatted numbers amongst the grand monuments of stone at the top of the hill, or ragged little affairs at the bottom where the destitute were stacked up in unmarked graves. I wondered how many of those latter unfortunates were helped to that end by my own hand.

I wondered a great deal about that sort of thing. I wondered where on that slope from rich to poor I'd be buried when I died, and what sort of monument – if any – would be erected over my grave. I wondered what sort of funeral I'd have, and who would attend, and what they'd say. I wondered if anyone would really be worse off if I was over there in the cemetery instead of over here in the workhouse.

I wondered what it would feel like to have my consciousness slip away under the draught. To feel the last of my thoughts and worries fade into nothingness, and know that I was letting go of them forever. There was something very peaceful about the idea. Something alluring, even.

I was actually holding a bottle in my hands – watching the hypnotic dance of the white grains as I tilted it this way and that – when there was a knock at my door. I quickly stashed the bottle out of sight before answering. Hungry for company as I might have been, I still wasn't entirely pleased to discover the Reverend John Gilder on the other side of it.

After a few forced pleasantries, he came – as usual – to the crux of the matter.

"May I remark that you're looking a few degrees below your usual radiant self?"

I hesitated, on the edge of saying that he was quite mistaken and that I was perfectly fine, thank you, but in the end I said instead, "I feel like I'm dying inside my head."

He frowned. "Physically dying, or spiritually?"

"Spiritually, I suppose."

"Then you're talking to the right man. I can help with that."

I shook my head. "I don't need a sermon. I just... can't abide this place. This job. There's so much death. So little else."

"I know that feeling."

"Do you?"

He nodded. "I was ordained in '66. Just in time for the last great typhus epidemic. My parish covered some of the worst slums in Leeds, and they were thick with it. Quite the baptism of fire, as they say."

"It sounds it."

"Have you ever experienced the slums, Miss Summers? I mean, *really* experienced them? Breathed the congested air? Seen how people live, day after day?"

"I have."

"I hadn't. I came from a privileged family; I had no idea. And so many sick, so many dying. You wouldn't believe how many people there were dying, hidden away in damp cellars and smoky, overcrowded rooms."

"I would. My old mistress, Blackshroud Cartwright, was there. She told me about it. Quite vividly."

"Ah, you're Esther's girl, are you? I should've known. You have something of her straightforward goodness."

"You know Esther?"

"Got to know her all too well back in '66 and '67. When I'd given what spiritual comforts I could, it was Esther following behind to dole out her more effective medicine. And it was Esther who shook me by the shoulders – quite literally – when I said I couldn't keep on doing what I was doing. She told me to get a hold of myself. Reminded me that I didn't have it too bad, compared to the people we were helping.

"So please don't despair, Miss Summers. I know you don't have an easy job, but God knows you have an important one. And things get better. They did for me. God often gives us our greatest tests when we're young, to make sure we're strong enough for a lifetime's service."

He continued talking about God for some time, and my attention drifted. But his words had already had their effect. I felt a little better.

The next day, I got out of my room and had a good productive pace around the grounds. When we were young, Francis had been captivated for a while by the idea of logical reasoning. He'd spent several weeks breaking down every comment and instruction into premises and analysing them. This phase proved most irritating to us all, especially as most of his reasoning seemed contrived to conclude that his own participation in household chores was highly illogical. But I'd learned a few things from him, and I now applied some abductive reasoning to analyse the causes of my own recent malaise. When I got back to my room I wrote them down on a piece of paper:

1. *I don't like this workhouse;*
2. *I'm too idle for my own good, too much of the time;*
3. *I'd like to be able to help people without killing them;*
4. *I'm not happy about what happened to Mr McGough, or about facilitating the suicide of future patients in the same situation;*
5. *I'm lonely.*

The next task was harder: finding a cure to match the diagnosis. In the end I wasn't completely successful. I didn't come up with a viable escape plan from the workhouse. But I did have a plan to partially deal with points two through five, and I hoped that would be enough.

"Sir," I said to the master, cornering him later that week. "I wouldn't mind a word. About any future cases like Mr McGough's."

"I thought I'd already made myself quite clear. You're to respect their wishes. I'm sorry if I made it sound like a cold commercial decision, but I also believe it's the correct Christian course of action. People who are suffering here so extremely should not be forced to linger."

"As a Christian, then, you surely won't object if I ask them to speak to Mr Gilder about it first? He's good at this sort of thing. Better than I am."

"Hmm. I suppose I can't see any objection."

"Thank you. There was another thing. You're aware that before I trained as a blackshroud, I trained as a nurse?"

"Yes. At the General Infirmary, was it not? The medical superintendent would walk hot coals, I've heard him remark, for a few good ladies with that background around his hospital."

"That brings me to my suggestion. You see, I find myself with a fair amount of free time, and—"

"Certainly not."

"I haven't even made the suggestion yet."

"I anticipated it. You *cannot* take up nursing when you're not otherwise engaged, so put it out of your mind. It would be grossly inappropriate to have a blackshroud tending to patients. Quite unthinkable."

"Actually, that wasn't my suggestion. I was going to ask to borrow the inmate nurses from time to time, to give them some basic training."

"Hmmmm." His dark eyes gazed into the distance as he thought it over. "It sounds reasonable. I'll have to run it past the superintendent, of course, but I'm sure he'll find it acceptable."

The superintendent clearly found it highly acceptable, because less than a fortnight later I was delivered my first group of students.

They weren't all pleased to be there. "I've been nursing half my life before I ever set foot in this workhouse," one of them announced. "Why should I take lessons from a blackshroud barely out her crib?"

She had a point. But I held my ground. I *did* have things to teach them. I'd been trained – or at least, half trained – in one of the country's most prestigious hospitals, under the most modern principles of Miss Florence Nightingale. None of my students had been formally trained at all. So I taught, hesitantly and clumsily at first, but gaining confidence as at least some of my audience looked attentive.

Most of the old hands refused to listen, and after a few weeks the superintendent stopped sending them. But others flourished. Millicent Barden, for one, followed my every sentence with an earnest nod and a frown of concentration, and improved dramatically over the course of a few months.

It was during those months that a widow in her thirties, a Mrs Haddock, came to me. Like Thomas McGough before her, she wished to die only to escape her poverty, rather than any physical suffering. I sent her to talk to Mr Gilder, but to my disappointment she came back to me the very next day, saying she was still much of the same mind. I was left with little choice, and provided to Mrs Haddock her final relief.

"Liberty can be a hard thing to administer," Mr Gilder said to me afterwards as the tears dried from my cheeks. "Fundamentally, it's about letting people make their own decisions. And that means letting them make bad decisions too, or you haven't really offered them liberty at all."

My life in the workhouse settled into a steady rhythm. Not a comfortable rhythm, but far from an intolerable one. Then May came around, and the day that changed everything.

It was an occasion a blackshroud usually has no involvement in whatsoever: a funeral. And no ordinary funeral. The deceased was one of the foremost men of the town: an industrialist, a councillor, a chairman of this and that committee, and a long-standing member of the Leeds Board of Guardians. His portrait in the boardroom was one of the largest and most prominent. He was to be buried in Burmantofts Cemetery, opposite the workhouse he'd helped to build, and the master had decided to make a good showing.

By midday, everyone in the whole complex capable of standing on their own two feet was doing so, lining up in the sunshine behind the blacked iron railings that fronted Beckett Street, waiting for the procession to arrive. First the mourners would pass the industrial school, with its poor, pauper and orphan pupils lined into fidgety ranks by its masters. Then they'd pass the infirmary lodge, where some of its more mobile patients stood on one side and a scattering of staff (including myself) on the other. Finally, they'd turn in through the cemetery gates opposite the workhouse proper, where the able-bodied inmates stood in forlorn rows, neatly categorised by sex and quality.

That was the plan, anyway.

When the procession arrived, it was a fine sight. Four horses with tall plumes pulled a hearse piled high with flowers and wreaths. Six men – the master amongst them – walked either side as a guard of honour. Behind snaked a long line of top-hatted gentlemen in solemn black, while a brass band at the rear played a mournful march.

The hearse was just approaching the lodge when a cart came rattling down Beckett Street in the opposite direction. It was a rustic number, piled high with sacks of potatoes and churns of milk. We all expected the driver to pull over, and to stand with hat in hand as the procession passed. But he didn't. He cracked his whip, clearly intending to bull straight through.

The master wasn't a man to put up with this sort of belligerence. He stepped out from the others and held up a palm. "Whoa there. Show some respect and—"

He never finished the sentence. His feet caught something, and he stumbled and fell. The driver tugged hard on the reins, but it was too late.

The master had fallen on the opposite side of the hearse from me, so I didn't see the tyre almost slice him in two. For that, I am grateful. I *heard* it happen, and that was more than enough.

There were a few moments of shocked silence, except for the band, who hadn't realised anything had happened and continued playing. Then the funeral disintegrated into screams and sobs and whispers.

There's a certain class of person who will always run towards any emergency whether they're remotely qualified to help or not, a class to which I unashamedly belong. To my relief, several better-qualified people had also run to the master's aid, and by the time I reached him he was quite hidden from view behind a dense knot that included the infirmary superintendent, his assistant, and a doctor and a surgeon who'd happened to be amongst the mourners. But after a minute or two this knot unravelled and the superintendent beckoned me over.

"He's beyond any of our help," he said, "except yours."

I knelt down by the dying man. His fine clothes had been ripped open by the doctors, revealing a bare, hairy chest and below that... a mess I didn't much like to look at. I looked at his face instead. Still the same proud, black brows and dark eyes, now looking darker than ever against the sudden paleness of his skin.

"Sir."

"Blackshroud." His voice attempted its usual authority but cracked slightly.

"You seem to have got yourself into some bother, sir."

"So it appears."

"They... don't think you'll make it, sir."

"So I heard."

"Would you like my help?"

I had the impression it was only by a colossal effort of will he was holding himself back from wailing like a newborn child. He closed his eyes, took a few deep ragged breaths, and opened them again.

"Yes. I think that's probably for the best."

A coarse voice cut across the street. "Whatever you're doing, can you get on with it?"

I rose to my feet and faced the carter. "Excuse me, sir?"

"I said, can you get on with it? Very sad and all I'm sure, but can you move him off the road? Some of us are trying to get places, here."

There was a babble of outrage from the gentlemen behind me.

"What?" protested the carter. "Not my fault if he threw himself in front of me, is it?" He rapped his knuckles against one of the big milk churns behind him, which gleamed in the midday sun. "Now I've got these sitting spoiling while all this hubbub's going on. *He* may be a goner, but this milk in't. Come on, move it already!"

Several of the gentlemen were now advancing on the man, shouting furiously, apparently with the intention of flogging him senseless with his own horsewhip.

"Everybody!" I shouted as loud as my lungs could manage. "*Silence!*"

There was a brief moment's pause. I leapt on it before it passed away.

"Mr Stanley," I said to the workhouse porter, "please run to my room and fetch my bag. Mr Crooke, if you wouldn't mind calling in at the lodge and securing a suitable chamber. I'll not have his final moments played out on a public road in front of a gawping crowd."

"About bloody time," growled the carter.

I spun on him. "And as for you, you shall convey the man who *you* ran over to that room once we've procured it. And you shall do so with your mouth firmly closed."

He gave me a foul look as though he were about to protest, but then got down from his cart with a grumble.

"Mr Gilder, you'll go with him and make sure he's made as comfortable as possible. I'll also need you and Mr Crooke to sign witness. Mr Cunningham, please refasten the master's clothes, he looks quite unseemly. The rest of you, you have a great man's funeral to attend, and you mustn't let this tragedy delay it any further."

I clapped my hands twice, and people started moving.

Barely five minutes later I was alone with the master, helping him drink his last drink.

"Am I a good man?" he asked me, his brows creased with pain. "Sir?"

His eyes stared desperately into mine. "Am I a good man? I've always tried to be a good man."

"Of course you're a good man, sir."

He mumbled something, and then slipped away without another word.

"'His suffering was shortened, we are glad to say, by young Blackshroud Summers,'" I read to the bank manager from the *Yorkshire Post*, "'who descended upon the scene like an angel of mercy. With a quite remarkable force of character she imposed order on the chaotic scene, and the sufferer was moved with maximum expediency and dignity to a place of privacy for his final moments. All present were highly impressed by her conduct, and she is surely to be considered a credit to her honourable profession.'" I folded the paper and offered it to him. "Care to read it for yourself?"

"No thank you, I read it on Monday. The *Mercury* was even more effusive."

"Reputation," I said, pointing at the paper. "This is a *gift* of reputation."

"You wish me to reconsider your loan."

"Naturally."

"Hmm..." He leant back in his chair, stroking his fingers across his chin.

One fine blowy day that June, I stood waiting outside the familiar grandeur of the General Infirmary. I was waiting for someone in particular. I saw her step out of the doors and lean against a pillar with a dazed look, and I hurried over.

"Millicent? How did it go?"

"They said yes, ma'am! They're going to make a nurse out of me!"

"That's splendid news!" I embraced her, but she was frozen rigid with shock. "I'm sure you'll make a far better nurse than I ever did. Just watch out for a ward sister called Haines; trust me, you don't want to get on the wrong side of her."

"Yes, ma'am. But what about you, ma'am? I heard you're moving on too?"

"That's right. I'm moving into my own surgery next week, if all goes well."

"Here's hoping it does, ma'am."

I embraced her one final time and we parted, to face our new and separate lives outside the cold, hard walls that had sheltered us for so long.

Chapter 7

I never liked the name "Blackshroud Summers". Summers is just too *sunny* for someone in my profession. Winters would have fit better. Still, I managed to put my name to good use when I rented my first surgery on Somers Street. It was a shabby and narrow sort of building, and Somers Street itself was a shabby and narrow sort of street, but my hope was that "Blackshroud Summers of Somers Street" would lodge itself nicely in people's minds. I took out some small but widely-scattered advertisements with exactly that wording and waited for customers.

My first visitor wasn't a customer, however, but a competitor: Blackshroud Mercy Shepherd, whose name was so improbably apposite I sometimes wondered if she'd chosen a husband purely to contrive it.

"I just thought I'd stop by to introduce myself," she said.

Not only did she have a better name for a blackshroud, she looked more like one too. She was a round-faced, motherly figure, with a big beam of a smile and crinkles around her eyes that made her look like she was always laughing. One could well imagine her fussing over the blankets on your death bed, giving you a sympathetic "there there", and offering something nice to drink to make everything better.

"It's so lovely to meet a new face in the trade," she said with one of her biggest smiles. "I'm so sorry to call at the back door, but I couldn't work out where the front is."

"This *is* the front."

"Really?" She made a point of gazing up at my surgery's crumbling facade. "Well, how very... *charming*. I suppose we all have to start somewhere, don't we?"

"We do. Won't you come in?"

"No no, I wouldn't want to trouble you. Besides, I'm so terribly busy; you know how it is, I'm sure." She looked up at my frontage again. "Then again, maybe you don't."

"It was *lovely* to meet you." I put as much venom into the word "lovely" as I could find.

"And you," she said warmly. "It's been quite refreshing. And don't let yourself get too down about all this, dearie." She waved a hand to vaguely indicate my surgery, myself and my entire business. "I'm sure you won't be here for too long."

Her horse, carriage and groom waited in the street. The carriage was a smart, sober, well-appointed number; the horse was a vigorous-looking stallion with a fine coat. The groom, who rather fit both descriptions, opened the door for her, and she gave me a parting wave out the window as they clattered away.

I fumed for an hour or so. Then I stepped out into Somers Street myself and looked over my building with a critical eye.

It wouldn't do.

And so, I started work on excising the shabbiness from my shabby new surgery. Over the next few weeks painters, carpenters, glaziers and signmakers all came to lavish their attentions on its weary frontage, and inside I spent most of what was left of the bank's money on wallpaper, carpets, curtains and furniture for my hallway and parlour, along with a few carefully-chosen works of art that looked like they might have cost a fortune but actually only cost quite a lot.

In the end, I was able to stand again in Somers Street and this time regard my surgery with something like satisfaction. It looked clean, neat, and almost expensive, giving the impression of a comfortable, prosperous, and most importantly *respectable* home and business. That was, however, a thin facade over a precarious reality. If you were to step through the narrow ginnel between my building and the next, you'd come to a dirty, muddy yard where you could look up and see the back of it in all its shabby shame. Peer through the cracked panes into my private rooms, and you'd see spartan spaces with bare patches of plaster, buckets positioned under a leaky roof, and packing crates serving as chairs.

In truth, I'd spent far, far more than I should have on the refurbishment, and by the time it was complete the money was still only flowing in one direction: out. My landlord didn't help matters at all. When he came to inspect his property, he was so delighted by the changes that he promptly raised my rent to adjust for its increased value.

"You should've nutted him if you ask me," my assistant, Eliza, told me.

Eliza was a niece of Mrs Battersby, recommended to me with the words, "She's a good girl at heart." On reflection, this should have served as a warning. There may well have been a good girl somewhere inside, but if so, she was deeply buried under a whole lot of Eliza. When asked to do anything at all – for example, to step outside and check the bell was still working – she'd let out a decadent sigh as though she were the most terribly put upon servant ever to suffer under her mistress' thumb, and then like as not get distracted on the way and forget all about it.

But, I didn't have much to ask her to do. For two months, not a single customer rang that bell. In retrospect, it wasn't too surprising. Let me explain the problem.

When a family is in the terrible position of needing a blackshroud, the decision is usually a simple one. "It was Blackshroud X who put Mother to rest," they might say, "let's call her in again for Father." Or, if they don't already have personal experience, someone else they know will. "Blackshroud Y was most kind and respectful when my brother died," a neighbour might say. "Why don't you call on her?"

Therefore the common witticism that a good blackshroud doesn't get repeat customers is completely wrong. Most custom is – however indirectly – repeat custom. And for a new practitioner, that's something of an intractable issue.

But, one Sunday afternoon in early September, the bell did finally ring.

I leapt to my feet and ran to the mirror, hastily trying to pull my dress and hair into some sort of arrangement. "Eliza!" I squeaked. "Door!"

She muttered something under her breath before tramping sullenly into the hall. I met the woman in the parlour. She was shrouded in a long hooded coat, and cast nervous glances towards the windows.

"Eliza, you may leave us," I said when she showed no sign of doing so. She scowled, and left the room with a slam. I could tell by the light under the door that she remained crouched behind the keyhole, but decided to ignore it. I probably would have done the same in her position, after all.

"I need someone to attend on this address," the woman said, handing me a slip of paper. "Tonight."

"I can do that. Who would I be attending?"

"It's..." she took another look around the room, as though she feared spies hiding behind the occasional tables. "I need someone *discreet*."

"Discreet, in what way?"

"I'd need you to arrive after dark. On foot, and knock quietly. And without wearing that." She pointed at my dove and dagger.

"But, why?"

"We'll pay double your usual rate."

That was quite enough for me to stop asking questions. I promised I'd be there, collected my bloated fee, and showed her out.

"Maybe they want you to murder someone," Eliza suggested unhelpfully. "Or maybe it's a murderer who's dying, what's spent his life on the run from the law. Or a pirate. Or—"

"Leeds is not so full of pirates and murderers as your imagination would suggest, Eliza. I'm sure there's some perfectly reasonable explanation why they want some discretion."

But privately my mind was also racing with murderers, pirates and even more scandalous things. When I arrived that evening at the address on Gower Street – my dove and dagger swapped out for cloak-and-dagger furtiveness – I was quite disappointed to find a modest, well-kept back-to-back house which could hardly have looked more innocuous. And indeed, when I was hurriedly admitted I discovered only an ordinary family with an elderly mother, who was dying slowly in immense pain. This I ended, perfectly legally, before leaving the house just as discreetly – and just as baffled – as I'd arrived.

The mystery didn't get resolved until a couple of weeks later, when John Gilder called in at Somers Street to see how I was getting on.

"I suspect they belonged to one of those odd little denominations that thinks your profession a sin. You must know the type. Life is sacred, to kill is to kill, and all that."

"Then why hire me?"

"The same reason as anyone else. Humanity. But this way they reserve the right to tell people that the old woman died in her sleep, as God intended. You must have been ideal. People might have recognised Blackshroud Shepherd, or Weston, or Cartwright. But you? Almost nobody knows who you are."

"Yes. And that's rather the trouble."

On my way back from the butcher's the next day I had an unexpected encounter. A patchy old man leading a patchier grey stallion fell into step with me on Park Lane.

"Ma'am," he said with a polite tip of the hat. I gave him a nod in return, and thought it the end of the interaction. I was wrong. "'Tis apt I should cross paths with one of your calling today, ma'am."

"Is it?"

"'Tis. 'Cause this old fellow's on his last walk." He gave the horse a sad pat on the neck. "Off to the knacker's, we are."

"I'm very sorry to hear it. What does it have to do with me?"

"Only that you're in the knacker's trade yourself, as it were."

"I most certainly am *not*."

"Begging your pardon, ma'am."

We walked in silence for a few dozen yards, while I eyed up the beast.

"What's wrong with him?"

"He's old, ma'am, and tired. No good for no kind of hard work no more."

I was, I reflected, rather in want of a horse. But certainly not this sorry specimen. He was too ragged. Too slow. Too weak. Most unsuitable, I told myself as I looked into his big, soft, watery eyes.

"How about very light work?"

I arrived back at Somers Street with my new purchase following meekly behind. Eliza stared as though I were leading a fire-breathing dragon.

"What is *that?*"

"This, Eliza, is a horse. Could you clear some space in the yard, and find something to tie him to?"

"You're never keeping that mangy old thing?"

"I most certainly am. A respectable blackshroud doesn't walk everywhere. She has a horse and carriage."

"But you don't have a carriage!"

"Now at least I have a horse."

She rolled her eyes. "As long as you're not expecting *me* to look after the damned thing. Do you have the least idea how much it costs to keep a horse? It's a bloody liability!"

That night, lying awake in bed, I heard Eliza sneaking out into the yard. Peering through a window, I could just make out her stroking her fingers through Liability's mane, whispering to him softly as she fed him sugar lumps stolen from the tea tray.

A carriage and groom were completely beyond my finances, but riding around town on horseback just wasn't *respectable*.

I settled on a compromise between the two extremes and purchased a one-seat gig, just narrow enough to squeeze down the ginnel into my back yard. It was a squeaky, rusty wreck of a thing, but I had it mercilessly oiled and scraped then repainted in all-concealing black, and I paid a signwriter to put my name and address on the sides in prominent gold letters, to make it a kind of rolling advertisement.

Liability looked a fine sight harnessed to it, with a tall black plume rising from his head, at least if you didn't look at either gig or horse too closely. I couldn't resist picking up the reins and taking him for a parade circuit of central Leeds. He really was a tired old thing, only capable of a sedate pace, but by good fortune that was the only appropriate speed at which a respectable blackshroud should travel.

When I came along Boar Lane to the junction with Briggate, I discovered an unsuspected perk of my profession. This junction had become such a notorious free-for-all – the occasional runaway pig included – that lately a policeman had been stationed there to impose order, and as I approached he raised his hand to indicate that I should stop. But then, noticing what was written on the side of my gig, he changed his mind and waved me on. He even raised his helmet to me as I passed by.

At the next junction, outside the Corn Exchange, there was no policeman, and yet I found I still had a magical right of way. Liability started to the right before I persuaded him to head left instead, resulting in an unnecessarily sweeping leftward turn that managed to get in the way of absolutely everybody. It was the kind of manoeuvre that should have attracted a volley of interesting obscenities from all concerned. But instead, the drivers merely took off their hats and let me pass, much the same as though I'd been leading a hearse. I gave them a slight, dignified nod of the head as I swept by.

It didn't quite work on everyone. As I rounded the corner from Vicar Lane onto Lowerhead Row for the homeward stretch, only slightly mounting the kerb, I had to pull sharply on the reins to avoid running down a familiar black-laced figure.

"Keep that beast under control!" she hollered in my vague direction.

"Esther!"

"*Girl?*" She looked between me and Liability in horror. "What are you doing tethered to that monster?"

"Isn't he a beauty?"

"A *beauty?* That evil-eyed brute? What were you thinking? Did you never listen to a single thing I told you about horses?"

"No! Go on, give him a pat. He's a big softie."

She kept safely out of biting range. "Enough of your nonsense. I have a patient to attend."

"Yes, me too," I lied. "I'm just so *busy* these days."

"If you're attending a patient, why are you heading *towards* your surgery?" She took a step closer. "Do you take me for a fool, girl?"

I gave the reins a sudden shake. "Liability, *attack!*"

Esther leapt backwards with a panicked porcine squeal, toppling over the kerb and landing in a puddle. Liability gazed at her curiously as he eased into gentle motion up the road.

"Come back here, girl!" she shouted from the ground. "Don't you *dare* ride away from me!" But that's exactly what I did, giving her a cheery wave as I went.

I was still laughing about it when I got home. As I recounted to Eliza the squelching splat of a sound she'd made as she landed in the puddle, there were tears streaming from my eyes. But Eliza returned me an icy look. "You acted like an absolute louse," she said.

On reflection, I conceded she might have a point. I bought Esther a basket of cakes by way of apology, and sent Eliza round to deliver it. And while she was out on that errand I took another look over my finances. The situation was bleak. My reserves were so low that the basket of cakes had made a not insignificant hole in them, and what was left was disappearing as rapidly as the cakes themselves probably were on their way to Tenterhook Yard.

In retrospect, thank Heaven for Major Dodgson.

Mrs Dodgson called in at Somers Street while I was out taking Liability on another adventure. "A woman was here," Eliza informed me on my return, flicking a pencil between her fingers. "Wants you to kill her husband."

"A customer?" I hurried out of my coat. "Where? When?"

"Tomorrow night. Springfield Place."

"What number?"

She shrugged. "Dunno."

"Don't know? Whatever do you mean, you don't know? Didn't she give you a number?"

"Probably. I can't remember."

"Didn't you write it down?"

"Nah."

"Do you have any idea how many houses there are on Springfield Place?"

She sucked thoughtfully on the pencil. "Or did she say Springfield Mount?"

"Oh, wonderful." I sat down wearily. "Did you at least take her name?"

"Of course I did. It was Elizabeth, same as mine."

"And her surname?"

"It began with a D. D or a B."

"How about her husband's name?"

"I guess it's the same as her name."

"I meant his *first* name."

"Oh. No, no idea."

"And what did she look like, this Elizabeth B or D?"

"Sort of..." she waved the pencil as though trying to draw the woman in the air... "that sort of shape."

"So to summarise, Eliza, tomorrow night I need to call at every house in Springfield Place *and* Springfield Mount and enquire after a Mrs Elizabeth B or possibly D and then twiddle my finger in the air and say she's 'that sort of shape'? You've got *nothing* else for me to go on?"

"Course I do! Cats. She loves cats. Couldn't stop talking about cats."

I could have strangled Eliza. Especially because Springfield Place and Mount alike were very respectable sorts of streets, home to exactly the respectable sort of client I most wanted to have, and least wanted to lose because my assistant couldn't even write down a simple address. As I led Liability down Springfield Place the following evening I peered left and right through twilight-quilted gardens at one big terraced townhouse after another. I was on the lookout for a telltale gaggle of mourners and wellwishers haunting a front step. Failing that, I was on the lookout for an unusual concentration of cats.

In the end, I didn't need either clue. As I approached, a serving girl hurried out to meet me at the gate.

"Blackshroud? They're expecting you. This way please."

I left Liability tethered outside with his nosebag and followed her in.

Elizabeth Dodgson was certainly fond of cats. A slinky black and white creature insinuated itself around my ankles as soon as I stepped into the hall. In the kitchen – where Mrs Dodgson waited – another three were to be found: a petite tabby prowling through the table legs; a big floppy ginger tom sprawled unhygienically in a mixing bowl; and a well-groomed Siamese peering superciliously down from a high shelf above the copper pans.

"My apologies for not receiving you properly," said Mrs Dodgson. "I've been perfectly beside myself with worry over Montgomery."

"That's quite alright. I can only imagine what you've both been going through."

"He just hasn't been himself since he got into that fight with that rascal from over the road. A nervous wreck. Barely touches his food."

"A fight? He was injured, then?"

"Not seriously, I don't think. Or at least, it didn't look serious at the time. A few scratches and he was limping off his front left paw for a couple of days." She gave the ginger tom in the mixing bowl a scratch behind the ears, and he purred in reply.

"Montgomery is a *cat?*" I said in vexation.

"Well of course he is. What else would he be?"

"I'm sorry, I thought we were talking about your husband."

"Oh, *Henry*. Yes, I'd better take you up to see him, I suppose."

Major Henry Dodgson was a weathered, grizzled man who'd been tucked out of the way in a spare bedroom, along with a cat-shredded old armchair and a rusting mangle awaiting repair. He turned a weary eye to me as I took a seat by his bedside, next to a propped pair of crook-handled walking sticks.

"While you're still here, Mrs Dodgson," I said after introducing myself to her husband, "I'll need you and Mary to witness consent." I pulled the green-bound book from my bag and flipped it open to the first blank page. "This just needs your signatures to say that you've—"

Before I could finish the sentence, she'd plucked the book from my hands, a pen flashing into her fingers as though from nowhere. "Yes, yes, I know how these things work," she said as she splashed her signature across the page and handed it to her servant to do the same.

"Mrs Dodgson! You're supposed to be witnessing your husband's signature. He has to sign *first.*"

"You'll have three signatures on your page, I can't really see that it makes much difference." She retrieved the book from Mary and returned it. "If you don't mind, I have some pressing business to attend to. Victoria has been scratching something dreadful and I need to comb her for fleas. Blackshroud, you're welcome to join me for tea downstairs when you're finished here. Come, Mary." She turned to leave.

"Elizabeth, my love..." said a weak voice from the bed. Mrs Dodgson stopped and frowned at her husband.

"Yes? What is it?"

"Just... goodbye?" He raised a trembling hand out towards her.

His wife regarded the hand, but made no movement towards it. "Yes. Goodbye, Henry," she said crisply and whisked away, closing the door firmly behind her.

In my time with Esther I'd seen plenty of relatives of the dying. I'd seen them sobbing. I'd seen them angry. I'd seen them hysterical. I'd seen them quietly stoic. But I'd never, ever seen anyone so completely indifferent as Mrs Dodgson. Even the serving girl had looked more affected by the situation.

"Blackshroud?" said the Major.

There are, very broadly, two types of patients on their deathbed. One type is those who just want to get the unpleasant business over and done with as quickly as possible. The other type likes to talk first. Major Dodgson was a talker. He talked about his time in the Crimea. He reminisced about mountain climbing in Snowdonia. He rambled at length about his beloved garden, and told me how finding himself too infirm to tend to it had been one final indignity too many.

He didn't talk about the one topic I was most keenly curious about: his relationship with his wife. In later years, with more experience and confidence in my profession, I might have raised the question myself. I've learnt that people in their last moments are usually more than happy to dispense with small talk in favour of the things that really matter. But I was new enough to it back then that I skirted the delicate issue and let Major Dodgson slide into some very small talk indeed.

He complained in detail about a minor dental problem he'd been having. He recounted an argument with a neighbour about a fence two years before. When he started talking about the various pros and cons of several strains of brassicas I finally realised he was talking just to put off taking the draught, of which he was understandably terrified.

"Major," I said, patting his hand, "it's been wonderful listening to your adventures, and thank you for opening my eyes to the many benefits of purple sprouting broccoli. But do you think you might be ready for the draught now?"

He gave me a look like a man tied to railway tracks might give to the locomotive steaming towards him. "I... I... can't we wait?"

"We can, of course, if you wish. But I can't help sense a certain reluctance about you, Major. Are you completely certain the draught is what you want?"

"I... I..."

"Because there's no turning back once you've taken it. It's something you should do only if your heart is absolutely, resolutely set on it. Is it?"

"I... no. No, now it really comes to it, I can't say that it is."

"Are you certain?"

"Yes, I suppose that... well... yes. Yes, I think I shall live a little longer."

And that was that. I packed my bag, closed the door on the Major and his new-found acceptance of life and went down to give his wife the good news.

"Ah. I see," she said without so much as a raise of an eyebrow. "Would you care for a cup of tea? We're quite out of milk and cream, I'm afraid – my darlings have had the lot – so it will have to be black." I declined politely, but something of my surprise must have shown on my face, because the next thing she said was, "I'm sorry, I must seem dreadfully cold to you."

"No no, not at all. We all react in different ways."

She waved that aside as the empty platitude it was. "The fact is, this has all happened before. Henry has had sixteen appointments before tonight, with two different blackshrouds."

"I don't quite follow."

"It happens the same every time. When the moment comes, he shies away from taking the draught as sure as Monday follows Sunday. It's become quite the routine." She shook her head and absent-mindedly stroked the nearest cat. "I'll see you again the same time next week?"

"You will?"

"Oh yes. You see, come the morning, Henry will be moaning again that he has nothing left to live for and would rather be dead. He'd have you round here every night, if we had the money for it."

Just as she predicted, when I returned to Springfield Place the next week I again found Major Dodgson welcoming my presence, complaining bitterly of the misery and indignity of his reduced condition. But again, when it came to actually taking the draught, a panic rose in him and he made another hasty retreat.

On my seventh weekly visit, Mrs Dodgson came with me to her husband's bedside to say, "Mary's made shepherd's pie. I've told her to bring you some up when you're done."

"Damn it, woman, I don't need pie. I'm dying, don't you understand that?"

"Of course you are. I'll go ahead and tell her to keep some warm for you all the same. *Just* in case."

The Major survived that meeting to enjoy his pie. And I enjoyed receiving my fee every week, collected – as always – in advance. The Dodgsons provided me with the beginning of a steady income. But even so, I wasn't earning enough to balance my outgoings. By Christmas, my reserve of capital had dwindled to a few shillings, and I was making plans for which bits of furniture I'd send to be pawned first, and wondering whether I'd have to send Liability to the knacker's after all, or if I could somehow contrive to send them Eliza instead.

On New Year's Day I suffered a major blow. I arrived at Springfield Place as usual, and found I wasn't expected.

"But what happened?" I asked.

"I can't explain it," Mrs Dodgson said with a frown of puzzlement, sitting at the kitchen table with her unhappy-looking Siamese cradled in her arms. "I called round your surgery yesterday and told your girl you wouldn't be needed. Didn't she pass on the message?"

"Evidently not. But I meant, what happened with your husband? Has he passed away? Or has he decided more firmly to live?"

"If only. No. No disrespect to you personally, but our finances aren't what they used to be and economies must be made where they can. To put it bluntly, I've found someone cheaper. She's with him now, as a matter of fact."

"Cheaper than *me*? But that must mean..."

A door opened and closed upstairs, and a heavy tread sounded on the stairs, along with the indignant yowl of a cat being kicked out of the way after getting friendly with the wrong pair of ankles.

"Blackshroud," Mrs Dodgson said, rising to her feet as Esther bulged into the kitchen. "I trust Henry was no bother?"

"Nothing I couldn't handle." She caught sight of me and scowled.

"Then we'll see you again the same time next week?"

"Next week?" Esther turned back to Mrs Dodgson with a perplexed look. "Why? Who's dying next week?"

"My husband."

"Your husband? Then who in God's name was that upstairs?"

"That's my husband."

"You have two of them?!"

"What? No!" Mrs Dodgson shook her head as though to shake out the confusion. The Siamese wriggled in her arms but didn't manage to escape. "Let me explain. My husband, the Major, the man you were with, will change his mind about the whole business by the morning."

"It's a bit late for that, don't you think?"

Mrs Dodgson froze, her face turning pale. "You... you don't mean... is he... is he *dead?*"

"What on Earth did you think I was doing up there? Reading psalms? Of course he's dead!"

"...Oh. But I didn't think he'd ever... Oh. Oh, Henry..." Mrs Dodgson's face crumpled. She dropped the Siamese, who darted away out the door. Then her legs collapsed under her. The servant Mary appeared just in time to catch her as she fell, and held the newly-widowed woman as she wept.

I felt it was time to make a quiet exit. Esther followed, and pulled me aside as soon as we were on the road.

"What in Heaven was all that about? And what in Hell are *you* doing here?"

I gave her a quick account of my history with Major Dodgson.

"She could've saved a lot of time and money by just calling me in the first place," Esther said.

"But what did you *do* in there?"

"My job. That one just needed a bit of a nudge."

"A *nudge?* What's that supposed to mean?"

"I told him to stop being a silly bugger and drink his medicine."

"But that's not..." I took a deep breath to quell a rising temper. "We're not supposed to *push* people into taking the draught. It's unprofessional."

"Unprofessional? *You're* calling *me* unprofessional?" Her face flushed a vivid shade of pink I'd never seen it before. "And what do you think *is* professional, might I ask? Strutting round town in your fancy carriage with your fancy beast? Putting on your bloody airs and graces? Knocking honest folks over on the street, then sending a servant out to do your apologising with a half-eaten basket of prissy cakes?"

I crossed my arms and stood my ground. "It is *professional* to respect a patient's wishes."

"Which wish? His wish to die that came from weeks of sober thinking, or his wish to live that came from a moment of fear?"

"Everyone has the right to change their mind. And we have a *duty* to let them."

"It's not like I held his nose and poured the stuff down his throat! But I'll bet you were right happy every time he turned tail, weren't you? Didn't try too hard to calm him down? Not when he's paying you a nice fat fee every time you call round, eh?"

That pulled hard at my nerves. Perhaps because there was some truth to it.

"Oh *shut up*. You're hardly a shining example of our profession, are you?"

"At least I know that a good blackshroud doesn't get repeat customers."

"I do *not* need to take lectures on how to be a good blackshroud," I snarled, "from *Bloody Esther*."

Her left eye twitched. Her nose wrinkled. A tense wobble rippled across her pink face, and she made a strange noise at the back of her throat. I braced myself for a heavy salvo of verbal abuse, but none came. Instead she just shook her head, turned her back on me and walked away down the street.

"Esther?" I called as she went, but she disappeared round the corner without looking back.

I had a long, thoughtful walk back home, leading Liability on foot instead of riding behind. When I'd tethered him in the yard Eliza came out and said, "There's some blackshroud turned up to see you."

"That'll be Esther," I said, my spirits rising at the chance to fix things between us. But it wasn't Esther. Mercy Shepherd waited in my parlour, sprawled into the best chair with a leg draped impudently over one upholstered arm.

"What a charming place you have here. I was simply eaten by curiosity to see if the inside meets the expectations of the outside, and lo and behold, it does. In every way."

"What do you want, Shepherd? If you're looking to end the misery of your existence, I'd be very happy to help you with that."

"Goodness! Your manners are as good as your girl's. Just a friendly visit, from blackshroud to blackshroud. How are you? Getting any patients yet?"

"Plenty. In fact I just got back from seeing to someone, over on Springfield Place. Very good family."

"It wasn't Major Dodgson, was it?"

I spluttered. "How do you know about him?"

"Used to be one of mine. And what a cash cow *he* turned out to be. Until the wife decided to look for someone cheaper." She looked me pointedly up and down. "I see she succeeded."

"Well, you'll be pleased to hear he finally died tonight."

"Oh good lord, you actually gave him the draught? Anyone with a lick of sense would've milked that man until he met his natural end. Ah well. At least you'll get a healthy commission for the funeral."

"What? I've nothing to do with funerals."

She gave me a look as though I'd said I'd nothing to do with speaking or breathing.

"But funerals are where the money is, dear. People always spend much more on funerals than they do on us."

"I'm not an undertaker."

"But you can *refer* people to an undertaker. An undertaker who has, of course, agreed to pay you a nice fat commission for doing so. Really, didn't your mistress teach you anything?"

"Well..."

"Ah. Yes. I forgot. Cartwright."

"Isn't it all a bit... grubby?"

"Of course not. You yourself give commissions to doctors for their hopeless cases, don't you?" When I didn't reply she stared at me open-mouthed. "You *don't?*"

"No!"

"But dearie, however are you getting any patients?"

I sighed. "To be honest, I'm not. Not many. Not enough."

"Oh, that's *terrible* to hear," she said, the words dripping with sickly insincerity. "I myself have quite the opposite problem, you know. I get so many patients I actually have to turn half of them away. You may be surprised to hear this, but I used to be really quite a cheap blackshroud. Not as cheap as *you,* of course, but still *quite* cheap. Nowadays I'm rather an expensive blackshroud. But I still get lots of the old sort of customers turning up, who can't afford my fees. I have to refer them all to old Mary Weston. She's so much more affordable."

She gave me a significant sort of look, as though she were trying to tell me something. I cottoned on, after a few moments of mental scrambling.

"I'm affordable. What would it take to refer them to me instead?"

"Weston pays me one and ninepence a head."

Mercy Shepherd left ten minutes later, having agreed over a firm handshake to send patients my way for a commission of two and threepence each. And over the next few weeks, patients did start to appear. Mercy's commission cut heavily into my profit margin, but I soon found that this was more than compensated by the commissions I was able to arrange for funerals with depressing ease. I became accomplished at pulling the relatives aside after the deed, and delivering a line like, "if you wish, I can engage a good, reasonably-priced undertaker on your behalf." In their grief, they nearly always said yes. After a while I even stopped feeling dirty for doing it.

Throughout January I lost even more money, having to pawn some of my artwork and ornaments to stay afloat. In February, I barely broke even. By March, enough money was coming in that I could buy my items back from the pawn shop. The drip of customers had become a slow trickle. As the months went on and my reputation grew it would become a steady flow. My financial troubles were over, for the moment. My greater troubles were about to begin.

Chapter 8

May of 1879 stands out in my memory like a mould-shrivelled orange in a bowl of fruit. It brought with it two encounters whose consequences would drift down my years like poisonous spores, infecting everything they touched. One was with a pebble. The other was with Gabriel Bogg.

Gabriel's is a name that has, in a way, become even more inextricably linked with me than even my own. Countless people from Penzance to Aberdeen – and probably from Fiji to the Falklands for all I know – who wouldn't know Caroline Summers to spit at will still summon a gobbet for "the blackshroud who killed Gabriel Bogg". As a man, however, Gabriel was almost as innocuous as the pebble that would cause the other great upset of my life. He was a pale young thing with untidy red hair, an overlarge forehead and a habit of holding eye contact with his shoelaces. He asked me to end his life. So I did.

Of course, it wasn't as simple as that. It never is.

I had this dream. One day, some world-bitten soul would trudge through my door, and instead of giving them the draught I'd say all the right things to make them see a little sliver of hope. I wanted, in short, to save a life.

So far, I hadn't found anyone who wanted saving. People didn't come to me unless they had real problems; most were already dying, or at least in a great deal of pain. Despite some people's perception, the suicide of healthy people is a very, very small part of a blackshroud's job. Gabriel Bogg was only the fourth such patient I'd had in the three years since the workhouse – or at least, only the fourth who was serious about it – and I fancied he might be the first one I'd save.

So I tried. I really did try. We met several times. I asked him to explain himself, and challenged what he told me. I talked about hope; he talked about death. I talked about love; he talked about pain. I told my best jokes; he didn't laugh. In the end, unhappy about it as I was, I didn't really have a choice. He was twenty-one, he appeared to be of sound mind, and he was very serious about dying. I gave him the draught, and while he drank was the only time I ever saw him look content.

And that, so I thought, was that.

Two days later a policeman arrived at my door.

Eliza let him in. "Miss S!" she hollered up the stairs. "Someone said you murdered someone! Did you?"

The policeman got through three cups of tea and a plate of biscuits while he cast a lazy eye over my paperwork. "It's a funny thing, accusing a blackshroud of murder. Next I'll be pulling in a taxman for larceny, then locking meself up for affray."

I didn't find anything very funny about it. I had to stand in front of a coroner's jury and defend myself, and they didn't find it funny either. But neither did they find any suggestion of wrongdoing. A verdict of Lawful Euthanasia was returned, and for the second time I allowed myself – quite wrongly – to imagine the business was over and done with.

The letter from Mrs Bogg came two days later. "I want to meet the woman who murdered my son," it said, along with a time and the name of a church.

I've never been fond of churches. My parents sent me off to Sunday school every week to make a good Anglican out of me, but it didn't stick. The only thing I learnt was the knack of daydreaming while still looking attentive. Esther, too, made an effort to correct my religious apathy by dragging me along to her chapel every Sunday. That didn't work either. But it did teach me another valuable lesson: that attending services is a good way for a blackshroud to advertise, and to establish herself as the sort of upstanding, spiritual pillar of the community that people look to in a crisis. And so, I went to church. I went to several churches, in fact, of different denominations. And the art of discreet daydreaming proved a key asset in all of them.

Mrs Bogg's church wasn't part of my usual rota. I had the odd feeling of stepping into enemy territory. The Sunday service was well over, but a few devoted stragglers remained, and furtive eyes turned towards me as I passed up the aisle. "That's her," I heard one woman say. Another hissed something in her husband's ear, and I thought I heard the name "Gabriel". A bolder voice even called out, "For shame!" but I didn't turn around to see whose.

The vicar intercepted me. "You'll be here to see Mrs Bogg? She's on the tower."

"She's *where?*"

"On the tower. If you wait here, I'll fetch her."

I glanced around at the whispering pews. "No need. I'll go to her."

He led me up a tight, steep spiral stair. It seemed to wind upwards an improbable distance, passing by a door with the rhythmic clunking of a clock, until it finally emerged into a tall, breezy space. The vicar, wheezing, pointed at a slender ladder rising up between a great ponderance of bells, wheels and ropes to a small patch of daylight above. I climbed up alone.

The roof was a flat square of lichen-greened lead, with tall pinnacles rising from the corners. Leaning with her elbows on the parapet was a short and stocky woman with vivid red hair to match her son's. She didn't turn to face me, so I went to join her. From up there, Leeds was a heaving ocean of black slate roofs, with tall chimneys rising like the masts of ships.

"Gabriel loved to sit up here. He was always sneaking up. The vicar turned a blind eye, bless him. He had such a soft spot for Gabriel. He did a lovely funeral." She pointed at a patch of green amongst all the red and grey. "See that? That's where my little boy is buried. Take a good look. You put him there. *You* killed him."

"I didn't kill your son. I only helped him to die."

"Oh?" Mrs Bogg turned to face me, her eyes fixed on mine like the gunsights of a cannon. "And what, pray tell, is the difference?"

I flinched under that stare, but held my ground. "There's a big difference. It was *his* choice to die. Not mine."

She shook her head. "My Gabriel was a good boy. A smart boy. He didn't want to die. He was just having a bad day, that's all. He had everything ahead of him. His whole life. You stole that from him."

"I took nothing he didn't want to be taken."

"You *murdered him!*" She'd been speaking so far with a strange, quiet calm, but these last two words she screamed, taking a step towards me. I resisted the urge to take two steps back. "He came to your door – my poor little angel – and you *murdered him!*"

"Mrs Bogg. Please listen. Gabriel was suffering. I helped him end that suffering."

Her hand shot up to point accusingly a bare inch before my nose. "Don't you *dare* say you 'helped' him! Don't you *dare!*"

I hesitated, unsure what I could say that might calm her down. I thought of telling her what Gabriel had told me: how life to him had all the pleasure of toothache; how he'd spent years counting down the days to his twenty-first birthday when he could finally be rid of it. But she never would have believed it. Every mother considers herself an authority on her own children, no matter how mistakenly.

I thought of telling her that Gabriel was so firmly resolved to die that it was inevitable; if not by my hand, then by his own. That if it was going to be done, at least I'd allowed it to be done with dignity and without pain. But I didn't think she'd listen to that either.

I thought of telling her that her son wasn't just having a bad day. That he never would have come through it, never would have made peace with his life. But I didn't because

I wasn't certain of that. No-one could ever be certain. Not completely.

I thought of telling her that I'd done everything I possibly could have to talk Gabriel around. But I wasn't certain of that either.

In the end, all I said was, "I only did my job."

"Then your job is the Devil's work! Your job is *evil!*" And she shoved at me with both hands.

I'd like to make it very clear that she did *not* push me off the tower. She was just lashing out in grief and frustration, and didn't push me even nearly hard enough to topple me over the edge. If my foot hadn't chanced to encounter the pebble, and hadn't skittered out from underneath me, then the push would have achieved exactly what it was intended to: very little indeed. And so it's the pebble, not Mrs Bogg, which I blame for what happened.

The only thing I remember from the fall is Mrs Bogg's receding face staring down over the parapet, perfectly mirroring my own astonishment.

I've had dreams about falling: a sickening clench of the stomach as the dream-world drops out from beneath me, making me lurch awake with a start. The dreams that followed my actual fall were just like that, except I couldn't wake up. I just kept falling, falling, crying out for someone to catch me.

When I did finally wake, it wasn't much of an improvement. I was at least lying in a bed, but the bed felt like it was made of broken glass and nails sticking into my skin in a thousand places. It took a few moments for my addled mind to realise that the bed was soft linen, and the pain all my own. I tried to scream, but my chest wouldn't let me.

"Easy there, Miss Summers," said a female voice.

I forced my eyes open. A familiar ceiling looked down at me. Not my own ceiling; mine was full of cracks and spiders' webs, and this one was high and grand and immaculate. But it was familiar nonetheless. The various ceilings of my life spun through my memory until I placed it. This was a General Infirmary ceiling.

The recognition was something of a comfort, until I forced my head up a little and saw exactly which room I was in. It was Ward Eleven.

"They told me you wouldn't come round," the voice said. "It would've been better for you if you hadn't."

A hunched figure in black sat at my bedside, with a well-polished dove and dagger glinting from her breast. Blackshroud Mary Weston had a face like a skull, with dark sunken eyes and pale skin stretched tight over her cheekbones.

I tried to sit up, but the attempt produced nothing more than a stab of pain. There was pain in my legs, pain in my back, pain in my chest and pain in my neck. How bad was I? I tried twitching my left hand, then my right. I felt my fingers move. Good. I twitched my left toes. A fresh shiver of pain, but they moved. I twitched my right toes.

Nothing.

Swallowing a rising panic, I eased my head up off the pillow and looked down. There was red blood, and the hard white of bone sticking out where nothing had the right to be sticking out at all. My head fell back down with a moan.

"I can make this stop, Caroline." My eyes slid sideways to meet Blackshroud Weston's. She was rolling a small blue vial of white powder between her skeletal fingers. "No more pain. No more suffering."

I managed to shake my head. Her jaw clenched.

"Take a look at yourself. Here, go on, here's my mirror. Take a good look." She held up the mirror, and I clenched my eyes shut. "You're on your way out of this world. You know you are. The only choice you have left is between a long, painful end and a quick, quiet one."

I wanted to tell her that she was wrong, that I could still live, and I tried to do so but couldn't make my voice work. It

133

was like there was a steel band around my chest. I just shook my head instead.

"You're being most unreasonable. Think it through. Even if they somehow managed to patch you up, do you think your life would really be worth living? You'd be a cripple, Miss Summers. Look at your leg. Look at your *face*. Do you want that life? Of course you don't. Now be a good girl and let me call in some witnesses. All you have to do is nod."

I shook my head more vigorously. I'd occasionally wondered, before, what I'd choose if I were ever faced with these sorts of prospects. Now I knew. I wanted to *live*. No matter what that looked like, or how slim my chances.

"Well, that is a shame. If you're not enough of an adult to make the right decision for yourself, I'll simply have to make it for you." She leant back in her chair and pulled out a half-knitted lace scarf on a pair of needles. "I don't need your consent to let nature take its course."

I stared at her, mouthing silent objections, begging her with my eyes, but she'd turned all her attention to her knitting. For a while there was no sound in the room but the click of her needles and a steady drip from under the bed.

I was dying. I could feel it. My strength, my very life, leaking out of me drop by slow drop.

"Lie back. Don't try to fight it. It will all be over soon."

Perhaps that was for the best? The doctors of the Infirmary – some of the finest medical minds in England – must have seen me when I was brought in, and had sent me here to die in peace. Who was I to doubt their prognosis? Should I accept my fate and die with grace?

No. They'd told Weston I wouldn't come round. But I *had* come round. I had to get to them. I had to make them reassess. Taking as deep a breath as I could bear, I tried to shout.

"Nnnghk!" escaped my lips in a strangled whisper.

"You know," Weston said without looking up, "I've always been a *good* blackshroud. Never rich. Never fashionable. But good. And people respected that. I got along. I managed. For forty years, I managed. And then *you* showed up." She gave the scarf a vicious stab. "Undercut my prices. Connived with Shepherd to steal my patients."

There were two doors from Ward Eleven. One led into a busy hospital full of doctors and surgeons and medicines. The other led into the morgue. Blackshroud Weston had clearly made up her mind about which she wanted me to leave by. If I wanted to take the other door, then I was going to have to make it through on my own two feet. Gritting my teeth against the pain that was sure to come, I tried to swing my legs off the bed.

I hit the floor like a rolled-up carpet, my head hitting the boards with a thump that sent the world spinning. Under the bed I could see a pool of fresh red blood; on the other side the legs of Weston's chair slid back, and a pair of black shoes and stockings took a purposeful step forwards. I managed to roll over, screaming silently with the pain of it, to face the door. I reached out a hand, palm flat against the floorboards, and dragged myself six inches closer. And then again. Just once more...

Weston's bony arms caught my shoulders. "Let's have less of this, Miss Summers. A *good* blackshroud known when it's time to die. Come on, let's get you back in that bed."

She was stronger than she looked, and in my reduced condition I could no more resist her than a mouse could resist the spring jaws of a trap. She pulled me up, but as she did so she happened to bring me momentarily close to the door. I swung out with my left arm, banging three times on the wood before I was dragged back to the bed, trying again to shout but managing no more than a pitiful mewl.

A set of footsteps paused in the corridor outside, and after a moment there was a sharp knock. The door opened without waiting for permission, revealing the straight-backed and immaculate figure of Nurse Haines.

"*What* – in all creation – is going on in here?" Her eyes widened as she recognised me. "*Summers?!*"

I tried to tell her but my voice still wouldn't work, and I gobbled like a goldfish instead. Weston imposed herself quickly between us.

"Miss Summers is dying, nurse, and *trying* to do so in peace. I'd ask you to go about your business, and leave me to go about mine."

The two women stared each other down for a few long seconds, until Haines gave a slight nod and turned back towards the corridor. But just before Weston could close the door again she swung back, her eyes fixed this time on me.

"Miss Summers, do you need my help?"

And this time, finally, my voice found its way out in a weak croak as it shaped two well-practised words. "Yes, Sister."

What happened next was a bit of a blur. Moving ceilings, and faces with sideburns and spectacles leaning over me to say "hmmm" and frown. My consciousness was slipping away, and I ignored all the faces to focus my dwindling reserves of attention on staying awake.

But I remember the theatre. I remember the surgeon, with a blood-browned apron over his suit, lining up a row of knives and a big silver saw on a table, as though setting it for dinner. And then one more face was leaning over me, and a cloth pressed against my nose, and the smell of chloroform cut into my nostrils like daggers. The world faded away completely, and I was once more falling.

I landed very slowly, drifting seamlessly from sleep into a morphine-addled slumber that was half-way between daydream and nightmare. When I finally roused into something approximating wakefulness, I was lying in a ward with a man sitting at my bedside.

"Francis," I said weakly. I ached all over.

"Well well. Awake at last? What a shame. I was getting quite used to our conversations being strictly one-sided, and frankly, it was something of an improvement."

I tried to sit up. I failed, and groaned.

"Take it easy. You've earned it. I managed to get a whole week in bed after I fell out of that tree in the garden, remember? Look, I've still got the scar." He rolled up his sleeve to show me. "I know you love to do one better than your brother, but really, wasn't jumping off a church taking things a *bit* too far?"

"How... how bad am I?"

"You're not going to be winning any beauty contests, but honestly, when were you? Also..." he hesitated. "I'm not sure what the best way to say this is..."

"Spit it out."

"Well, you know how we used to have to do chores for Mr Kirkby when we were young, because he had that peg leg, and you got all grumpy about it and said you wished *you* could get a peg leg too?"

"*What?*"

"Well... congratulations?"

"Oh no..."

I forced my head up and looked down at my legs. Well, at my leg. The right one was completely missing from just above where the knee should have been.

"No, no, no..."

"Cheer up, I always thought it was a very substandard limb anyway. You're probably better off without it."

"Francis, they cut my *leg* off! What am I going to *do?*"

"Lie back and take advantage of everyone's sympathy, that's what I'd do. And don't worry about that business of yours. I've arranged to cover the rent on your surgery – *and* your hospital bills – until you're back on your foot."

"But that's—"

"No no, don't worry about it. I'm in a partnership now. Sparrow and Summers, doesn't that just sound fine? And I can't think of a better use for my new riches than indulging my daredevil little sister. The first thing I'm going to do when you get out is buy you one of those enormous crinoline dresses."

"Why?"

"So that next time you jump off a tower, it'll act as a parachute and you can float gracefully to the ground."

Francis came to visit me every day for the next two weeks before returning to London. I had other visitors too. My parents came dutifully, and John Gilder took some time out from the workhouse to talk and to read me choice passages from the bible. I could have done without the bible readings, but the talking was nice.

The person I saw the most, however, was another old face from the workhouse: Millicent Barden. She attended to all my needs very reverentially, even when I was beastly to her. And I'm afraid I *was* beastly to her, calling her all sorts of foul names when she wouldn't give me the morphine I wanted. She just responded to every outburst with a calm, "Yes, ma'am."

I usually got the morphine anyway. My old roommate Clara had charge of the next ward over, and sometimes stole through to see me. She was always happy to do a favour for an old friend.

By July I was finally well enough to walk out of the hospital. Well, hobble out, with a wooden crutch under each arm. The movement was awkward and painful. It took me ten minutes to get down the Infirmary steps, even with my mother's aid. There was of course no question of returning to Somers Street to pick up my career there. My dove and dagger had been lost somewhere in the fall, and I chose to take it as an omen. That life was over. Instead, my parents took me back to Wetherby to start my new life as an invalid.

So began the period I like to refer to as my Great Sulk. I settled into a comfortable chair with a view over the garden, where I could keep an eye on Liability, who'd been rescued from Somers Street and tethered to the horse chestnut. I barely left that chair for the next three months. My father's entreaties to get outside and practise my walking went mostly unheard. I sat in grumpy silence, shunning conversation and glaring at the hated crutches. I rubbed patent ointments and creams into my stump to try and stop the aching and itching, but nothing worked. Nothing except laudanum, which I drank in copious quantities, but it was a pale substitute for the morphine I still craved.

I had few visitors, and what few did arrive I snapped at until I had no visitors at all. Finally my mother, deciding that marrying me off might be the only way to get rid of me, invited a fresh batch of suitors to the house. They were a poor lot. One was a greasy gambler up to his armpits in debt. Another was the wrong side of sixty, with breath like a sewer rat and manners not much better.

"You're going to have to lower your expectations," she said when I objected. "You're damaged goods now."

At the start of October I got an entirely unexpected visitor. Esther sank into the chair across from me, after lifting the doily from it between finger and thumb and tossing it aside with a wrinkle of the nose as though it were a species of ornamental slug.

"I know why you're here," I told her.

"Really? Then do enlighten me."

"You're here to persuade me to take up blackshrouding again."

She raised an eyebrow. "Am I?"

"Of course you are. Well I'm not going to. So there."

"Bloody glad to hear it."

I blinked.

"With you laid up here moping, and that ghastly old witch Weston finally struck off, I've got the bottom of the market almost to myself. Times have never been so good. You can stay here as long as you like, girl, as far as I'm concerned."

"Then why *are* you here?"

"I want your surgery."

"Somers Street? Whatever for?"

"It's for my apprentice."

"Your *apprentice?*"

139

"Miss Winn. You'd like her. Snotty family. Snottier than yours, even. Just earned her dove; on the first try, too, and *without* finishing off her examiner."

"Why does she need Somers Street?"

"Well it's not as if you're using it, is it? And it's in a proper posh part of town. It might look a rat's nest at the minute, but it could be very nice if it was done up a bit."

"It *is* done up!"

"If you say so. I was thinking a big gilt sign at the front, maybe put in one of those bay windows, and a nice garden at the back in place of that muddy hole. Finally make it look like a classy establishment, really give Miss Winn a leg up in the world."

"And why does *she* get a leg up, when all *I* got was one little watch?"

"Because she's a *real* blackshroud, Miss Winn is. You only have to look at her. There was no point spending money on *you*. You never had the stomach for it, that was clear as anything. I said to myself, I said, 'this girl's a flake, Esther, why waste your time on her? She's just going to drop and run at the first hurdle.'" She gestured to me on my chair. "And here we are."

"I lost my *leg!*"

"And bloody sad I am to see it, but do stop whining on so. There's still lots of things you could do. Stitching knickers, perhaps, or wiping babies' bottoms. I'm sure you'd suit fine at that kind of work. Better than you ever suited at blackshrouding, that's for sure."

I rose to my foot. It wasn't an easy process. First I had to twist to reach my crutches. Then, holding them both in my right hand, I used my left to push myself up out of the chair. There followed a balancing act as one crutch was transferred from the right to the left, and both eased into place beneath my shoulders. But I made it, and it was well worth it to be able to loom over the still-seated Esther.

"I was an *excellent* blackshroud. A better one than *you* ever were."

Esther rose too. She was a couple of inches shorter, but that never seemed an obstacle to her ability to look down at me.

"The only reason I ever took you on, girl, was out of respect for old Martha White. And it's a kindness she never lived to see what a sorry specimen you turned out to be."

I swung a crutch at Esther's head. It was a clumsy swing, and she dodged it with the slightest step backwards.

"*Out!*" I snapped. "Get *out* of my house! I will *not* be spoken to like that!"

"Sure I didn't want to stay anyway."

I tried to chase her out, but I was a slow and shambling creature, and Esther was able to leave in an unhurried and dignified manner despite my best efforts. When she was gone, and I stood trembling in the hallway, my mother emerged from the shadows.

"Thank goodness that beastly woman is gone. Do you need a hand back to your chair, dear?"

"No. I need you to gather my effects from upstairs. And have Father harness up Liability and bring him round the front."

"But... where are you going?!"

"It's time I went home."

The lamp was just being lit at the end of Somers Street as a weary Liability pulled me round the corner. There stood my surgery, as though I'd never left it, except for some tall weeds in the ginnel and a thick layer of sooty grime coating the windows. And a woman, wrapped up thickly against the cold, perched on my front step.

Mrs Bogg stood up to glare at me as I approached. "I knew you'd be back," she said. "Your sort never gives up."

"I hope you're here to apologise, Bogg."

"Oh! You expect *me* to apologise to *you?*"

"I lost a *leg* because of you!"

"Bother your leg. I lost my *son* because of you."

"Do you have any idea how hard it was to convince the police that you *didn't* push me off that tower? I didn't have to do that, you know."

"Do you think I'm going to *thank* you? After you murdered my son?"

"No, but—"

"I wish you'd died. I'd have gladly gone to Hell for it, knowing I'd sent *you* there before me."

I shook my head. "Why *are* you here?"

"To haunt you. This is where I am now. Right here. Outside your door, to tell everyone that you're a murderer. To tell *you* you're a murderer, in case you ever forget it."

"But... why? What do you possibly hope to achieve?"

"My son is dead. It's too late for him. But one day, another mother's son will come to you, and maybe I can save *him*."

I was too tired to think of a good objection to that. So I left her to her vigil, secured Liability in his stall and headed inside.

The place was in a state. Five months of dust covered every surface, and garlands of spiders' webs hung from the ceiling. But oddly, the dust didn't look completely undisturbed. A footworn trail led down the stairs, and I followed it into the kitchen. There, ensconced in a chair by the fire, surrounded by empty but unwashed jam jars with the spoon still in, sat Eliza.

"Evening, Miss S. You're back."

"What... what are you still *doing* here?"

She shrugged. "Where else would I be? No-one never fired me."

"But—"

"By the by, you owe me five months' salary."

I gestured around at the mess. "Why haven't you at *least* kept the place clean?"

"I do what I'm told. No-one told me to do nothing."

"Well, here's me telling you to do something. Clean up this mess. *Now.* In fact, before you do that, why don't you make a nice hot pot of tea. I'm badly in need of one."

Eliza sighed and rose to her feet, making her ascent from the chair look even more arduous work than my own had been. She slouched over to the drawer and started rummaging.

"I reckon you might want this back," she said, pulling out something silver and lobbing it my way. I caught it. "Went round that church you fell off to look at the hole you made in the grass. Found that."

I opened my palm to look at the object. It was my dove and dagger.

The following day I managed to hobble all the way over to Tenterhook Yard, stopping twice to rest on the way. I banged on Esther's door with a crutch, and the window slid open above me.

"I want you to know that I'm back in business," I shouted up as her face appeared over the sill. "Miss Winn shall have to find her own premises."

Esther wrinkled her nose. "Who the Hell is Miss Winn?" she said, before slamming the sash shut.

I stood there staring up at the empty window for a minute or two. Then I turned and hobbled away, swearing *"Bloody* Esther!" under my breath as I did so.

Chapter 9

A ragged curtain was pulled across the window, admitting only a thin sliver of daylight that fell across the pale face of Walter Wrangthorn.

"What happens... after?" he asked me.

It was a question I got a lot. People expected – perhaps not unreasonably – that having witnessed so many deaths, I might have gained some theological insight. But they were wrong. Nothing I'd seen had given me the slightest hint that anyone was really going to a better place. For all I knew there was no Heaven, no Hell, just a quiet oblivion while the body rots and the person fades into memory, until eventually even the memory is gone, and all that remains is a forgotten name chiselled into a neglected headstone.

Of course, I said nothing of the sort to Mr Wrangthorn. "There's a place at God's table set for us all."

"And my Betty? Will she be there? Will I be with her again?"

"I'm sure she's waiting for you."

"I can't leave my boys. Whatever will they do without me?"

I'd had the displeasure of meeting Mr Wrangthorn's two adult sons downstairs, and a seedier and more shiftless pair I'd rarely seen.

"They looked like fine lads to me, just like their father. I've no doubt at all they'll find their feet."

A blackshroud quickly masters the professional lies of her trade. People don't want truth on their deathbed. They want comfort.

I prepared the draught and offered him the glass. He eyed it cautiously.

"Will it hurt?"

"Oh, no. It's just like falling asleep."

Unfortunately, Mr Wrangthorn proved to be one of the small number of people for whom the draught wasn't remotely like falling asleep. Instead of relaxing into its dark embrace, his body shook and sweated in reaction against the poison. He shot me a wide-eyed stare of accusation, froth dribbling from the corner of his mouth.

"There there," I said, squeezing his hand and resting my other on his shoulder. "Don't try to fight it. Everything's going to be alright. Calm now, Walter, calm. That's it."

A messy death, but the draught did its job in the end. And before I left him I wiped the froth from his pillow, cleaned the shit from his bedclothes and arranged him in an orderly state, with his eyes closed and his hands resting one atop the other.

"He died very peacefully," I told his sons downstairs.

By the time I pulled back into Somers Street, the autumn sun had retired behind the rooftops and the wind was just beginning to bite. I looked forward to sinking into the chair by the fire for the evening, once Liability had been settled into his stall. I could put my foot up, indulge in a generous spoonful of laudanum, and let it soothe me into a pleasant doze before bed.

But first I had to run the gauntlet of Mrs Bogg.

She had a stall, like a little newspaper stand, except the only thing it sold – and those free to anyone who'd let her press one into their hands – was a stack of pamphlets, proclaiming in an excess of capital letters how I was the most evil woman ever to have lived. The proprietress, in mourning black, stood behind her stall like a preacher behind a pulpit. A small audience of ragged women had gathered around in curiosity, and Mrs Bogg was pronouncing her son's story unto them.

"I knew, when it happened. I just fell to my knees, right there in the street. There was this pain in my chest, right here," she clasped her hands over her heart, "and there were tears coming down my cheeks. Suddenly there was this light, from above.

Bright white light, it was, and the sound of weeping. It was angels. Angels weeping for my Gabriel."

The story seemed to get more elaborate every time it was told; the crying angels were a particularly recent addition. I was never quite sure if it was pure invention, or just her changing memory of events. Either way, her tale stopped abruptly when she noticed me approaching, and her face clenched into a sour stare.

"Here she comes," she called to her disciples. "The murderess herself, back from her latest victim." The women murmured vague noises of disapproval.

So far, her campaign to warn off my customers hadn't had the intended effect. Rather, she was acting as a quite effective advertising service for me. Thanks to her very visible campaign, *everybody* in Leeds now knew who I was, what I did and where to find me. But none of that stopped me from praying the woman would pack it in and go home.

As I passed she picked up a framed photograph and pointed it at me like a rifle.

"Look. *Look.* Look at him, damn you!"

It was a portrait of Gabriel. It was badly blurred, giving him a strangely spectral quality. Only his eyes were sharp, looking out with a doleful plea as though even death hadn't ended his torments. I didn't much want to look at it, and turned away.

As I was leading Liability into his stable, Mrs Bogg's verbal torrent was still audible from the street behind me. Eliza came slouching out the back door to meet me.

"Miss S."

"For the last time, Eliza, it's not Miss S. It's Blackshroud Summers, or just ma'am."

"Whatever. You just missed a man."

"Oh good. Men are so bothersome."

"I said you'd go round at once, soon as you were back."

"Joyful news. Oh well. Who, where and why?"

She scratched her head, a vacant inward look flashing over her eyes. "Um..."

"Oh for Heaven's sake, please not this *again*. How many times? Take their name and address and *write it down*. How hard can it be?"

I wasn't sure why I still employed Eliza. I was easily in a position to hire someone more competent. But somehow I just couldn't bring myself to fire her. With time and experience, I kept telling myself, she'd shape up. It was a delusion that hadn't showed any signs of realisation so far.

"He was... sort of... ordinary."

"'Sort of ordinary'? Remember last month when Mr Meadows called round and the only detail you could recall was that he was 'tallish'? And I said it was the least helpful description you'd ever provided? I think you've just bettered it."

"Well, I'm sorry, alright? He was ordinary, that's just what he looked like. And he said he knew you."

"I know a lot of people, and most of them look at least marginally ordinary."

"And he had a really ordinary name. No, two really ordinary names."

I searched my mind for past contacts of unexceptional appearance with two common names. "George Smith? Samuel Green? Joe Barker?"

"No, his second name wasn't a second name, it was a first name."

This statement took a few seconds to interpret. "Arthur James? Albert Edward? Richard Williams?"

She snapped her fingers. "William. That was the first name."

Something clicked in my mind. "Not... not William Johns?"

"That's him! William Johns!"

I looked at Liability, considering leading him out of his stable for another walk, but the old boy looked just as weary as I felt. With a wistful thought for my fireside and my bottle of laudanum, I left him in Eliza's care and picked up my crutches.

I happened to have an address for William Johns; after Mother got wind of my refusing his proposal, she'd sent me it "just in case". The address was in Burley, a mile and a half away. A mile and a half is a short walk on two legs, but a very long one on just one. Every step felt less like walking than like pulling myself over a stile, and the weight of my bag on its strap didn't help anything at all. By the time I arrived my shoulders were aching, my back was aching, my leg was aching, and somehow even my *missing* leg was aching. A stranger opened the door and told me that Mr Johns didn't live there any more, but he had a forwarding address in Woodhouse. Another mile and a half away.

When I reached *there* I was just about ready to collapse. I rapped on the door of the house – a spotless new-built brick terrace, identical in all regards to every other house for streets around – and tried to look like I wasn't leaning on the wall as I waited. I hoped that William Johns hadn't summoned me all the way out there just for a social nicety, or worse, an attempt to pick up where he'd left off, in the hope that my reduced condition had rendered me less particular. Blackshrouds aren't supposed to help people die by beating them over the head with crutches, but I was just about ready to if he began talking about his prospects again. However, when the door opened I was guiltily relieved to see his face pink and wet with the stains of grief. I knew where I stood now. This was a professional call.

He'd filled out since I'd seen him last without quite running to fat, and his hairline had receded by half an inch in a way that suggested that baldness lay some way in his future. Inviting me in, he reached for a plate from the Welsh dresser – one of a matching set with rather garish pictures of lolling-tongued spaniels – and arranged biscuits on it with shaking fingers. He showed no sign at all of having noticed my new scars or missing limb.

"It's good to see you again, Mr Johns," I said, ignoring the biscuits. But he didn't seem to hear me. Turning to the fireplace, he picked up a poker and started worrying the coals to no particular purpose.

"Mr Johns?"

"I need you to help her," he said in a small voice without looking at me. "There's no-one else who can now."

"Help whom?"

"My wife."

Mrs Johns was to be found upstairs, a slight doll-like figure laid out in a bed so deep and soft that a heavier woman might have sunk without trace. She was a weepy creature, and it took several attempts to get her to stop sniffling long enough to give coherent consent in front of two of her neighbours. Even when they'd signed and gone, she wouldn't take the draught until she'd told me – between fits of sobbing – all about how gentle and kind a husband she had, and how lucky she was to have him, and how happy he'd made her, and how sad she was that her silly problems were taking her away from him so soon into their marriage. In fact, she went through five complete rounds of this monologue, as repetitive as a mechanical music box. I kept saying things like, "go on," and, "please, take as much time as you need," but privately I was growing increasingly impatient with the warble of her voice. Just as she seemed in danger of winding herself up for a sixth cycle, I managed to gently nudge her to get on with it and drink her medicine, and she faded away into a welcome and permanent quietness.

She gave me cause for thought on the long limp home. I'd rarely seen anyone who seemed more satisfied with their husband. And William Johns could have been *my* husband, if I'd only said yes when he'd asked. A whole different life would have opened up for me. I wouldn't have trained as a blackshroud – he'd never have had with that – but he would have looked after me. No crutches, no missing limbs, no hostile women camped outside my door. I might have been happy, in a domestic sort of way, darning his socks and dusting the china. I might have had children already. I might even have grown to love him.

I tried to shake the idea out of my head. There was little use speculating about might-have-beens. True, Mr Johns was technically available again, but having just finished off his first wife I felt I'd very firmly precluded myself from any prospect of becoming his second.

It's a problem of my profession: it offers very few opportunities for meeting people. Or rather, I meet a lot of people, but in the worst imaginable circumstances for striking up a romance. And even if I did succeed in getting acquainted with someone socially, marrying a blackshroud wasn't to most men's taste. A wife with a profession was bad enough, but a professional killer was unthinkable.

It sometimes seems that we blackshrouds enjoy an honorary exclusion from the female sex. This has its advantages to be sure, but it also has its challenges. Perhaps it's not surprising that so many of us are lifelong spinsters. Although, this isn't always for lack of opportunity; the calling does attract the sort of stubbornly independent woman who disdains the very idea of marriage. Like Esther, for example.

"I'm just as much a maiden as the day I was born," she'd once announced without warning over the breakfast table. I'd almost choked on my porridge, even before she'd added, "and I plan to stay a maiden till the day I die." She'd waited until I slurped another big spoonful before saying, "No man's stirred my loins, and no man ever will," and that time I *did* choke on the porridge, coughing and spraying it across the tablecloth.

"Esther. *What* possessed you to say such a thing?"

"Look at that mess, girl! What's come over you?"

"What's come over *me?* I'm not the one talking about loins over breakfast!"

"I should think not! Blasted silly business. God blessed me with a mind free of that sort of nonsense, and I'm forever grateful to Him for it." She watched me take a hearty gulp from a glass of milk, and timed her next sentence carefully. "Here's my advice for you, girl: turn the men down and keep your panties up."

I'd never dared tell her I hadn't been a maiden since I was sixteen. The culprit was one Sidney Stuart from Gashouse Lane, a handsome young rapscallion with ermine hair and the morals of a weasel who'd of course been my absolute idol. He'd taken me for a few memorable adventures under the arches of Wetherby Bridge before dropping me unceremoniously in favour of some doxy from Collingham. In retrospect, I can only thank my blessings I didn't end up in a family way. Otherwise my life might have played out very, very differently.

Since then I'd grown less stupid and more careful. No-one since Sidney had been given the chance to make me a mother. In fact, no-one had been given the chance to do anything at all, apart from those two brief kisses with Jacob Arthington. And now that I was damaged goods, on top of everything else, I had to assume that my romantic prospects were behind me.

I took a deep breath of the chilly air as I hobbled into Somers Street, my whole body trembling with fatigue. Mrs Bogg had retired for the night, but she'd left Gabriel's photograph to welcome me home. *You should have got out while you had the chance,* his eyes seemed to say. *You could have been at peace now. Like me.*

Instead of opening the door I stepped round the back and bent over Liability's trough, splashing the cold water all over my face and letting it stream down my neck and soak into my dress. Liability nuzzled my wet cheek. I slumped my head against his dear old muzzle, and felt better. A little.

Inside, the first thing I did was reach for the bottle of laudanum. I measured out a teaspoonful in shaking fingers and swallowed it down. By the third spoonful my fingers had stopped shaking. By the fifth a beautiful numbness had started to wash out all my aches and pains and worries. It wasn't as permanent a medicine as the draught, but it was a most effective one all the same.

A month and several bottles of laudanum passed by before the incident with the photographer.

It wasn't too often I had to deal with photographers, back then: they were mostly an affliction of middle class deaths, and I got very few middle class clients. But Emmeline Hook was most certainly one of them. She owned a townhouse on one of the old streets of Leeds that still carried a proud Georgian grandeur, even if the royal purple wallpaper had long faded to lilac, and the rich carpets worn threadbare by the feet of children and grandchildren. And all those feet had marched their owners back to the family home from far and wide, to pose together for one precious picture.

The old matriarch sat pale but rigid in her wicker throne, her frizzy grey hair pinned back beneath a white crown of lace, croaking instructions to her battalion of offspring that were obeyed like royal decrees.

"Howard, move a little to the side there, your elbow's blocking my face. Olive, do stop snivelling, anyone would think it was you dying and not me. Philip, be *still* child, you'll come out a smudge if you wriggle like that. Do you want to spend the rest of your days as a smudge? Noah, no need to look so damned cheerful, I've still time to cut you out of my will if I've a mind to."

There were so many of them it took an age to squeeze them all into shot. With some effort and cajoling, children were knelt in front of adults, gaps between siblings who weren't on speaking terms were forced closed, and an ill-favoured nephew was shunted in behind Big Ernest's left shoulder where he was barely visible.

"We're nearly there," said the photographer from beneath his black sheet. "Everyone just huddle a *little* bit tighter."

I wasn't in his photograph, so I was free to watch him at work. When he emerged from beneath the sheet he proved to be a clean-shaven man not much above thirty in a neat silver waistcoat. Not a tall man by any standards, but with a meticulously well-groomed look that covered every aspect of him except his hair, which protruded in unruly auburn wisps as though he'd just stepped out of a strong wind. As he knelt behind his camera he glanced sideways, his eyes meeting mine. I gave him a smile. He flashed me one back, then returned his attention to his machine. His fingers darted in quick, precise motions, whipping the cover from the plate.

"Be still, now, everyone." The babbling crowd of relations stiffened and hushed, contorting their faces into what they imagined were expressions of dignified neutrality. "Stiller. Like statues. I want to see lichen growing on your feet, and pigeons settling on your shoulders. That's it. Good. Now, everyone say 'prunes'."

"Prunes," intoned the family.

His fingers slipped the cap from the camera's brass eye. An unearthly silence and stillness followed while he counted down a few long seconds under his breath, then the cap was back on.

"And... relax."

I found an excuse to talk to him later, when the family was in the long process of saying their goodbyes to old Mrs Hook, one by one.

"Still here?" I asked, feeling more like a nervous fifteen-year-old than I'd have liked.

"Mrs Hook has asked for a second photograph."

"Not... a post-mortem?"

It's thankfully a forgotten artform these days, but back then it was still very much in fashion to photograph the dead. I imagined with some distaste the camera's lens leering over Mrs Hook's lifeless face framed by the white cushions of her deathbed. Or – worse still – the family portrait recreated, only now with the the once-vibrant old matriarch staring silently out from amongst her dynasty with cold, vacant eyes.

He wrinkled his nose. "Oh no, no. Not that. I much prefer to work with the living, even if the dead are better at sitting still. Mrs Hook has requested a deathbed photograph, yes, but *before* the event. A pre-mortem, you might say. With her blackshroud."

"*Me?*" I flustered. I'd never been in a photograph before. "Why me?"

"It's a general rule of my trade: any picture can be improved by the addition of a beautiful woman." He shot me a suggestive little smile, quick as a camera flash.

I felt a blush prickle over my cheeks and hoped it wasn't noticeable, but was fairly certain it was. "Well! Really!" I said rather pathetically for lack of anything better that came to mind.

He nodded. "Really."

"You know, it can be considered improperly forward to tell a woman she's beautiful before even telling her your name."

"My apologies, allow me to do things in the proper order. My name is Quicksilver." He bowed. "And you are beautiful."

"Why thank you." I shifted on my crutches. "You do tell some very pleasant lies, Mr Quicksilver."

"Not *Mr* Quicksilver. Just Quicksilver."

"What an extraordinary name."

"It's my professional name."

"And what's your unprofessional name?"

"You'll find out if you ever get to know me unprofessionally." That dratted little smile again.

He was, I mused, a most forward, predatory little man. Not my type at all. Quite inappropriate. The proper thing to do was to make my excuses and move away. Instead, I moved a few inches closer. "And how does one go about getting to know you unprofessionally?" I said with an inappropriate little smile of my own.

At that point I was interrupted by one of the Hook brood, who subjected me to a dreary conversation about money. By the time I'd escaped him Quicksilver had slipped away, and I didn't get another chance to corner him.

Mrs Hook was borne upstairs in her wicker chair by two of her sons and laid in a bed between moth-bitten, wine-red drapes. One last round of emotional outbursts from all present, and I was finally able to shoo everyone else out of the room. Everyone, that is, except Quicksilver and his camera.

"Thank God," said Mrs Hook, "I thought I'd never be rid of them." She allowed her rigid muscles to slump at last, all at once looking another decade more ancient. But her eyes were still sharp and vivid, and they flickered back and forth between me and Quicksilver, who stood leaning on his equipment. "Everything I say and do in this room is confidential, correct?"

"For my own part, entirely," I said. "However, do remember the photographer is also present."

"Oh, I already know *he's* confidential. Come here, Quicksilver."

"Emmeline," he said in a soft voice, and came. Tears sparkled in his eyes. He dropped to his knees by the bedside, grasping Mrs Hook's limp hand in his own, and to my utter astonishment planted a long, tender kiss on the back of it.

I cleared my throat uncomfortably, not sure what was happening or what I should be doing about it. My discomfort deepened considerably when Quicksilver stopped kissing her hand and kissed her full on the lips. It was a hot-blooded, passionate kiss, like between young lovers in their first flush, and it was unearthly to see a kiss like that between a dying woman and a man fifty years her junior. I was hypnotised by the sight for a good thirty seconds or so before I remembered myself and turned to look out the window, studiously watching the smoke billowing from chimneys across the street.

"My angel," Quicksilver cooed behind me.

"My pretty one," Mrs Hook purred back.

"I know you've told me to stop asking this, but are you *certain* you won't change your mind?"

"It's a bit late for that now, isn't it?"

"No. It's the *perfect* time. Think how much you'll enjoy telling that rabble outside they'll have to wait a bit longer for their inheritance. I'll personally escort them out the door for you, quite rudely, and then we can have one more wonderful night together. Or a lot more. As many as you can desire."

"How many times? My spirit may be young, but my flesh is old, and my bones are old, and they're telling me they need to rest."

"When did *you* ever listen to what anyone told you?"

"And you think I'll break a lifetime's habit and listen to you of all people?"

"I just don't want to lose you."

"But this is what *I* want, and I'm a selfish old woman who gets what she wants. As you well know. If it helps, I think I might have done this years ago, without you to keep me entertained."

He made a sound that was three parts laugh to one part sob, and I heard them kissing again.

"Go on now, out with you, or they'll start to gossip."

"The photograph—"

"Bother the photograph."

I turned back to face them as I heard him step towards the door. With one hand he straightened his jacket while the other wiped one small tear from his face.

"This is goodbye then, Emmeline."

"Goodbye, Quicksilver."

"I—"

"It's alright. There's nothing more to say." She smiled. "You've done good. You can go now. Go!"

He nodded, closed his eyes, and took a deep breath. When he opened them again, his face had assumed its previous professional neutrality. He picked up his equipment, turned, opened the door, and left.

Mrs Hook now finally turned her attention to me. "Sorry you had to witness all that. You were the only way I could contrive it. That gaggle out there would never have left me alone in a room with a strange man." She rolled her eyes. "Who knows *what* might have happened."

"That's... quite alright."

"He's a devil, isn't he?" She said this as though it were a commendation. "Five years, I've been keeping him. If only I'd found someone like him at your age, instead of that yawn of a man I married."

"I'm... glad you found someone who makes you happy."

"You disapprove, don't you? I can see you disapproving. It's all over your face."

"It's not my business to approve or disapprove. People's private affairs are their own affairs."

"Really? Well, I'm an incurable old gossip and I love nothing more than prying into other people's affairs, the more private the better. In fact, why not die doing what I love? How are *your* affairs, Miss Summers? Any promising men in your life?"

I felt the blush coming back, deeper than ever. "Not... not really."

"Not really?"

"Not at all."

"Well that's a shame. A young flower like you."

"It's difficult. In my position." I tapped my dove and dagger with a crutch handle.

"I can imagine. May I matchmake for you? It's another bad habit I'm rather partial to."

"Really, there's no need to do that."

"Dying woman's prerogative."

I sighed. "If you must. Who did you have in mind?"

"Quicksilver, of course."

"*Him?*"

"He's *very* good. And very discreet."

"Mrs Hook! I do hope you're not serious."

"I've never been more so. And if you want him, you'd better jump on him quick; he's in demand, that one. With me gone he has an opening to love someone else. A Thursday evening opening, to be specific. He's marvellously expensive, but I trust a woman in your position can afford that."

"In demand? Thursday evening? I don't understand."

"My dear, wasn't I clear? Quicksilver is a *professional* lover."

I looked about for Quicksilver after the death, but was disappointed. Next Thursday evening came along and I entertained a fantasy of heading round to his studio and seeing if he really did have an opening, but of course I did no such thing. Instead I stayed in and looked over my accounts, trying to let cold hard numbers push all the girlish silliness out of my head. It worked, for a while, and laudanum worked even better. But the next week I faced an ordeal that tends to make even the most committed of spinsters dream wistfully of lost love: a wedding.

Francis was getting married. The bride was a pretty young flower named Blanche, who tripped over the skirts of her dress half-way down the aisle and fell flat on her face. Not an auspicious start to a marriage, perhaps, but it did afford Francis a splendid opportunity to dash forward and act the gentleman. He offered an arm to help her back to her feet and whispered a few quiet words of reassurance when she stammered out apologies to everyone for making such a scene.

During the ceremony, Francis kept sneaking sideways glances at her, breaking out into a little grin each time. I couldn't help but remember a day from our youth when he'd spotted a beautiful swirled marble lying lost in the gutter. For hours afterwards he'd kept pulling the thing from his pocket and taking a peek at it, as though to remind himself that he really did own such an exquisite object. He had the very same expression, slightly disbelieving of his own good fortune, as he looked at his bride.

After the wedding they posed for a photograph. They took a while to compose their faces into stern aloofness for posterity; Francis kept collapsing into giggles when he was asked to stand still, and he set Blanche off giggling too, and then they had to start all over. I nudged my way to the front of the spectators and my heart skipped a beat as I saw the photographer for the first time. He was half-hidden under his black sheet, but I was sure I recognised those legs. What I couldn't work out was what Quicksilver was doing down there in London, of all places?

Francis and Blanche broke out into a new fit of laughing, clutching each other with tears rolling down their cheeks. While everyone was distracted watching them, I hopped over and placed a discreet hand on the sheeted figure's shoulder, squeezing softly. "You never answered my question the other week," I said, quiet enough for only him to hear. "How does a girl like me get to know a man like you *unprofessionally?*"

"Eh?" He threw the sheet back, revealing himself to be an entirely unfamiliar man with a thick beard and eye-watering halitosis. "Sorry love," he spat in a voice loud enough for everyone to hear. "Thanks for showing an interest, but I'm a happy married man."

I turned what must have been an interesting shade of beetroot, mumbled something incoherent and hurried away. I kept an embarrassed distance from the rest of the congregation after that, until it was time for Francis and Blanche to go start their new life together. Before she stepped into the carriage she tossed her flowers out over the crowd. Blanche, quite in contrast to her appearance, had the throwing arm of a Greek javelineer; the bouquet shot well over the heads of the grasping bridesmaids with a fine spin along its axis, arcing perfectly towards where I hovered at the back of the throng. Why not, I thought, and reached up to catch it. Unfortunately, catching has never been one of my talents and I fumbled it, the flowers landing in a muddy patch beside me with a soft splat. I bent to pick them up, but before I could do so I was rugby tackled out of the way by Francis' new sister-in-law, who brandished the bouquet over her head like a prize trophy.

"You can't push a cripple around like that!" I protested from the floor. Using one crutch I hauled myself back upright; the other, I wielded like a club. "Not unless you're looking for a *fight...*"

I advanced on the bouquet thief.

I didn't see my brother again until the morning, when he and his new wife accompanied us to King's Cross to see us off.

"One of the many uses of a wife," he said, gesturing to where Blanche stood locked in conversation with our parents, "is as a decoy to draw off attentive relations and let a man have a private chat with his sister."

"Really? And has she found any uses of a husband yet?"

"Honestly, I think I'm mostly ornamental."

"Like a garden gnome without the beard?"

"Sounds about right."

I gave him a prod between the ribs. "You look after that girl, or I'll come visit. That's a threat."

"Please, you must visit! I want Blanche to get to know you properly. I'm afraid she's gotten the impression you're a bit of an animal."

"What? Why does she think that?"

"Well, if I remember correctly, you and her little sister had to be pulled forcefully away from each other, both screaming like wildcats. And that was *after* you propositioned the photographer. I couldn't be more pleased with your performance, dear savage little sister, but Blanche has more delicate tastes."

My skin crawled. "About that thing with the photographer. I thought he was someone else."

"Quite understandable. However is a woman to guess that the man concealed behind the camera is in fact the photographer? He could easily be, say, the handsome young coachman engaged in a game of hide-and-seek?"

"You're going to tease me about this for years, aren't you?"

"Until the day I die. And on that subject, I hope you're more careful to identify the right person in your professional life than you are in your love life. 'Sorry I killed your uncle, I thought he was someone else,' doesn't quite cut the mustard."

"Francis!"

"Alright, alright, enough teasing. For today, at least. Really though, are you alright?"

"I'm fine. Business is doing pretty well these days."

"I didn't mean business. Are *you* alright?"

"Me? Yes. I'm fine too. Perfectly happy."

I tried hard to convince myself of the truth of that on the long train ride back up to Leeds, despite Mother peppering me with pointed comments like, "it's so nice to see *one* of my children married," and, "I wonder how long it'll be before I'm *next* invited to a wedding?" By the time I arrived back at Somers Street the early November night had already fallen, and I felt weary down to my bones.

Mrs Bogg was asleep at her post, snoring peacefully. I let myself in. There was a sound of giggling from upstairs; Eliza had invited Alfie the greengrocer's lad round again. I didn't officially know about Alfie, and didn't feel like breaking the illusion now, so I moved quietly about the kitchen, trying not to make a clatter as I searched for my laudanum. Eliza had hidden it again, but I eventually located it under the tea cosy and reached for a teaspoon. Then I thought better, and put the teaspoon back in favour of a tablespoon.

I eased myself into the chair by the fire, doing my best to ignore the rhythmic squeals of bedsprings from the room above. Instead I focused on keeping the tablespoon steady as

I filled it almost to the brim, looking forward intently to the peace it would bring me.

All at once, the thought arrived that there might be an even more effective medicine for my troubles than laudanum.

"Sod it," I said out loud, and poured the liquid back where it came from. I hobbled over to the safe and clicked it open. Reaching past the bottles of the draught I grabbed a few heavy coins and slipped them into my purse. After checking myself in the mirror with a grimace, I sneaked out of my home as quietly as I'd arrived.

It was a Thursday evening, and I had someone to see.

The studio – set well back from the main road with the words "Quicksilver Photographic" painted on a small oval sign – was dark behind frosted windows, but a soft orange light slipped through the curtains of the floor above. I stood rooted to the spot outside, wondering if I really dared knock on that door. It was too big a step. I wasn't that sort of a girl. I was a respectable blackshroud, with a reputation to uphold. What if people found out? I'd be the gossip of every street corner. My business would disappear. It simply wouldn't do. I should turn around and go back home. That was the sensible course.

"I believe I said, 'Sod it'?" I told myself sternly, marching myself up to the door with two purposeful swings of my crutches and rapping loudly.

When Quicksilver answered he didn't ask why I'd come. He just gave me one of his devilish little smiles and offered me a hand. I took it, and let him lead me into the warm upholstered womb of his private chambers. There I surrendered myself to the pleasures of his clever fingers, and closed my eyes dreamily as he whispered the sweet professional lies of his own trade into my ear.

Chapter 10

My dearest Miss Summers,
*   I am arranging a small social gathering*
of blackshrouds, and would be delighted if you
would honour us with your presence. A room in
the Oak in Headingley has been booked for the
purpose; I hope to see you there on the eighth of
May, at five.
*   Yours in friendship,*
*   Blackshroud Selina Abbott*

I stared at the card as though the postman had instead delivered a keg of gunpowder or a stuffed octopus. I turned it over, to see if the reverse held any more information that might redeem the object. It did not.

"Look at that," said Eliza, craning over my shoulder. "A party! Sounds fun."

"No, it really doesn't."

Blackshrouds don't socialise. We're solitary creatures, like cats. When we happen to meet there's usually a lot of snarling and unsheathing of claws until one of us backs down. A roomful doesn't make a party. It makes a free-for-all.

"Can I go if you're not?"

"What? Of course I shall go. It would be unthinkably rude not to, since I've been invited. Unless an urgent patient turns up that night, of course."

"Eh, probably won't happen."

"Oh, I don't know. I can always invent one."

But in the end, despite my misgivings, I did attend. It was a morbid curiosity that carried me, of the sort that drew crowds to the Colosseum to watch Christians fed to lions.

"If I'm not back by midnight," I told her, "gather a dozen strong men to form a rescue party."

The village of Headingley was quiet as I stepped off the tram, or at least it was once the contraption had clattered away up Otley Road. The smoke, smells and clangs of Leeds weren't welcome out here. A well-buttoned gentleman in black stepped out of the churchyard of St Michael's with a bonneted lady on his arm. He greeted me with a tip of his hat, and the couple promenaded away down the well-swept street.

I have to admit a personal distaste for the place. It stems almost entirely from its most famous landmark, the Shire Oak. Legend has it that the tree, in its youth and vigour, was a meeting point of some significance in Saxon times. Now, however, the once-mighty oak was no more than a ruin. A few dead, rotting branches grasped into the air like black skeletal fingers; a tortured scream of twisted wood, looming over the heart of the village. Only a few fungal growths of green leaves marked the thing as still living at all. If ever there was a tree that needed a blackshroud, it was that one.

And Headingley had no shortage of blackshrouds on that night. Inside the inn I was shown to a private space with a fine view over the bowling green, and tables set out for two dozen with silver and good china. Only four of the places were already filled by my fellow professionals. To my immense relief there was no sign of Esther. Selina Abbott sipped alternately at a bowl of soup and a glass of white wine, while Mercy Shepherd sat gulping down what looked like a whole calf's head with roast vegetables and a pint of porter. The other two I didn't know; I was introduced to Fanny Burgess of Halifax and Lettice Luther of Pontefract. Selina offered me some wine. I declined.

"Are there many more coming?" I asked.

"Oh yes!" said Selina with a gesture around the room. "Half the West Riding got an invite. But I hope they don't *all* make it; I only ordered ten decanters of wine, and *someone* has been through half a decanter already." She glared at Mercy, who carried on shovelling cow into her mouth with perfect indifference.

Selina didn't have cause to worry. As the hour ticked on from five towards six, our number remained stuck firmly at five. We sat around just one of the tables in prickly silence, broken now and then by Lettice saying, "Well this is nice, isn't it?" or by Mercy accidentally inhaling a roast potato through her nose and spluttering. Selina drummed her fingers on the table, looking through the windows with increasing anxiety.

"Oh!" she said at last, jumping to her feet. "That's Blackshroud Ambrose's carriage!" And she rushed out the door to meet it. Two minutes later she was back with a new slump in her shoulders. "Ambrose sends her apologies. She's been called to attend the Earl of Batcliffe's household."

"Stuck-up cow," spat Mercy. "It's not enough that she gets the gentry. She's got to make sure everyone knows about it."

"You don't see me chasing after earls or bishops or the like," said Fanny. "And if I did happen to get one, it wouldn't even signify."

"Absolutely," agreed Lettice. "I'd treat them just the same as I treat any other client."

"And I certainly wouldn't *gloat* about it."

"I wouldn't even take them on," said Mercy. "I'm a humble blackshroud for humble folks, and that's good enough for me."

"Well said. What do honest folks like us need with nobs like that anyway?"

"Much better off without them."

Selina nodded at the wisdom of this and looked around at the empty tables. "No-one else is coming, are they?"

"No," said Mercy. "And you know what that means?"

"What?"

"It means we've got ten decanters to get through between the five of us. Ladies, let's get drinking."

* * *

We discovered, somewhere part-way through the third decanter, that we were all very good friends. It was an uneasy friendship that rather fell apart into tears and accusations during the fourth, but by the fifth we'd forgotten what it had all been about and were firm friends once again.

It was the start of the sixth decanter when the footman arrived. Fanny was just finishing off a delightfully tasteless anecdote about an old bachelor who proposed to her on his deathbed, and the applause and laughter was loud enough that none of us noticed our visitor until he cleared his throat loudly.

"I need a blackshroud," he announced.

"I'm a blackshroud," said Mercy, attempting to rise to her feet but staggering and sitting down again with a bump. "But I'm a drunk blackshroud. Fanny, you go with the man."

"Why should I do it? I'm a drunk blacksmith too."

"Caroline, what about you? You might be more... more soberer."

The footman looked uncertainly from face to face. "Maybe I should try elsewhere...?"

"That might be for the best, sonny."

"Do any of you ladies know where I *can* find a sober blackshroud? Sir Edwin Carrcroft is dying."

"Sir Edwin *Carrcroft?*"

"*Sir* Edwin Carrcroft?"

Barely two minutes later we staggered out onto Otley Road, breathing the cool night air and trying to think sober thoughts. We piled into the carriage pulled up under the ominous shadow of the Shire Oak. There was a lot of elbowing and arguing before we managed to fit ourselves in with myself, Selina and Lettice – as the three slimmest – wedged uncomfortably into a seat meant for two. The footman closed the door, looking deeply unhappy with the situation.

"This is ridiculous," I said. "We can't all help him die."

"Quite," agreed Selina. "You all get out and leave him to me."

"And why you, might I ask?"

"Because a certain quality of client expects a certain quality of blackshroud. Blackshroud Ambrose – *my* former mistress – is always being called to treat lords and sirs and whatnot."

"*She* is. *You* mostly treat farmers and tinkers."

"I should do it," said Mercy. "I've more experience than any of you."

"I think I might be most soberest," I countered, rather self-defeatingly.

"This is hopeless. We'll just have to let Sir Edwin choose for himself."

The carriage raced through the quiet streets of Headingley and turned into a drive by a small lodge. The Carrcrofts' home came into view as we rolled up the curve of the drive, an angular edifice of grey stone squatting uncomfortably in the bosom of its manicured grounds.

The butler met the five of us in the entrance hall. He was as grey as the house, and almost as old. Behind him, the entire household, from the housekeeper down to the stable boy, were dressed in their best black and arrayed in a neat line across the hall. We all made an effort to pull ourselves up into the proper image of well-mannered, well-bred and above all well-behaved ladies.

The butler gave a low bow, with an audible creak of his back. "Thank you all for coming. My lady is on her way from her other estate, but has begged you not to wait on her if Sir Edwin is in distress." His eyes sliced across us. "Why are there five of you?"

The footman hurried to the butler's side and whispered, "I'm sorry sir, but they're all—"

"Blackshroud Mercy Shepherd," Mercy stepped forward to announce herself with a curtsey, cutting him off. "*I* am Sir Edwin's blackshroud. These four are simply here to witness the great man's passing."

"Although if Sir Edwin should prefer a different one of us, we'd all be most honoured," put in Fanny.

A couple of wrinkles deepened on the butler's brow. "This is extremely irregular. I shall have to consult Sir Edwin." He glanced at a door.

"No need," said Mercy, pouncing for it. "I can take care of everything from here."

But we weren't letting her take the prize *that* easily. "Let's *all* go see Sir Edwin," Fanny said, and we jostled behind Mercy into the room.

I, on my crutches, was the last through the door. "We'll let you know if we need anything," I said as the butler looked set to make some objection. "Thank you." And I closed the door firmly in his face.

Sir Edwin Carrcroft lay in a bed in the centre of the room, a pale and sagged figure with weak, bleary eyes. The room was dark, with thick curtains drawn over the bay window, letting in only a stray gloom. White sheets covered most of the furniture; I spotted the pedals of a piano peeking out from under one.

"Which of you is the blackshroud, then?" said Sir Edwin, his voice a weak rasp.

"Whichever of us you'd prefer," I said quickly before Mercy had time to assert herself again.

"Oh. Blast. Not more decisions. I thought I was finally past making decisions."

We gathered around him, perched on chairs and sheeted tables, and murmured simpering words of reassurance, sympathy and condolence.

"You know," he said after a grating cough, "it's good to hear some voices in here again. This used to be the drawing room, you know. We'd have quite the parties in here. Music. And dancing. The most interesting people in all of Yorkshire. Until Amelia and that ghastly doctor decided I was too ill for parties. Then they turned it into this dreadful mausoleum. Everything under sheets. The only thing not under a sheet is me, and I suppose that's what you're here to correct."

"Now now Sir Edwin," I said, "it's your decision and you don't have to listen to anyone else. Not even your doctor. Not even your wife. You don't have to die if you don't want to."

"Do stop talking rot, Sticks." The other four looked at me with a smirk of triumph. "Death is coming whether I want it or not. Which I don't. But I'd rather your potion than this slow wretched fading." He closed his eyes and let out a papery sigh. "I only wish I could feel the sun on my face one last time, before I go."

"You can." Lettice stepped over to the bay window and threw back the curtains with a sweep of her arms. There was just enough left of the evening sun to fill the room with warm golden light. She helped Sir Edwin to sit up in bed, letting the sunlight shine upon his face.

"That's it. What a wonder of a woman you are."

Lettice had a superior smile on her face as she knelt down by the bedside and took Sir Edwin's hand. "Are you ready? If you are, I can send these other four away."

"I'm nearly ready. So nearly. It's just... it's a ridiculous thing, but... I think I'd be more ready, if I had a drop of whiskey to steady my nerves."

Mercy, with uncanny efficiency, located the sheet covering the drinks cabinet and pulled out a bottle of good Scotch and a few glasses.

"Splendid stuff!" he said when the glass was raised to his lips, after coughing a couple of times. "That's what I call service from a blackshroud. Now I can truly die a happy man." He eyed the rest of us sideways, a glint of cunning in his eye. "Although, I would *so* love to hear the sound of music one last time..."

Selina whisked the sheet off the piano.

It turned out that Selina could play rather well, and that Lettice had a very good singing voice. The pair started off with something from *La Sonnambula* but when this didn't prove to Sir Edwin's taste quickly switched to *H.M.S. Pinafore*.

Fanny and I looked on glumly, feeling hopelessly outmanoeuvred, as he nodded along happily in his bed, sometimes singing the odd snatch of lyrics that he knew. Mercy kept his glass well filled with golden whiskey no matter how much he spilled. But our own chance to endear ourselves came when Sir Edwin announced that wouldn't it be wonderful if he could *dance* one more time? And so the two of us heaved him out of bed, and – with his right arm secure over my shoulders and his left over Fanny's – we whisked the invalid around the room in a series of swings and swirls; or at least, as close to swings and swirls as three inebriated people with three working legs between them can really manage, which as it transpired was a sort of slow, ill-coordinated shuffle.

"I am the monarch of the sea!" he croaked as loud as his failing voice could manage. "I am the ruler of the queen's na-vy!" There was a knock on the door and the butler's voice expressed an enquiry of concern through the wood. "Go away, you bothersome man!" croaked Sir Edwin. "I've never felt more *alive!*"

It was ten more minutes before the door finally opened. Mrs Amelia Carrcroft, still in her travelling clothes, stepped into the room looking perfectly furious, the staff peering in cautiously behind her.

"What – in the *world* – is going on in here?"

By that time the party was over. Selina sat slumped with her head on the piano keys and an empty glass slipping from her fingers, snoring contentedly. Mercy was leaning over Sir Edwin's bedpan with a queasy look on her face. The other three of us were standing around his bed, looking down at the dead man in a state of some shock. He'd died quite quickly, in the end. Of a heart attack.

Professional habit took over. I stumbled towards the newly-widowed Mrs Carrcroft in something less than a straight line and bowed my head respectfully.

"He died very peacefully," I told her.

Chapter 11

The most famous blackshroud in England is Belinda Mort. She was, for many years, one of the most exclusive and respected practitioners in London, seeing to dukes and diplomats, princes and poets. Unknown to everyone at the time, she was also a cold-blooded murderer, dispatching her illustrious clients against their will after obtaining their consent through trickery or outright forgery.

Fortunately, Belinda Mort was an entirely fictional character. The first issue of *The Mayfair Murderess* appeared on shelves back in 1848 and then a new one dribbled out relentlessly every fortnight for nearly two years. In each story Belinda would find a new and more colourful way to finish off her latest victim, and then use ever more audacious ruses to cover her tracks. It was lurid, tasteless stuff, and of course it flew off the shelves as fast as they could print it. The series came to an end when the anonymous author finally had Belinda caught and sentenced for her crimes, in a token nod to morality which fooled no-one.

The fictional Belinda may be dead and buried, but she is alive and well in the popular imagination. Most of us in the trade very much wish she weren't. Before Belinda, blackshrouds were a revered group, generally regarded as above suspicion. Now, there's a little bit at the back of everyone's mind that wonders if our black books are hiding any black secrets.

And not without reason. One of the great secrets of my profession is this: blackshrouds kill people – illegally and immorally – quite frequently. But not like you're probably imagining. No spiking people's wine with the draught; no forcing it down their throats while they kick and struggle. Nothing spectacular enough for *The Mayfair Murderess*. No, *real* murder by blackshroud is a less dramatic but much darker business.

Imagine you have an elderly relative you're keen to get rid of. She's costing you precious time and money to look after, and the sooner she dies the sooner you can get your inheritance. Imagine also that she's rather weak of mind, with a tenuous grip on who people are and what's going on around her.

"A lady's coming to see you today," you might tell her. "A nice lady. She's going to give you some medicine. Some good medicine, that'll make you feel better. Now listen, because this is important: when she asks you some questions, you have to say yes. You got that? Yes."

I've met a few cases like this. Confused older people who nod along happily to everything I say, but understand what's happening about as well as an elephant understands a piano.

"Of course she's of sound mind," the relative insists when I state the contrary. "Sharp as a needle underneath all that, you know. Been telling me for months how she wants to be with her husband up in Heaven. I'm sure you'll see she's sound if you have another talk to her. How about you take an extra few shillings for your understanding? No? How about an extra pound?"

I've never, ever taken their money. But others aren't so particular. There have been several cases where I've stormed away with some very sharp words for a would-be murderer, only to see the name of their victim appear in the obituaries column some days later, having been taken out by another blackshroud who I'll not name here.

But I can't claim too lofty a moral high ground. Because I myself, just once, was directly involved in a killing just as grisly and sensational as anything that ever graced the woodpulp pages of *The Mayfair Murderess*.

It was January of 1881, and the setting couldn't have been more fitting for a murder. A heavy smog hung over the town;

a pea-souper so thick that the warehouses crowding the riverbanks were no more than vague outlines in the murky haze. The lamps across Leeds Bridge had been left burning through the day, and each carried a sickly aura hovering in the foul air around it.

"This way, ma'am," the girl said, hurrying over the bridge. I hastened after her, pausing only to cough into my sleeve. I didn't know the girl's name, or where she was leading me. She'd only said the matter was of the utmost urgency. I was beginning to regret leaving Liability to wheeze in peace back on Somers Street; I could travel much faster and further on my crutches than I once could, but it was still achingly hard work after the first half-mile or so.

We passed by the South Market, took a couple of twists and turns into narrow side streets, and when we reached a certain secluded court she knocked twice on a white-painted door. Inside, I looked around in surprise. The building, from its exterior aspect, had looked like it might be a modest but respectable lodging house, but there was nothing remotely modest nor respectable about its interior. The place had the look of a private bar or club, but decorated with a tasteless excess of red velvet and white lace. Two women in dresses rather too revealing leant against the bar. One whispered something to the other as they regarded me, and both broke out laughing. Off in a corner, a greasy middle-aged man sat ensconced in a floral upholstered chair, enjoying the company of another young woman who had draped herself over his lap.

A very prim lady with sculpted silver hair materialised and greeted me stiffly, introducing herself as Miss Featherstone. I noticed her flash a subtle gesture to the girl in the corner as she did so, who whispered something into her client's ear. He gave a gap-toothed grin and lumbered to his feet, letting the girl lead him by the hand up a bald wooden staircase. Miss Featherstone watched them disappear around the corner before turning back to me.

"I fear you may have been called on a false errand, Blackshroud. Please allow me a moment to find out what's behind this."

She pulled the girl who'd brought me there off to one side. They spoke in whispers, but not so quietly I couldn't overhear.

"What's *she* doing here?"

"You said to fetch the blackshroud!"

"I said to fetch Blackshroud *Cartwright!*"

"Well I couldn't find her, could I?"

"Excuse me," I interrupted, walking over, "but if it helps, I was trained by Blackshroud Cartwright. Anything she can do for you, so can I."

Miss Featherstone exchanged a look with the girl. "Would that include... *discreet* services?"

"Absolutely," I said, having no idea what she meant but not willing to concede that Esther might be capable of anything I wasn't.

"In that case, there's a man upstairs who needs your attention. His name's Nathaniel Bennett. We found him crying in the street. We took him in and tried to comfort him, but he keeps asking for a blackshroud."

"I'd better see him then."

She nodded. "Good. Sophia, see her up."

I hobbled up the stairs behind Sophia to a corridor of closed doors. I was bursting with curiosity to peep through keyholes and see what sort of things were going on behind, but I was shepherded swiftly past them to the one at the very end. A woman in a pink dress stood guard outside it.

"We found him crying in the street," she recited as I approached. "We took him in and tried to comfort him, but he keeps on asking for a blackshroud."

"Um... right. So I heard."

She opened the door. I stepped inside. She closed it quickly behind me.

"Hello? Mr Bennett? I'm Blackshroud Summers." A man lay in the bed, but he didn't reply. "Sir? Can you hear me?"

He couldn't hear me, because he was dead. A quick glance was all it took for me to be quite certain; I have some experience in these matters.

He was tucked neatly into spotless white linen, dressed in fine worsteds and silk tie, his eyes closed as though asleep. Everything was a little *too* neat, *too* spotless. Real deathbeds are rarely clean or tidy, until the blackshroud arranges things on her way out. I couldn't avoid the conclusion that this scene had been arranged already.

Of the eclectic mix of faults I can lay a claim to, one is a tendency towards snoopiness. I find myself sitting in a lot of people's bedrooms while I wait for them to stop breathing, and I never can resist sliding open that top drawer, or turning the page of that diary. Here was a situation that was crying out for some quality snooping, and I was more than willing to step up to the challenge.

The first and most pressing question: how did this man die? Could he simply have dropped dead of his own accord? He was middle-aged and fat as a bull seal, after all, and there was no obvious sign of blood or struggle. I bent over him for a closer look. He had a full head of red-brown hair that fell down over the pillow like autumn leaves over snow. Amongst it, I spotted a few darker crumbs. Dried blood. Combing through his locks, I uncovered a heavy wound on the left side of his head, with protruding shards of white where the skull had shattered.

A few good minutes of snooping later, and I'd identified not only the location of the death but also the murder weapon. The location was marked by a splatter of dark red across one wall like the map of some cursed archipelago, which they'd tried to hide from sight – without much success – by repositioning a wardrobe in front of it. The weapon was a small but surprisingly heavy statuette of a naked woman in an indecent pose, suspiciously clean except for a spot of blood that had been missed in the crux of her cleavage.

Deciding there was nothing much more to be discovered, I turned to face the door and took a deep breath. Corpses I didn't mind, but I wasn't looking forward to the conversation that had to happen now.

Miss Featherstone imposed herself in front of me as I left the room. "Is Mr Bennett still of the same mind? A tragedy of course, but Sophia and I are ready to bear witness if he's sure."

"Mr Bennett is already dead, as I think you well know."

"Nonsense. The man was quite well when I saw him. Perhaps you'd like to check again? And take this for your trouble." She dropped a few coins into my palm. I looked down. They were shining gold half sovereigns.

"That man in there has been violently murdered. This is a matter for the police, who I fully intend to inform."

"There's no need to get the police involved. And no need to worry. I know a very good undertaker who's *very* discreet." More half sovereigns were pressed into my palm. "Now how much more does *your* discretion cost?"

After only a few moments' greedy hesitation I handed the coins back. "My morals are not for sale, Miss Featherstone."

I enjoyed saying that sentence rather a lot, but it made several fine cracks appear in the old lady's porcelain face. "Please, Blackshroud. It'll be the end of my business if this gets out."

"*What* a shame that would be." I made to storm out but she caught my sleeve.

"Stop! Before you go, there's someone you should meet."

I let her show me into one of the rooms and then follow in behind me. As I did so I wondered if I'd just made a fatal mistake. No-one knew I was there except her and her girls. No-one was likely to have seen me step inside, through the smothering smog. I was cornered and out of sight, and there was nothing to stop them disposing of me alongside Mr Bennett now that I'd become an inconvenient witness.

Three figures waited inside the room, and stood as I entered. One was the girl Sophia. One was the girl in the pink dress. The other, her face disfigured almost beyond recognition by blossoming bruises and the wet shine of tears, was Millicent Barden.

"*Millicent?*"

"Ma'am!"

She stumbled forwards and wrapped her arms around my waist like a boa constrictor. I put an uncertain hand round her shoulders as she buried her face in my bodice and wept her heart out for two long minutes. Miss Featherstone and the other two girls quietly left the room.

"Millicent, what happened to you? What are you doing here?"

She unclasped her arms and wiped a sleeve over her eyes. "I'm sorry, ma'am, after all you did for me, ma'am, I really appreciate it, ma'am, you must be so ashamed of me...."

"Please, Millicent, you don't have to call me ma'am all the time. I consider you a friend. Call me Caroline."

"Thank you, ma'am. Um... Caroline."

"That's better." I took a seat, and gestured for her to join me. "Now, why don't you sit down and tell me all about it?"

The sad tale unfolded, with lots of sobs and apologies and – despite my insistence – ma'ams.

The trouble had started a few months before my accident, and reached its conclusion a few months after. One of the young doctors had taken a shine to Millicent. Nature had taken its usual course. Suddenly the doctor wanted nothing more to do with her, and denied any responsibility for the matter. He had, however, provided her with the name of an abortionist of some disrepute. That operation achieved its primary aim, but was botched badly enough that Millicent found herself a patient in her own hospital. There was no hiding the cause of her injuries. She'd been promptly dismissed for amoral behaviour. The doctor, naturally, received no penalty worse than a slap on the back.

"They said the Infirmary was no place for a prostitute," she said, blinking back fresh tears. "So I found somewhere that was. Once I got over the shame of it, ma'am, it's much better than the workhouse. Better than mill work, even. I earn enough to live decent, and Miss Featherstone looks after us, and treats us alright. It's just some of the clients I don't much like."

The late Mr Bennett had seemed a perfect gentleman until he'd got her on his own. Then he'd turned into a snarling beast, giving her the bruises that now covered her face. When he'd wrapped his hands around her throat and choked her, Millicent had lashed out with the handy statuette.

"I didn't mean to *kill* him," she said, trembling. "Honest I didn't! I was just so scared. I've never been so scared. But Miss Featherstone, she said she'd make everything go away."

And that was where I came in. A bent blackshroud, two bent witnesses and a bent undertaker, and everything looked like a good, honest, legal suicide. I cursed the woman for dragging me into this mess, instead of taking the more traditional expedient of just quietly dumping the body into the river at midnight.

"Please, ma'am, won't you help me?"

"Millicent." I took her hand. "I can't be involved in a conspiracy. I need to tell the police."

She jerked her hand away. "No ma'am, please! They'll put me in gaol and leave me there, ma'am, if they don't hang me! I can't go to the gallows, I can't! I'd rather you gave me the draught now, ma'am, than go to the police. Honest I'd rather."

I opened my mouth to tell her she had nothing to fear – that what she'd done was a clear-cut case of self-defence – but the words died on my tongue before they came out. Mr Bennett had clearly been a wealthy man, who would have wealthy friends to hire wealthy lawyers. Millicent was a fallen woman. In theory that made no difference in the eyes of the law, but I wasn't so naive to imagine it made no difference in practice.

"*Please,* ma'am," she begged.

* * *

I emerged from the brothel with new entries in my green and black books and a new weight of coins in my purse. I rehearsed the new truth in my head. Mr Bennett had been found crying in the street. The women at the brothel had tried to comfort him, but he kept asking for a blackshroud. So they'd called me. I'd talked to him, tried to bring him round into some sense, but found that he was quite adamant and of perfectly sound mind. So I'd given him the draught, and he'd died very peacefully. It was all witnessed and signed for. Miss Featherstone had done a very fine impression of his signature, copied from some papers found in his pocket.

As I limped home the evening felt strangely unreal, an effect helped along by the murky haze which still hung over the town. What had I just done? It was dishonest. It was criminal. It wasn't the sort of thing that I, as I liked to think of myself, would ever have done. It was more the sort of thing that—

I stopped dead, my hands tightening on my crutches, a neglected snatch of conversation intruding back into the front of my thoughts: "I said to fetch Blackshroud *Cartwright!*" I turned myself around and started towards Briggate, my crutches striking the flagstones like war drums.

Esther and I hadn't talked much recently. I still saw her occasionally, when we had the misfortune to pass on the streets, but mostly we exchanged little more than a few civilities which had a tendency to slide rapidly into incivilities. It had been a few years since I'd last set foot in Tenterhook Yard, but the grubby little passage hadn't changed a jot. I thumped a fist on her door.

"Esther!"

The window above groaned open, and Esther's scowling face peered down at me like an unusually grotesque gargoyle.

"Well well, if it isn't Her Ladyship."

"Let me in, Esther, I've got something to say to you."

"Whatever it is you can say it from down there. Or are you scared someone will come along and see you talking to the likes of me?"

"I've got something to say that *you* won't want overheard any more than I do. Now hurry up and open the Goddamned door."

"Alright, alright, keep your knickers on, I'm coming."

The inside of Esther's surgery *had* changed. It was dirtier, darker, untidier, with lines of her habitual movements visible in the dust that lay unswept on the floor. She filled the kettle and hung it over the fire before settling into her usual sagging chair.

"For Heaven's sake, girl, stop clattering back and forth and sit down. Can't you sit still for a few minutes at a time? All that endless pacing was bad enough when you didn't have two floor-thumping sticks. Now it's like hosting a stampeding wildebeest."

I stopped pacing, but didn't sit down. "I need to talk about your 'discreet services'."

"My what?"

"Using your position to hush up unnatural deaths."

"All a blackshroud's deaths are unnatural."

"You know what I mean."

"I'm quite sure I don't."

We eyed each other in silence for a few long seconds.

"You've a reputation for shady business."

"All a blackshroud's business is—"

"I'm talking about *crime*," I interrupted. "Disposing of inconvenient bodies."

"I'm not a bloody undertaker."

"You know full well what I'm talking about. It's illegal and immoral."

"I've never done anything immoral."

"I notice you're not denying the 'illegal' part?"

"What's legal and what's right aren't always the same thing. I'm surprised you haven't found that out already."

"I *have* found that out." I pulled the ill-gotten half sovereigns out of my purse and threw them into her lap. "Here. I don't want it. They wanted you. You have it."

She looked at the money, and looked up at me. "What are you blithering on about now, girl?"

So I told her everything, about the brothel and Mr Bennett and Millicent. Esther rose to her feet, the half sovereigns scattering over the floor.

"*Imbecile* girl!" she bellowed, and slapped me hard across the cheek. I reeled backwards, stunned, and opened my mouth to speak but Esther got in first. "I didn't train you to cover up murder for cheap whores!"

"But—"

"Oh, I know I've got a reputation. Bloody Esther, she *must* be crooked as a crankshaft, mustn't she? But I thought *you* knew better, girl."

"I—"

"*Be silent!* Let me tell you something. I may have broken a few laws in my day, but never the ones that count. I never gave the draught to no-one who didn't want it. And I never, *ever* covered up a murder. Oh, I've been asked. Many a time, I've been asked. But I've always told them where to go. Because I'm an *honest* blackshroud. Not like *you*."

"But I *am*—"

"I thought I told you to be *silent? Damn* it, girl. *Shame* on you. I thought you were different, but you're no better than Shepherd or Weston after all. Moral backbone of a plate of jelly. I wash my hands of you."

"You what?"

"I said I wash my hands of you. I disown you. I don't want my good name sullied by yours. Get out."

"But—"

"Out! Out of my sight! I can't stand the sight of you. Out! *Get out!*"

I got out, and quickly, the door slamming shut before I was even fully out of it, making me stagger into the yard and nearly fall. Shakily I straightened my skirts and took a deep, calming breath. A group of drinkers outside *The Tenterhook* watched me curiously, their conversation fallen silent.

"Gentlemen," I said to them with a crisp nod.

Esther's upstairs window creaked open again, and a small shower of golden coins drizzled over my head, rolling over my shoulders and trickling onto the cobbles below. The window slammed shut. The drinkers stared.

"You're welcome to those," I told them, and walked away. Behind me I heard a loud bustle as the men scrambled and wrestled over the golden gift from above.

"They ought to lock you up for what you've done," Mrs Bogg shouted as I limped past. "They ought to put your head in a noose."

Just that once, I found that gritting my teeth and ignoring her wasn't enough. I whirled on her, putting my face two inches in front of her own, one crutch brandished like an axe.

"Will you shut your twisted mouth and leave me alone?" I snarled. "You ignorant, bitter little woman!"

She didn't even flinch, just let her lips curl into a smile. "Go on. Hit me. Bash my head in. That'll shut me up, won't it? One more murder can't be so hard, for a woman like you. Then everyone will know what you're really like."

The blood pounded in my head, and for a moment I thought I really might. But prudence won a narrow victory and I backed off, without breaking eye contact.

Inside, and after a cup of tea that failed to calm my nerves, I hobbled around the kitchen in agitation. One leg of the table was propped up by the *Modern Guide to Practical Blackshroudery*. "A blackshroud is a mountain," it said to me. "Her virtue stands tall and unassailable; unyielding against the winds of compromise."

"Shut up," I said out loud, and whacked it with a crutch.

Would anyone find out what I'd done? The discreet undertaker would make sure the head wound wasn't easily visible, I was sure. No-one would know that Nathaniel Bennett had met a violent end, even if they saw the body. Unless they were *looking* for a wound.

It was my duty to report the death to the coroner. The coroner had the power to order a post-mortem. If that happened, I was finished. But the coroner rarely bothered to investigate deaths by blackshroud. Not unless there was some reason for suspicion. Like if there was a complaint raised by a relative of the deceased, for example, that they didn't think everything was above board. I'd already faced one inquest over Gabriel Bogg. They'd picked apart every detail of the case, and I'd survived it only because there was no wrongdoing for them to uncover. But Nathaniel Bennett's inquest, if it happened, would undo me. At best I'd be expelled by the Worshipful Society. At worst I'd end up in gaol. I might even get a cell next to Millicent.

In the morning, my fitful sleep was disturbed by a banging and clatter from downstairs, and I was certain it was the police come to take me away. But it only turned out to be Eliza packing a large bag.

"I'm leaving," she announced rather abruptly.

"Leaving? But why? Where?"

"I got that job, didn't I?"

Eliza had indeed applied for a new position lately, as maid to a wealthy household, which she considered quite the step up. The wife had asked me for a letter of reference. I'd sent one back that was, on the surface, very polite about Eliza, but between the lines said she was rude, lazy, incompetent and generally not to be hired under any circumstances. It seemed her new employer wasn't one for reading between the lines.

"They said I could move in straight away," she said, brazenly dropping a teapot that didn't belong to her into her bag.

"I don't know how I'll manage without you." I stealthily retrieved the teapot while she was distracted emptying the pantry of cocoa and jam.

"What are you talking about, Miss S? I was useless."

"Well, yes. But I'll miss you anyway."

Privately, I was making bets with myself about how long Eliza would last in the less forgiving atmosphere of a big house. About two days, I reckoned, then she'd be back begging at my door. And so when, exactly two days later, I heard a timid ring on the bell, I couldn't suppress a smug smile.

But it wasn't Eliza. It was the Reverend John Gilder.

"John! It's so good to see a friendly face." I invited him in and made some tea, apologising for the lack of biscuits, which I still hadn't restocked since Eliza's rampage through the pantry shelves.

"I've just had a most stimulating conversation with the charming lady who lives outside your door," he said, settling into a chair.

"I would assume you meant Mrs Bogg, except you inexplicably used the word 'charming'."

"Perhaps charming isn't the right word. Hypnotising, let's say. Like a dancing flame that one can't quite take one's eye off. She has such extraordinary passion."

"Passion on the subject of how I'm an evil murdering witch?"

"Passion for the memory of her son, and for the value of human life."

"If you've come to try and sell me on Mrs Bogg, you've had a wasted trip."

"Actually, Caroline, I came to talk about someone else entirely."

"Oh?"

"My wife's brother."

"He's not needing my services, I hope?"

"No. That's the thing. It seems you've already provided them."

"I have? I didn't think I even knew your brother-in-law."

"Nathaniel Bennett."

My heart slipped in my chest. Somehow, I think, I kept an outward appearance of calm.

"Yes. I did treat Mr Bennett. He... um... never mentioned you were related."

"We were all rather surprised to hear of it. No-one in the family had the least idea he was so troubled."

"Some people keep these things well hidden. And family are often the hardest to confide in." I felt filthy for saying these things to John.

"My wife was so shocked she's calling foul play. We were actually all set to raise concerns with the coroner, but then I found out it was *you* who'd treated Nathaniel, Caroline, and I knew at once that there couldn't possibly be anything unseemly going on. I told Rebecca I'd talk to you first, and that I was sure you'd clear everything up."

He sat back, smiled, and looked at me expectantly, waiting for me to clear everything up. I willed my hands to stop shaking, took a deep breath, and explained. "The... establishment where Mr Bennett died..."

"The brothel," he provided.

"...Yes. The people who work there..."

"Whores."

"...Right. From what I've been told, they found your brother-in-law outside, crying, and took him in. He was suicidal and wanted a blackshroud, so they called me." So far, all true. I *had* been told that.

"Can I assume this a polite fiction to save Nathaniel's reputation, and that he was in fact at the brothel for the usual reason?"

"Yes. I'm sorry."

"I'm under no illusion about my brother-in-law. He wasn't a terribly pleasant fellow, and I wasn't terribly fond of the man. But I'm struggling to imagine him as suicidal. So please, what did he tell you? What had happened to him, to make him so?"

I shook my head. "I'm sorry. What my patients tell me is strictly confidential."

"I know, but please, it would put our mind at ease to know. And neither of us will tell another soul."

"I'm sorry, John."

"Rebecca will insist on an inquest, Caroline, if I can't provide her an explanation. I dearly don't want to drag a friend through that. Please. Anything you can give us."

Panic rose in my throat and I mouthed something inarticulate.

He leaned forwards. "Was it Emma?" he said in a softer voice. "Was he still not over his wife's death?"

I nodded, grateful for the lifeline. "Please don't tell anyone I told you this, but... yes. He talked about her a lot. He clearly loved her very much, and didn't want to carry on without her."

Mr Gilder pulled back with a sharp intake of breath. "Nathaniel never married, Miss Summers."

An icy chill crept through me. "I meant... that is to say..."

He rose to his feet and reached for his coat. "I never would have imagined you, of all people, telling the Devil's lies. I'm afraid you've left me little choice. I don't know what rotten business went on between you and Nathaniel, but I'm going to the coroner and by God we'll get to the bottom of it."

"*Wait!*" I shot out a crutch to block the doorway, cutting off his escape. "John. Please. I've valued your friendship over the years beyond what words can express. If you've at all valued mine, will you do just one thing for me first?"

It was a cold, breezy day, although I was glad of the wind as it had blown away the wretched smog, making everything look clear and crisp and solid. I paused uncertainly as we reached the white door.

"What's the matter now?" he asked.

"It's just... this is a brothel. You're a man of God."

"The Lord's work has taken me to worse places than this."

"Very well. Ask to see Millicent Barden. And *please* try to phrase it so you don't sound like a prospecting client?"

He was in there for a good hour. I found a seat by the market and pretended to be interested in the comings and goings of men, women and animals until he reappeared and sat down beside me. He looked noticeably paler.

"Dear God," he said. "I knew Nathaniel had a devil inside him, but I never imagined he was capable of... of that. That poor woman."

"You understand now?"

"I understand why you did what you did. But no matter the motivation, I cannot sanction your actions. We cannot pervert the good laws of England for the benefit of another. It is but the smallest step from perverting them for the benefit of ourselves."

"You're going to report me, then?"

He sighed. "I should. It is my clear duty. But I can see the evils that would follow if I did. To Miss Barden. To my wife. To you, most of all. And it will not change the evil that has been done already."

"So... you're *not* going to report me?"

"No. I'm not. Even though it will involve lying to my own wife."

I let out a heavy breath. "Thank you, John."

"Please don't thank me. It's the Devil's own business." He stood up. "I only do this in honour of the friendship we've enjoyed. But you may consider that friendship over. Nathaniel isn't the only person today whom I've found to be so much less than I thought they were."

"John—"

"Don't. I find it difficult even to look upon you right now. I imagine I shall find the mirror a similar challenge for a long time to come." He gave me a stiff bow of farewell and turned to leave, but then paused. "Perhaps Mrs Bogg was right about you," he said over his shoulder. "Perhaps she was right about all of you."

* * *

I didn't find out what he meant until the morning after next, when Mrs Bogg herself knocked on my door.

"You won't see me here again," she said.

"I won't?" The news was a sudden ray of sunlight through the clouds that had gathered around me. "I'd say I'm sorry to see you go, but really, I don't think I could manage it with a straight face."

"Don't you go thinking you've won. You most certainly have not. And don't you go thinking I've forgiven you, neither. But the Lord spoke to me, and He said, 'She's not worth it. She's small. Just a nasty little Belinda. She's not the *real* enemy.'"

"Oh no! *God* said that about *me?* Gosh!"

She looked like she might bite me.

"Go on then," I said, "do share more of His message. Who *is* the 'real' enemy?"

She pointed to my dove and dagger. "Blackshrouds. The lot of you. A coven of murderesses. Moral filth. Someone ought to wash you all off the streets."

"And you think you're the woman with a big enough mop?"

"Your friend Mr Gilder set me up with some other mothers who've lost sons. And, he's said I can address his congregation."

"And what are you going to tell them?"

"God's truth. That only He gets to decide when we die. That life is sacred. That to end it before His chosen time is a mortal sin."

I shifted my posture into one that I hoped looked suitably contemptuous. "You really think you can overturn centuries of tradition with *that* old argument?"

"Yes." Her eyes were unwavering and unblinking. "I do."

"Everyone's leaving me."

It was Thursday evening, and I was sunk deep in one of Quicksilver's most indulgent chairs. The man himself was perched on an arm of the chair, running his fingers in slow circles over the back of my left hand. One of his photographic backdrops was propped behind us – the one with the foliage design – as though we were sat in a misty, out-of-focus forest.

"Not everyone."

"Everyone. Esther left me. John left me. Eliza left me. Hell, even Mrs Bogg left me."

"Isn't that last one a good thing?"

"It ought to be. But somehow the street seems so empty without her. Do you know, yesterday – you remember how cold it was yesterday – I actually shouted down to Eliza to take her out a cup of cocoa. And when I remembered neither of them were there, a sort of frosty feeling crept up through my stomach. It really made me understand, how alone I am now."

He stopped circling the back of my hand and kissed it instead. "You're not."

"It's like I'm a monster." I eyed the stump of my right leg critically. "Some shambling, deformed thing that sends everyone running as far and as fast as they possibly can."

"You are a beautiful and mesmerising woman, Caroline." Both of his hands closed around mine and I turned to meet his eyes. "And not everyone is leaving you. *I'm* not."

I gave him half a smile for his efforts. "You don't count. You only stay because I pay you."

"Just because a relationship is professional, doesn't mean it can't also be personal."

He went back to stroking my hand, and I sat letting those words circle through my mind, letting them outline the germ of an idea. An idea of how to make some small good come of all the rotten events of the past week.

I fumbled to my foot, reaching for my crutches. Quicksilver lent me an arm with a puzzled frown. "Caroline?"

"Sorry, my dear, but I have to leave. There's something I need to do."

"Can't it wait? I have quite the evening planned for you. Something..." his fingers twined with mine... "exquisite."

"Next week. It's best I get this done now." I extracted his hand from mine and planted a small kiss on it.

"But whatever is so urgent?" he said as he handed me my coat.

"I have someone to save."

Millicent's face was still a painter's palette of bruises, although the vivid blues and reds had faded to more subtle tones. I closed the door behind me.

"Ma'am? Is everything going to be alright, ma'am?"

"Yes, Millicent. Everything's going to be alright."

"*Thank you*, ma'am!" She seemed about to fling her arms about me again, but stopped herself and bobbed an awkward curtsey instead.

"Actually, Millicent, I have something to ask you."

"Ma'am?"

"I find myself in need of a new assistant. It's light work, and it includes board and lodging. It's not much, but it's got to be a whole world better than working here."

Millicent looked at her feet. "I'm not sure I'd be much good at that, ma'am."

"I think you would be. In fact, I suspect you may turn out to be the best I've ever had."

"You... you really think so?"

"I really do." I didn't tell her what a very low bar that was. But as time proved, Millicent was a courteous, dutiful and intelligent assistant, not to mention a trusted friend, and I honestly struggle to imagine anyone who could have done the job better.

Mrs Bogg never returned to her vigil outside my door. In time, I – and many others – would come to dearly wish she'd never left. Her sermons found an audience. That audience became a following, and then, as the years went by, a movement.

Belinda Mort had done much to undermine the reputation of English blackshroudery. Mrs Bogg was to undermine its very existence.

Chapter 12

The bell rang, for the third time that morning. I threw open the door and said, rather testily, "Yes? What is it, then?" Testiness isn't a good quality in a blackshroud. She should rather be, as the *Modern Guide* would have it,

> *a reservoir of patience, from which any volume*
> *of calm water may be drawn without risk of*
> *it running dry. Her world is a small one. It*
> *comprises only herself and her client. Her own*
> *woes and vexations are set aside before she steps*
> *over the threshold of this world, and not picked*
> *up again until she emerges back into the privacy*
> *of solitude.*

That's all very worthy advice, and something I've tried to adhere to, but my calm water does have its limits. On that particular day I was in the late stage of purchasing a house, which is an entirely bothersome business, and I'd been busy writing bothersome letters to bothersome people and was feeling very testy indeed. I wanted to sit and fester in my own vexations, and not have to drop them to be burdened with someone else's.

"Yes? What is it, then?" I didn't really have to ask. The man outside was clearly a patient. He had a drooping look to him. Drooping eyes. Drooping shoulders. Like a pot plant in dire need of watering.

"I need you to kill me," he said.

I was on the verge of telling him – still rather testily – that I didn't kill people, only helped them to die, when something stopped me. I recognised the voice. And, when I looked more carefully, I recognised the man. All of a sudden, the bothersome letters vanished from my mind and my world narrowed to just me and him.

"Mr Arthington?"

I must here commit something of a narrative sin, and draw you away from the failings of a young blackshroud and towards the failings of an old memoirist. Because the story of how Jacob Arthington came to become that broken figure on my doorstep – a story that begins long before the kiss outside the prison gates – is a most important and fascinating one, but one I've had the most wretched time turning into a coherent sequence of words. I've tried this way and that, and the resulting manuscripts have been crumpled into balls, torn into shreds, burnt, shouted at, and in the case of one particularly unfortunate draft, tied to the washing line and publicly flogged with the handle of an umbrella. I am not, and never have been, a reservoir of patience.

The trouble, I slowly came to realise, is that this part of the story isn't *my* story at all. I wasn't there. And any small literary talent I may have discovered seems only to extend to describing the events of my own life. The solution, then, was obvious: Jacob must tell his own story, in his own words. Fortunately – although I say this at the risk of rather spoiling the ending – Jacob is still with us to do so. And, although he insists he is a hopeless writer, the following account is a far more agreeable yarn than any of my own obliterated attempts. Trust me.

My name is Jacob Arthington. I was born on the 28th of June 1838, the same day Queen Victoria was crowned. My father took this as an omen of good things to come. "You, me lad, are meant for better things than this," he'd tell me as he led me by the hand to the privy block we shared with twelve other families.

I guess I have been the lucky one, compared to my five brothers. Two of them were dead before I was born. The other three followed by the time I was eight. My father wasn't a man to shed tears. Not when anyone was watching. He'd just suck on his pipe and he'd say, "Least our little prodigy's still here and well."

Prodigy. He really believed it, and all. Maybe because I was quiet and kept my own company, made him think I must be clever. He wasn't rich. He was a bricklayer. But he was sober and he was thrifty, and he put by just enough to keep me out of work and send me to school.

Mr Wharram had one golden rule in his classroom and it was silence. Silence as he read from the bible. Silence as we wrote our lines. Silence as he lashed us, else we'd get half a dozen more. I never had much trouble being silent, so I didn't get the cane too often. But all the same, I took none too well to school. So I bunked off.

Mr Wharram never told my father I wasn't in class. Must've figured he'd stop paying him to teach me, if he knew I wasn't being taught. So I was left to myself. In fine weather I'd walk out of town and into the fields, poking at hedgerows to see what crawled out. In wet weather I'd a spot by the canal, under a bridge. I'd watch the barges, or enact naval battles with pebbles in the weeds. When my father asked what I'd learned that day, I made something up. Like how treacle was made from black beetles. Or how German was just English but backwards. Always impressed him. Never went to school at all, my father.

I was a proper disappointment when I left school to get my first job, doing grunt work for a firm of painters and decorators. "All them years breaking me back to pay for your schooling. And for what?" I moved out of the house as soon as I could. We never saw much of each other after that. He died in '63, and I didn't find out till '65.

I stayed with the firm for near on twenty years. Did quite well with them, in a modest sort of way. My father had looked down on the trade. "It's a man's job to build walls and a boy's to paint 'em," he'd said. But I took a fair bit of pleasure in it. There's a rhythm in good brushwork. Strokes something in the soul.

I let down my father's memory in one more way too. I didn't get married, didn't carry on the family name. But though I'd no wife, I did have friends, of a sort, and I always looked forward to Saturday drinks in *The Tenterhook*, to mark the end of the working week.

It was there, in '74, I got talking to Johnny Purvis, and he put me a proposition that'd change my whole life.

"That place we've been doing, out Knostrop way." He'd pulled his chair up close and was talking in an odd sort of voice, somewhere half between a growl and a whisper.

"What about it?"

"Proper posh place that."

"Yeah."

"They must be right flush."

"Right enough."

"Gold, jewellery, paintings, the works."

"I'll bet."

"Wouldn't mind getting my hands on some of that."

"Me neither. But they don't leave it lying about while we've the run of the place, do they?"

Johnny laid out his plan. He'd borrow the keys from the supervisor and get copies made. We'd wait till the work was done and the house restocked. Then we'd turn up one night, let ourselves in, and let ourselves out.

"You in, Jacob?"

Sometimes I've wondered what would've happened if we'd got away with the caper. If the house had been as empty as we thought. If that servant hadn't managed to sneak up behind me. Or if Johnny had come to my rescue, instead of cutting and running. Perhaps things would've turned out no better than they did in the end.

I admitted everything, without naming Johnny of course, and pleaded my guilt to the court. They gave me six months with hard labour.

You might think six months was getting off lightly. If so, you haven't been inside. Those six months felt as long again as all thirty-six years of my life so far.

The diet was mean. The guards were meaner. The bed was as hard as the walls. I could put up with all that. But the crank nearly broke me. It was a square wooden box with a big iron handle, sat on a table in my cell. The handle was connected somehow to a counter, so the guards could check I'd turned it the proper number of times. If I hadn't, I didn't get to eat. It wasn't easy to turn. I think it was churning up a big pile of sand or something inside the box. And there were some screws in the back the guards could tighten to make it even harder work if they'd a mind to. I was careful never to get on the wrong side of the guards. Sometimes they tightened the screws just the same.

Took me ten hours of the day to turn the crank its full lot. Ten hours a day, six days a week, for six months. Arithmetic was never my strong point, but I reckon I must've turned that handle a million times and another half million on top. Only blessing was, at the end of it all, I was so tired I could sleep another ten hours. Didn't leave so many hours for sitting there in my cell, listening to the silence.

The gaol's rule of silence would've made old Mr Wharram proud. We ate in silence. Exercised in silence. Prayed in silence. The only sounds were the whir of the crank, the shuffle of footsteps, the jangle of keys. And the guards, who'd throw open a trap here and there to shout *"Silence!"* along with a ring of their baton on the bars.

Once a week, I'd get a visit from the governor, then the surgeon, then the chaplain. These were my only chances to speak to anyone. The governor would ask if all was well with me and I'd answer that yes, sir, all was very well, thank you. The surgeon would ask if I was healthy and I'd answer that yes, sir, I was very healthy, thank you. The chaplain would ask after my soul, and I'd answer that yes, sir, I was more at peace with myself than I'd been for years, thank you.

Wasn't true, though. I'd always thought of myself as someone who didn't much need anyone else. Someone who could live quite happy as a lighthouse keeper. Gaol taught me how wrong I was.

Can't remember how many weeks it was till I started talking to myself. Not many, I reckon. And it wasn't much longer till I wasn't talking to myself any more, because I'd imagined someone to talk to. She was a white feathered bird and her name was Sky.

"Come on Jacob," she tweeted in my ear one morning. I was sat on my bed, all sore and stiff and unwilling to raise myself. "There's no use sitting there like a pudding."

"What's the point?"

"You've got a breakfast to earn, that's the point."

"They can keep their bread and gruel. I ain't turning that thing one more time. I can't. I won't. I'd rather starve."

"That's silly talk, that is. Now stop acting like a vegetable and get on your feet, Jacob Arthington. That's it. Every turn of the crank is one turn closer to freedom. And don't you forget it."

We'd a lot of talks like that. And Sky always, always kept me going, even when I just wanted to curl up and weep.

The worst day came three months in. I was a few hundred turns off my tea. The crank came down to the bottom of its circle and I let it hang there.

Sky was perched on top of the box. "Jacob? What is it?"

"I... can't."

"Yes you can. Remember. We're counting down to freedom."

"But I'll never be free, will I?"

"Of course you will. As free as a bird, if you'll pardon the expression coming from yours truly. Whatever makes you say such a silly thing?"

"Me life were never much more than this, were it? Only instead of working a crank, I worked a brush. Ten hours a day. Six days a week. And instead of this cell I had a room what were barely much bigger. And a good deal colder."

"Now that's not really true, is it? I seem to remember you quite liked your old job, and your old room too."

"Only 'cause I never knew nowt better. And I won't even have *them* no more when I get out, will I? Where am I going to work? Where am I going to live?"

"However should I know? But I know you *will*. You'll find a way to spread your wings again."

I held the crank tightly, but I didn't turn it. "I've made a proper mess of everything. Threw away me chance at an education. Right disappointment I were to Father. Barely held down the meanest of jobs. No friends worth talking about. Never found no-one daft enough to marry me. I'm a failure, head to toe. What makes you think I'll ever be owt else, now I'm a convicted criminal to boot?"

"Because I know you better than that. Come on, Jacob. Leave the crank for a few minutes. Sit down. Let's talk this through."

I sat on the bed, put my head in my hands, and wept. Sky put a wing round my shoulders.

"You're not a failure," she said when the tears had stopped. "You've made some pretty bad mistakes. But you're going to learn from them, pick yourself up, and have a better future."

"I don't see no future."

"Then you are, as usual, suffering from a dismal lack of imagination. What have you always most wanted to do with your life?"

"I've never done nowt."

"Do stop being so self-pitying, or I'll give you a darned good pecking. What's your dream, Jacob?"

"Don't have none."

"You did. When you were a boy."

"That were stupid! I wanted to be a ship's captain."

"So you wanted to go to sea. That doesn't sound stupid to me. That's a real thing you could do."

"Now *you're* being stupid. Just imagine it! Me, going to sea. Me who's never been more than a dozen miles out of Leeds."

"And isn't it about time you changed that?"

I don't know how I'd have got through without Sky. Wouldn't, most likely. Either the asylum or the blackshroud would've been my end. But, she was always there, to lift me out of the darkness. And, slowly, as the end of my sentence came near, I started to feel hope. Under Sky's constant pecking, I'd begun to dream of a whole new life. A better life. A life at sea.

I walked out of Leeds Borough Gaol wearing my old clothes, but everything else about me was all new. The sunshine never felt so warm against my face. I dropped to my knees and stared up at that big, blue, open sky above me till tears filled my eyes.

"Mister? Are you ill? Are you hurt? I'm a nurse."

And there she was. Caroline. Right at that moment, she was the most beautiful woman I'd ever seen. Her hair caught the breeze and shone in the sunlight. And an expression of such kindness on her face. I let her take my hands and pull me back to my feet. And then, to my own surprise, I grabbed hold of her and kissed her, like a brute.

There was a great hullabaloo, and I ran off in shame. I got round the corner and stood there, cursing myself. The new Jacob looked to be an even worse turd than the old Jacob.

"Well don't just stand there, you big useless lump!" squawked Sky. "Get after her and apologise!"

So I did. And, though I deserved nothing of the sort, she accepted my apologies. She even let me take her for a meal. I think I did a frightful lot of talking. I'm a quiet soul, usually, but six months of silence had left the pressure of words building up inside, like a boiler without a safety valve. "I want to see jungles, and pyramids, and polar bears!" I remember myself saying. And she nodded as though it was some great wisdom, and not the blathering of a madman.

I left for Hull that same day, and Caroline gave me a kiss through the train window as it pulled away. I'd remember that kiss for a very long time.

Albert Dock was like nowhere I'd ever seen. An endless forest of masts and funnels and rigging, all creaking and clattering and sighing. I wondered which ship was going to take me away on my new life. Everyone but me seemed to know where they were going, and to be going there in a hurry.

I'd no money. No plan. I'm not exaggerating when I say I didn't know one end of a ship from the other. By all rights my dreams should've beached themselves right there and then. But by the best of luck, the first person I made myself talk to was Sigurd Henriksen, captain of the *Fuglen*.

"Why do you want to work on my ship?" he asked me with one foot on the gangplank.

"Just like the look of it, sir."

"And what other ships have you been on?"

"Hitched a ride on a canal barge once, sir."

"Can you speak Norwegian?"

"Can't say I've ever tried, sir."

"Can you cook? Carpenter? Mend clothes?"

"Not especially, no, sir."

"Do you have *any* skills that would be useful on a ship?"

"Yes, sir. I'm strong and I can work hard, sir."

"And let me guess, you're a fast learner too?"

"Not especially, no, sir."

He laughed at that. "At least you're honest."

"Try to be, sir."

He looked me over. Ran his fingers through his beard. "Well, I'm a fool for it, but I like the look of you, and I could use a sober pair of hands. Welcome aboard."

* * *

I stayed on the *Fuglen* for four and a half years. She sailed back and forth across the North Sea, so I never did see jungles or pyramids. But I saw a polar bear, just the once, when we ran up to Tromsø one unusual cold winter. And I saw other things. Blue fjords as tall as mountains. Whales making fountains amongst the waves. The Northern Lights, hanging there in the sky like dancing spectres.

I worked hard. I learned. Not fast, but I learned. Even learned what I thought was pretty decent Norwegian, although the crew pretended not to understand a word of it. I wasn't popular with the crew. Why would I be? I wasn't one of them. Wasn't a sailor. Wasn't from their country. Didn't join in their songs and back slapping below decks. And worst of all, I was the captain's favourite.

I never understood what Captain Henriksen saw in me. "You are English, and I am a devoted Anglophile," was how he explained it, the first time he took me for a private "colloquy" in his cabin. "I love everything about the English people and English culture. Except the food, of course."

I wondered if he'd seen my quiet nature, seen me standing staring out over the waves, and figured I must have the soul of a scholar or a poet hidden somewhere inside. Same mistake my father made. The captain was properly cultured, always asking if I was familiar with the paintings of Millais, or the novels of Eliot. I wasn't, of course. But he was never disappointed. For him, I reckon, all my ignorance was just another chance to teach. He loved to make his mark on people, and I was a blanker slate than most. And I liked hearing him talk about poetry and music and science and things, even if I never understood half of it. He'd got knowledge and he'd got passion, and they're always fine things to listen to.

I was much too embarrassed to admit I could hardly read or write. When he finally found out, I thought he'd be disgusted, but he just pulled out some paper and an ink pot and said, "We'd better fix that, then, hadn't we?"

The crew called me his "English pet". They made suggestions about what really went on in our colloquies. I didn't much care. It was an odd sort of friendship, me and the captain, but it was a good one. And they were happy enough years, for the most part. But those years came to an end on the third of March, 1879. There was a devil of a gale blowing. The *Fuglen* was trying for the shelter of the Tyne. Must've been dashed against the rocks. Try as I might, I can't remember the wreck itself. I remember rushing about below decks, struggling to keep my footing with the ship bucking and swaying something awful. Then the very next thing I remember is being in the sea.

I'd never been taught how to swim. And let me tell you, getting dropped in the sea in the middle of a storm isn't the best way to learn. But I didn't have much choice. I threw my limbs about, and somehow managed to stay above the water. But I knew it was hopeless. I couldn't see the ship. Couldn't see the shore. Couldn't see any of my crewmates. Couldn't even guess what direction they might be in. And the cold was pushing its way inside me, freezing me solid. Wave after wave poured over, and my head sank a bit lower after each one. With a weirdly calm mind, I knew this was the end of me.

"Swim, Jacob! Swim!" It was Sky, circling above.

"It's over, Sky. I'm done for." The cold had reached my bones. I felt numb. Felt nothing. It'd be so much easier, I thought, to stop fighting, sink down, let the sea take me...

"Wake up! Keep those legs moving! What would the captain say if he saw you giving up like that? What would your father say? Swim! You can do this! Swim with every last ounce of strength left to you, and then swim some more!"

I found some strength from somewhere. Fought to keep my head above the water. Swam till my arms and legs were all screaming. But not even Sky could keep the cold back forever. The sea was winning, and I was drowning.

But I didn't drown. There were voices, and hands, and I was pulled from the waves. The lifeboatmen wrapped me in blankets, fed me brandy, and rowed me back to Tynemouth. God bless those men, for it wasn't just me they stole from the sea that night but my crewmates as well. As I learned after I'd come round from two weeks of fever, only one soul went down with the *Fuglen*. Captain Sigurd Henriksen.

The first person to come see me once my mind was properly clear was a young solicitor's clerk, just off the boat from Christiania and looking a bit queasy for it.

"Captain Henriksen left you five hundred pounds in his will," he told me in Norwegian.

"What?"

He repeated it in English, but I still couldn't make sense of it. Took him a long time to persuade me he was serious. But he was. Within the week I was out of hospital with five hundred pounds in my pocket, and not the first clue what to do with it.

One thing was sure. I wasn't going back to sea. Just looking at it made me shiver all over, as I remembered my time in the waves. I wanted to be well away from it. And Leeds, the only town I really knew, was about as far from the sea as anywhere in England could be. I bought myself a first class train ticket, since I had the money.

"Five hundred pounds could last me, what, maybe six years, living rather grandly," I thought to myself.

"Six years of idling, and then what?" said Sky. "If you spend it wisely, you could set yourself up for life. Build yourself a business. Educate and train yourself to a job that you'll love and that means something."

In Leeds, the first thing I noticed was the smoke. You get used to it when it's always been there. But after years in the sea air it was a shock. The town seemed like nothing so much as a murky forest of chimneys, all pouring the muck up into the sky. Grey walls were turned black. White clothes were turned grey. I stood there on the street and coughed and coughed, till I reckoned that figuring out my future could wait till after a good stiff drink. Next day I lay in my hotel with a thumping head, and told myself the figuring could wait a bit longer, till I'd had a big meal and a bath. Couple of weeks later, I'd stopped thinking about my future much at all.

There was a whole side to life in Leeds I'd hardly known was there, as a working man. Concerts. Plays and operas. Museums and lectures and exhibitions. Now I was a rich man, I set about exploring all those things. I wanted to be like Captain Henriksen. He'd talked about paintings and operas and things like that with so much enthusiasm, it made me hungry to see them for myself. But I wasn't him. All that high-brow stuff just left me a bit baffled.

More to my liking were the music halls. I became a regular of the *Princess Palace* and the *Varieties*, and must've seen every bawdy song and novelty act going round town. And I found other things more on my level. Rugby matches at Cardigan Fields. Ice skating at the Horticultural Gardens. Even went up in a hot air balloon from Woodhouse Moor, though when I got back down I was shaking so bad I vowed to leave the flying to Sky from then on. There was good eating to be had, and I started to get a taste for wine. Best of all, I found out money could solve even the most personal of wants, if I knocked on the right door.

One year on from the sinking of the *Fuglen*, I counted what was left of my fortune. I'd spent nearly half of it.

"You need to settle down, stop drinking, and find a career," Sky told me.

"Bother that. I'm really living, Sky. For the first time in me life."

"Are you, though?"

"Yes! I can't go back to the bottom again, toiling six long days in the week. Just can't."

"You won't have a choice when the money runs out."

"There's always a choice. There's the blackshroud."

"You don't really mean that."

"I do and all. I'm going to enjoy me life as a rich man as long as I can. Then, when there's nowt but a few shillings in me pocket, I'll hand 'em to the blackshroud and die happy."

I didn't really mean it. Not then. But I started to, as the next year went on. Everything had changed, and nothing for the better. For the first few months, I'd properly enjoyed my new life. Times was, I'd get up in the morning with a grand feeling of excitement for a new day. Now, the thought of finding something to do with myself until I could lie down in bed again just made me feel tired. There was no more ice skating, no more hot air balloons, nothing like that. Stopped going to the music halls too. Some days I never even got out of bed. But the money kept running away faster than ever. I'd learned that wine wasn't just a nice thing to drink. It let me stop feeling much at all if I drank enough of it.

"Look at you," said Sky. "You're a blubbering wreck. Pull yourself together, man."

"Tomorrow." I took a big gulp of wine.

"You always say that. You never do. Jacob, please put down the bottle."

I took another swig, not enjoying the taste at all. "Why should I? Being drunk's the only time I'm happy these days. Don't you want me to be happy?"

"I do. And you can be. You've climbed yourself out of a darker hole than this. You can do it again."

It was harder and harder to believe that. In my prison cell, it'd been easier to find hope. I had hard things to blame for my misery. Walls. Bars. The crank. Now, I'd nothing to blame but myself. Heaven had sent me more strokes of fortune than I deserved, and I'd thrown them all away. I was a failure. A failed son, failed pupil, failed tradesman, failed criminal, failed sailor, and now just a failed man. I'd failed my father, failed the captain, failed myself. What was the point of carrying on? Some nights, curled and crying on my bed, I wondered if I might not even wait till the money ran out before I went to the blackshroud. Sky talked me out of that, at least. She kept my head just above the water, every time I looked sure to drown.

I marked two years since the shipwreck with a drink in my old haunt *The Tenterhook*. The end of the captain's money wasn't a prospect in the future any more. It was happening. I sat at the bar, stared at my beer, and figured through what I had to do.

I had to find a job. I'd no real skills except sailing and decorating, and I couldn't face going back to sea. Perhaps I could work in a decorating firm again? But I'd no good references, and a bad reputation. Not even the mills would hire a convicted thief. No, the only sort of job I'd get was the sort no-one else much wanted. Back breaking stuff, no better than turning the crank. It wouldn't pay for my fancy chambers. I'd have to take a mean little room somewhere in the slums. No more restaurants. No more wine. Just toil and squalor and want for the rest of my sorry life.

"I can't do it, Sky. Honest to God, I'd rather be dead."

I waited for Sky to tell me why I was wrong. But there was no answer.

"Sky?"

I was alone.

I'd come to think of Sky as someone real. Someone alive and separate. She wasn't, of course. She was part of me. The part that still had a bit of hope, that still believed Jacob Arthington was worth saving. And that part of me was gone. Perhaps it was time the rest of me went too.

I had another drink, and another. Then I staggered to my feet and asked the barman where I could find a blackshroud.

"Blackshroud Cartwright, next door. Hey, hold on there fella, before you go and get yourself killed." He caught my shoulder as I turned, and looked me in the eye. "How about another drink first?"

I had two more. By the time I made it out I was reeling. I wasn't so far gone as to forget my purpose, though. I found the door that said "E. Cartwright, Blackshroud" and gave a good hard knock.

For a second, my drunken eyes thought the woman who answered was Queen Victoria herself. Looked enough like her it was frightening, all dressed in black, even if she was a bit fatter than in the portraits. And she definitely didn't look too amused.

"Don't stand there gawping, boy, what is it?" she said, and the spell was broken, because it was the least queenly voice a man could imagine.

"I... want to d... to die," I said.

"You want to sober up is what you want. If you still want to die when the Devil's drink is all pissed out of you tomorrow, then come ask me again." And she slammed the door in my face.

Next day I was sober enough, but I didn't go back. I felt willing to give life one last shot. Stayed off the wine and beer. Took long, sad walks from one end of town to the other. Searched the rooftops for Sky, but didn't find her. And neither did I find any new reason to keep on living. The thought of the draught was a sort of relief, like the bell that rings the end of a long and tiring shift. My mind was made up. I would die.

I didn't go back to Tenterhook Yard, though. I was much too embarrassed for that. I found a different blackshroud. My stomach was twisting all up inside me as I knocked on her door in Somers Street.

"I need you to kill me," I said when I stood before her, my eyes on the doorstep.

"Mr Arthington?" she said back, though I hadn't told her my name.

And here's another of those odd turns of luck that's come up again and again to turn my life in strange directions. For, when I looked at her, I found I knew Blackshroud Summers. She was much changed. All propped up on crutches with her right leg quite gone, and looking a woman instead of a girl. But there was no mistaking her. She was my Caroline.

I think we were both a bit shook up by it. Weren't sure where we stood with each other. We both remembered that kiss, after all. But in the end, she was my blackshroud, and I was her patient. She sat me in her parlour. "Why do you wish to die, Mr Arthington?" She sounded like she really cared about the answer.

"Nowt left to live for."

"What happened to the man who wanted to see jungles, and pyramids, and polar bears?"

"You remember that crap I came out with?"

"I remember that day vividly." She gave me the littlest smile. I turned red and looked at my shoes. "And I never thought it was 'crap', as you would have it."

"Well it were." I gave her a history of the years since. The *Fuglen* and the shipwreck. The money and how I wasted it. My love of life and how I lost it. "And that's how it is."

"I'm deeply sorry to hear that Fate has treated you so poorly. I've often thought of you, since we first met, and hoped you were off in some exotic part of the world, having swashbuckling adventures and making your fortune."

"Not asking for your pity. Only for your medicine."

"I'm not going to give you the draught today."

I jumped to my feet. "Why? Why not? Please."

"Sit down." I sat. "I'm not going to give you the draught *today*. I want to discuss your decision first. To make sure you understand what you're asking for, and to make sure you've fully explored all alternatives."

"I do. I have."

"We'll see about that. And then I'll ask you to go away and think through what we've talked about. Drinking the draught is an irreversible decision, and not one to be taken lightly. If you still want it after a few days' reflection, then I shall respect your decision and provide it. No matter how tragic a waste I think your death would be."

"You reckon I'm making a mistake?"

"I've seen the light of joy in your eyes once before, Mr Arthington. And where the light has shone once, so the clouds may part to let it shine again. Now let me just call my girl to fetch us a pot of tea and some cake. She makes the most excellent cakes. We can have a nice big slice and talk everything through, most carefully. How does that sound?"

By the time I left it'd turned dark. I'd worked so hard to convince her I was hopeless. But she still kept on saying I had a future, if I wanted it. I tried to see what she saw in me. Tried to find that little window of hope. But it was too well hidden. Three days later I was back on Somers Street to receive my death.

I was much calmer the second time round. A peace had come to me, like I hadn't felt in a long time. It was all over at last. All my worries. All of it. And of all people, I was glad it was Caroline who'd be there at my end.

I knocked on the door. She opened it, dressed in gloves, coat and hat.

"Come along, Mr Arthington. We're going for a walk."

"But—"

"I said, come along."

I went along. She moved fast and easy on her crutches, like a leaping dolphin. Even with two good legs I found myself falling behind.

"Where are we going?"

"Less talking, more walking."

We were heading towards Woodhouse cemetery. For a while I was sure that was where she was taking me, to show me my grave before she put me in it. But well before we reached it, she turned off onto another lane. Then she turned again, down a driveway full of weeds.

"Well?" she said. "What do you think?"

It was a farmhouse. Or, more accurate, it used to be a farmhouse. Its farm was long gone under acres of brick and cobble, everything but this one little triangle of bramble and teasel. The house was a wreck. The windows were small and cracked. The roof was bowed. An old sign on the door said *Paradise Cottage.* I thought this a bit rich.

"What am I looking at?"

"My new home." She pulled a big silver key from her purse and headed for the door.

"You're going to *live* in this?"

"I certainly am. Isn't it a beauty? Come in and take a look."

Inside wasn't much better. Dust and leaves crackled under our feet. I looked up the stairs and saw daylight through a hole in the roof.

"I still can't believe it's really mine," she said. "See this wall? This is *my* wall. And that window? That's *my* window. And this cupboard?" She pulled at the door of a cupboard. It fell off its hinges in a big cloud of dust and damp. "Well, never mind the cupboard. Will you take the job?"

"Job?" I prodded an old boot in the hearth. Something brown and furry shot out of it. "What job?"

"Didn't you used to be a decorator? I want this house decorated."

"It don't want decorating. It wants demolishing."

"Nonsense! All it needs is some love and attention from a skilled professional. You just need a bit of imagination." She went from room to room, explaining her plans. Don't think she saw the cracks, or the cobwebs, or the mouse droppings. She was excited as a child, pointing out curtains and carpets and paintings that weren't there yet. And, just for a second, I saw it too. And in that second I fell in love with Caroline Summers.

"So how about it, Mr Arthington? I'll pay you, of course, and I'll pay for any materials and extra help you need. And you can live here until it's finished, if you want to. Or would you still rather be dead?"

I bowed. "I am your man, Miss Summers."

So, she went back to Somers Street while I went to buy some tools. I walked circles round the place, making plans. Suddenly, I had something to live for. And someone.

Wish I could tell you that was the end of my problems. It wasn't. Life's not so simple. Next day was a bad day. First job was to sweep out all the cobwebs and other mess. Easy. But the brush looked so heavy. I didn't want to pick it up, no more than I'd wanted to turn the crank in my prison cell. I went for a walk in the spring air instead. By lunchtime the brush looked to have gained another fifty stone or so. I let it lie and went to buy a bottle of wine.

I couldn't understand what I'd been thinking yesterday. The task was too much for me. I was useless. No good for no-one. Certainly not good enough for Caroline Summers. Being in love's no comfort, when you love someone so far above you it don't even bear imagining.

She came that evening and found me drunk and idle. I thought for sure I'd be fired. Instead, she just looked at me, disappointed, and said, "Let's try and do a bit better tomorrow, shall we Mr Arthington?"

Day after that, I managed to stay sober. Even swept one room clear. Little enough for a day's work, but when Caroline saw it she just said how much better the room looked already, and what a grand job I'd done, and how much she looked forward to seeing the rest of the house clear. Next day I swept out the rest of the house.

Things got easier. Slowly. There were bad days. Days when I could do nothing but weep at how useless I was. But Caroline always picked me straight up with a few words of understanding. In her own way, she did the same job Sky used to do for me. And as my own bad days got fewer, I noticed that Caroline had her bad days too. Days when life weighed heavy on her shoulders. Got me thinking that she wasn't as lucky as I'd been, because she'd never had a Sky of her own. And that maybe, if there was no-one better for the job, I should have a go at it myself.

"Penny for your thoughts, Miss Summers?" I said one night when a cloud was behind her eyes.

"What? Oh. Nothing much."

"Don't look like nothing much, if you'll pardon me saying."

"Well... perhaps not. But I'm sure I don't want to bother you with *my* troubles, Mr Arthington."

"There's nowt'd bother me less. Now come on. Sit down a few minutes, and let's talk it through."

She seemed a bit unsure, but then she sat, and started talking. When she started, she didn't much stop. She talked about an old man she'd finished off that morning, who'd been lonely and sad, and had made her feel lonely and sad too. Talked about the names and faces of her patients, and how she used to remember them all, but now she didn't, and she was scared she was getting hard hearted. Talked about what right she had to be doing such an important thing, as opposed to all the better people who could be doing it. Then she asked if I understood.

"Nah. I don't. 'Cause I've never had to do your job, Heaven be thanked. But I'll tell you what I do know. You're proper good at what you do. I know, 'cause when I were going to die, you made me not feel scared. And that's really something, that is."

Each night after that, I'd always make sure there was a tin of cocoa for when she came round, and some milk and sugar, and I'd warm us up a pan. Then we'd sit and we'd drink and we'd talk. Sometimes she'd lift me up. Sometimes I'd lift her up. And sometimes we just sort of leant on each other.

As the months went on, the old farmhouse looked more and more like a proper home. I threw myself into painting, carpentry, plastering and papering. I found better people to fix up the roof, to fit gas lighting, and to put in a modern indoor bathroom.

211

"For the garden at the front, I'm thinking, instead of the straight drive, we could have a path, with a bit of a curve," I said on one of Caroline's visits. "And we could put in some trees and shrubs round it. That way, when you look in the gate, you just see a bit of the house looking out between all the green. With some flowers round the door, maybe some ivy up the walls. Reckon it'll look right nice and welcoming, but sort of private at the same time."

"What a marvellous idea! You've got a real knack for this, Jacob." She'd stopped calling me Mr Arthington some time ago. "I didn't even know you knew much about gardening."

"I didn't. But I'm learning. And I'm thrilled to see it finished as much as you are."

That was true, and it wasn't. Paradise Cottage was what I thought about from when I woke up to when I went to bed at night. But I dreaded the day there was nothing more to do. Because then, I'd have to move out. And I'd have no more excuse to see Caroline.

That day came in February of 1882, almost a year after I first saw the cottage. It was changed completely. Still an old farmhouse, but its walls were repointed and its windows reglazed. A dove and dagger weather vane stood over the nice straight pyramid of the roof. White frost covered fresh dug flowerbeds, that'd bloom into jungles of colour with the spring.

I was changed and all. Didn't drink myself stupid. Definitely didn't want to die. But I felt pretty sorry for myself all the same, as I handed my key over to Caroline. I was still in love with her. But it was a hopeless love, and I knew it. She'd never have me. I was too lowly for her. Too crude. Too poor. Too old. Too many scars inside.

"Jacob. I'm beyond words. Everything you've done..."

"It were my privilege."

We looked at each other most awkwardly. There wasn't usually a silence between us, but there was one right then.

"I guess this is..." I stopped, because I didn't know how to finish.

"I guess so. Take care of yourself. You'll always be welcome here."

We parted. She headed for the door of her new home and I headed for the road. And then something swooped over my head. A white feathered bird landed on the gatepost.

"Are you seriously just going to walk away, Jacob Arthington?"

"Sky?"

"Ask her the question!"

"But she won't—"

"Just ask it!"

I turned back to the house. "Caroline..."

She paused with one hand on the door and looked round. I walked up. And before I could have second thoughts, I dropped down on one knee.

I haven't talked to Sky in years. I still see her from time to time, perched among the chimneypots, watching over me as I tend the flowerbeds. When I do, I give her a tip of my hat. Caroline gives a wave too if she sees me doing it. She never flies down to me, though. Happy to say, I don't need her to. But it's a comfort to know she's there, and she'll be right there to catch me if ever I fall.

Chapter 13

It was what we blackshrouds call a "big death". Passing-away parties on a lavish scale were very much in fashion in the 1890s, and Mrs Lupton's was, if far from the most extravagant, certainly amongst the most sprawling. Black-suited sons and grandsons nursed whiskies in the parlour. Nieces and daughters-in-law crowded round the dining table to laugh and cry over precious memories. The hall was thick with cousins; the stairs clogged with childhood friends. Neighbours circled each other in the garden, scooping up sandwiches from trays and wondering if it was too early to stake a claim on the hydrangeas. Out in the street, an even more casual crowd of well-wishers and hangers-on were mostly there for a tipple and a chin-wag.

Given the choice, I'd much rather have been out there on the fringes. But, as usual, I was trapped right in the baleful heart of the thing. Mrs Lupton gave me a sympathetic glance, as though to tell me she understood perfectly.

"You know," I bent down to whisper in her ear, "my job is to offer an escape from torments. If you want to get out of all this, just say the word."

"Oh no," she said back. "That wouldn't do. They've been to such trouble, arranging all this."

She bore her sending-off with admirable grace. As people came to gush and wring her hand she told each and every one that they were dear to her, even the ones who weren't. When gifts were thrust into her arms she didn't question what on Earth she was supposed to do with them now, but only said "thank you" very earnestly. She even just about managed to keep her smile from sliding into a grimace while her nephew – who fancied himself a poet – intoned an interminable tract in her honour.

And then, finally, one last indignity. Her husband wheeled her out onto the front steps where her son-in-law rang a glass, hushed everyone to silence, and asked if she'd care to make a speech.

"Thank you all for coming. It's so good to see all my friends and family one last time." The was a long pause while her pale eyes blinked short-sightedly over the assembled faces. "Why, some of you I haven't seen in years! Is that you hiding in the back, Susannah? What a surprise to see you here!" Someone who must have been Susannah gave a wave. Mrs Lupton's gaze narrowed, and her cracked voice hardened into a sharp point. "You never came to visit before I was dying. Was it the free drinks that brought you, or did you just want to gloat?"

A ripple of uncertain laughter trembled through the air and then died, as everyone tried to work out if she was being serious or not. Mrs Lupton's eyes moved from face to face before settling on a new target.

"And you, Mr Prothero! You've some nerve turning up here after you stole those urns from my garden. Yes, I know about that. I was much too polite to say anything, but now I'm dying I'm feeling very ill-mannered indeed. You're a thief and a liar. Get off my property! Go on, off!

"What do *you* think's so funny, Mrs Redknapp? Twenty years I've lived next to you, and twenty years I've pretended to listen to your spiteful gossip over the fence. And twenty years I've wanted to tell you to shut your mouth and keep it shut. Well, I'm telling you now. Shut it!

"In fact, all of you, shut up and clear off! All you second cousins and somethings-in-law and people who met me once in 1865. Out! That's right, *out!* Yes that includes you, Mrs Apperley! Leave an old woman to die in peace!"

215

There was a general exodus. Mrs Lupton watched the crowd slink and mutter away with a stare that could have sliced steel. But she wasn't done yet.

"That's a bit better. Now, who's left? Ah yes. My dear children. Stand up here where I can see you; that's it. Oscar, it's every mother's duty to love her son, but with you it's been such a challenge. You've a mouth on you and a temper to match, and I pity that poor wife of yours. And Louise, you're a good girl, but you never did have much of a head on your shoulders. You married a hopeless wastrel, you know. Yes I'm talking about you, David. And as for you, Samuel, I think you've caused me more worry over the years than the other two put together. You've frittered away every penny you've ever earned, and you can say it's misfortune as much as you like, we all know it's pure selfishness.

"And that brings me to my darling husband." Mr Lupton visibly flinched as his wife's wheelchair swivelled towards him. "You are the most *frightful* bore. Day after day, bent over your newspaper droning on about horses and share prices and Gladstone as if anyone in the world cared. I certainly never did. And did you know you snore like a strangled walrus? I used to fantasise about smothering you in your sleep. But I'm glad I never did. Because Heaven help me I love you, you ridiculous man." She reached out to take his hand. "I love you, and I love our children, and I love the life we've had together."

When I'd finally got her on her own she said to me, "Do you think I overdid it a bit?"

"Not at all. I thought you were magnificent."

Secrets have a way of coming out in a person's final hours. Perhaps, after a lifetime of hiding these little fires inside our souls, we realise we're more afraid of them being snuffed out unseen than we are of letting them free. Or perhaps we just realise they no longer have the power to burn us. Either way, they're rarely let out as explosively as Mrs Lupton's. The privacy of the deathbed and the confidentiality of the blackshroud are the more typical outlet. Especially when that blackshroud is incurably nosy, with a talent for easing such things from her patients, like a woodsman can draw flames from a dying pile of ashes by prodding at it with a stick.

A disappointing number of these secrets are repetitive accounts of adultery, invariably confessed as though it were a rare and exotic specimen amongst the menagerie of sins. But I've also had thieves and fraudsters. I've had a man with three wives, a man who's wife had been invented for tax purposes, and a man who – for reasons too convoluted to follow – had spent thirty years of marriage pretending to be French. I've even had an honest-to-God Russian spy, who told me in perfect Oxford English some truly jaw-dropping tales of his exploits during the Crimean War.

I've had murderers too. One sherry-breathed old gentleman admitted in wheezy gasps that he'd strangled a business rival in his youth, and watched another man go to the gallows for it. The guilt, he said, had left him a hollow shell. As for a mildewed lady who confessed to slowly poisoning her father, husband and brother just to get her hands on their money, she claimed no remorse for her actions whatsoever.

It wasn't my job to dispense justice. It was my job to dispense the draught, and the murderers received it just the same as the poor woman who blurted out, in deepest remorse, that she'd once laughed at a very vulgar joke she'd overheard about her vicar, and was terrified she'd go to Hell for it. I certainly never shared their confessions with anyone else. I simply collected them, holding their little flames as tight inside myself as I held my own secrets.

My missing leg had become one of those secrets, albeit a fairly widely known one. I'd had a prosthetic made – polished oak with ivory joints, no less – that let me walk quite freely with the aid of no more than a light cane. I'd taken to putting a matching stocking and boot on the wooden foot, so that my shortage of limbs was quite invisible to the untrained eye. And if I couldn't move quite as fast or as easily as I'd learned to with my crutches over the years, then that was a price worth paying for looking respectable.

If there was one thing that two decades in the trade had taught me, it was that an expensive blackshroud was a powerful status symbol. My new carriage, for example – a gleaming black and gold number, with two fine stallions tied in front – was always carefully parked where the neighbours would get a good look at it. It was all part of the service.

When I returned to it after Mrs Lupton's passing, my groom opened the door for me and I stepped inside.

"Thank you, Gingham."

"Home, ma'am?"

"No. I have some family business to take care of. Could you take me on to Wetherby?"

The first family business was at St James' Cemetery. I'd plucked a few flowers on the way, and I laid them dutifully on my parents' grave.

We'd never been particularly close. Especially not latterly; they hadn't approved at all of my marriage to Jacob, considering him far beneath the family's dignity. For a while they'd quite stopped speaking to me, and me to them. Only in their final months had we made some peace with each other.

They'd had quiet deaths, the pair of them. My father died with the help of a blackshroud – not me, thankfully – but it was a private, tender affair; just them, Francis and myself. My mother died an even quieter death a few scant weeks later, quite without help from anyone. We call these "small deaths". That's the way I want to go when it's my time: surrounded by the handful of people most precious to me and no-one else, without any great fuss.

The other family business was at my parents' old house. I knocked on the door and Blanche opened it. She and Francis had been living in Wetherby for a couple of years, ever since Sparrow and Summers had sunk without trace into a quagmire of debt, taking along with it their London home and most of its comforts.

"Caroline! How lovely to see you," she said, maintaining a safe distance between us as she beckoned me in. All my best efforts to present myself as a tame and friendly sister-in-law had so far been in vain. She still looked at me as though I might at any moment strip down to my underwear and pull a cavalry sabre out of my knickers.

"And you. You're looking radiant today. How is my dear brother? Is he here?"

"He's... up a tree."

This description proved entirely accurate. He was to be found in the garden, a considerable distance up the big horse chestnut.

"Aren't you a bit too old to be climbing trees?"

He looked down, removing several iron nails from his mouth before speaking. "Why hello there! How's my favourite little Grim Reaper?"

"Not as grim as the sight of a middle-aged man scrambling about in the treetops like a particularly paunchy monkey. Whatever are you doing up there? You do know you won't find any conkers until the autumn, no matter how high you climb?"

"I'm building a treehouse." He gestured to a couple of precarious-looking timbers he'd managed to nail to the branches at odd angles.

"I see." I checked Blanche was safely out of earshot. "If you're having troubles with your marriage, you know there are easier solutions than moving into a tree?"

"What? No. That's not it at all. I'm as much in love with my wife as the day I married her. She can move in with me if she likes. We'll have treetop picnics and befriend squirrels. It'll be romantic."

"She doesn't strike me as the treehouse sort. But then, *you* don't strike me as the treehouse sort. What's this about, Francis?"

He scratched his ear with a hammer. "Well... I always imagined that I'd build a treehouse together with my son, one day. But... you know... Blanche will be forty next year, and... well, I'm probably never going to have a son. I know that now. But I figured, at least I can still have the treehouse."

Both Blanche and I had been married for fifteen years without the slightest hint of a pregnancy. In my case I blamed my fall, or perhaps *thanked* my fall, because I was actually rather grateful for this particular misfortune. But Francis wasn't like me. He loved children, all children, even the really noisy or sticky ones. And his lack was a sadness that a whole forest of treehouses couldn't make up for.

"Why don't you come on up? The view is spectacular from here."

I shook my head quickly. A distaste for high places was another legacy of my fall, and just thinking about being up the tree made me want to grab hold of something solid. So Francis came down to me instead, and Blanche came out with a plate of sandwiches and bottles of ginger beer, which we sat down on the lawn to enjoy.

"How's your business going?" Blanche asked me politely, as she always did.

"It's mortifying." Blanche stared at me in bewilderment, but Francis chuckled.

"Word on the street is, you might be out of a job soon."

"If this is about Mrs Bogg's rabble, I don't think I need to be too worried. They may be making a lot of noise, but really, they're just a handful of nuts."

"I wouldn't be too quick to dismiss them. A handful of nuts, planted in just the right spot, has a tendency to grow into a forest. And forests can be hard to uproot."

"Pah," I said.

"Pah? Is that your best argument in defence of your profession, little sister? 'Pah'?"

"Yes. Pah."

He took a swig of ginger beer. "When the trees take over, you and Jacob are more than welcome to come live in my treehouse."

I had an encounter with some Boggites on the way back home. A group of men in caps threw stones at my carriage as it passed by. One of them knocked the hat clean off poor Gingham's head and he had to stop to retrieve it, while they pressed their hateful faces to the window and called me a murderer, a whore, and even less savoury names.

When I arrived back at Paradise Cottage I saw they'd postered my gate again. Both the gateposts and the walls to either side had been plastered white with big black letters reading *STOP THE SLAUGHTER*. Thick blocks of print below pointed out, between highly selective bible quotes, that blackshrouds were responsible for more deaths than tuberculosis, and that the government should pursue a policy of eradication.

While I was tearing these hateful objects down, Millicent bustled out the door to meet me.

"Ma'am! A man to see you, ma'am. I put him in the parlour."

"Thank you, Millicent. A client?"

"Not sure, ma'am. But he had a funny name."

"How funny?"

"Quicksilver."

Well. I hadn't expected her to say *that*. A cold shiver ran through me and I pushed past her, thanking Heaven that Jacob was away for the day – with some of his gardening friends, comparing begonias – as I went to face the shadow of my past.

I'd last met Quicksilver fifteen years before, the Thursday after Jacob proposed. I'd stepped into his studio and been greeted by the familiar acrid stench of his chemicals, a smell that has become indelibly linked in my mind with passions of the flesh. He flashed his devilish little smile and moved to take me in his arms, but I dodged away.

"I've... actually come to say goodbye," I said.

"Goodbye? But why? Is it me? Or have you come down with a sudden sense of propriety? Because I know a few sure cures for that particular infection."

"No. I'm getting married."

"*Really?*" He broke out into a grin. "Why, congratulations! I always knew a lady of your qualities wouldn't go unclaimed for too long. Someone's made quite a catch, the lucky fellow. Is he as pretty as me?"

I ignored that. "Do you realise that you could have asked me the question yourself, any time in the last two years, and I would have said yes?"

"Exactly why I never asked, my dear. I'm not really the marrying type. It wouldn't have worked out well for either of us."

"Yes. Well. I want you to know, it's... it's meant a lot to me, coming here. *You've* meant a lot to me."

"And you to me. But you know, we don't really need to stop just because you've got yourself hitched?" He took my hand in both of his and started stroking my palm in that special way he had. "I can be *very* discreet."

Weak-willed creature that I am, I succumbed to his seductions and spent one last wonderful night in Quicksilver's arms. After all, I wasn't married *yet*. But that was the last time. I didn't trust myself to go near him again. We saw each other, from time to time, in our professional duties or just passing on the street. I gave him a polite nod of the head, and he gave me one of his smiles. But we'd never approached each other, and never spoken. Until now.

The Quicksilver who waited for me in Paradise Cottage didn't look much different to the one I'd known so well, except his hair had turned grey and he'd gained a few extra creases around the eyes. Both of these changes suited him well. He'd also taken to wearing white gloves and a tall white collar, which didn't. Even so, he looked far more young and beautiful than a man of fifty had any right to be.

"Blackshroud Arthington." He rose to meet me. He still had that same dratted smile, and it still melted something inside me. The chemical smell of his darkroom tickled against my memory.

"Really, since when did you call me anything but Caroline?"

"Forgive me, but I thought I'd better call you by your professional name, since I'm here for a professional request."

"Oh dear. Who's dying?"

"I am."

"You? But... you look the very picture of health."

"Look again." He removed a glove. I grimaced. He put it back on. "Syphilis. I picked the blasted thing up years ago. Don't worry; it was after our time together. Of course, that was the end of *that* career. I've been nothing but a simple photographer ever since." I must have looked dubious, because he appended, "Well... alongside a few other interesting sidelines."

I motioned him to sit down, and waved to Millicent to bring tea. "Tell me about it."

"It's an evil thing, this disease; it's been gnawing at me gently for nearly a decade, but now it's developed a ravenous hunger. It's consuming me, inside and out. I want to die on my own terms, before it gets a chance to finish."

"It doesn't look... *so* very bad yet."

"No? It pains me, from the moment I wake up to the moment I fall asleep. Even walking has become an ordeal. I've had to remove the mirror from my bedroom, as I cannot undress in front of it without the bile rising in my stomach. How long should I wait? Until the disease disfigures my face as well? Until it takes my eyes? Or my mind?"

"Oh, Quicksilver..."

He waved off my sympathy. "I have led a blessed and beautiful life, Caroline, and have shared it with blessed and beautiful people. I knew the risk I was taking. There's very little I would change, if I had the chance. Please don't mourn me. I don't. I plan to die exactly the way I've always wanted to."

"And how's that?"

"I believe you refer to it as a *big* death?"

I tried to stop him from paying, but he was having none of it. "You always paid *me*."

"But I don't feel right charging you. You're a friend. More than a friend."

"Didn't I tell you once, that a professional relationship can also be a personal relationship?"

Consent was witnessed. Plans were made. He wanted to have the party – and the death – at Paradise Cottage rather than his own "dismal" studio, which I agreed to. We set a date over a month ahead, to give plenty of time to send out invites and put his affairs in order, and for me to find an excuse for Jacob to be absent. The only thing he insisted was that it be on a Thursday. "Thursday was always our night together," he explained.

The day arrived, and so did he, looking more cheerful than those about to die usually did. "I've been looking forward to today for a long time," he told me.

"Death is nothing to look forward to, Quicksilver."

"No no, not the dying, the *party*. One's own death is simply the most wonderful opportunity for a truly unforgettable party. A once-in-a-lifetime opportunity, quite literally. And best of all I will take no part in the tidying up and don't even have to worry about a hangover. Really, it's almost worth dying just for that alone. It upsets me terribly, you know, that most people squander this one and final opportunity in the most dreary ways imaginable. Ah, look! Here comes my first guest."

A dozen or so people drifted in over the next hour; it was a wet day, so we all packed into the parlour. And then, to my horror, my husband turned up.

"Whatever are you doing here? I thought you were going to be all day helping Francis rebuild his treehouse?"

"I were, but it were raining, and your brother wouldn't have me working out in the rain. I did tell him I didn't mind a jot,

224

but he weren't having none of it. Gave me a lunch and sent me packing. Thought you could use a hand with your guests." There was very little that could be done to dissuade Jacob when he had a mind to be helpful. And so, he was soon dressed in his best suit, rigidly ladling out punch to my former lover's guests, saying things I'd never ever imagined him saying before, like, "How do you do?" and, "May I offer my commiserations, good sir, on this most sorrowful of occasions?"

"Jacob," I hissed at him. "Talk normally, for Heaven's sake."

"I don't want to embarrass you," he whispered. "There's some fancy folks here."

"You don't embarrass me. At least, when you're not sounding like an elocution lesson. Behave."

He toned it down a little, while remaining rather over-formal and uncharacteristically grammatical, looking as much at ease as a starched flagpole. I sighed and turned to Quicksilver's guests.

They were an odd lot. Mostly men but a few women too, mostly in their middle age or older, and mostly comfortably middle-class. They'd all arrived individually – no couples – and none of them seemed to know anyone else. I struck up a conversation with a grey-bearded gentleman in a monocle.

"I hope everything is to your satisfaction?"

"Splendid, thank you. And my compliments to whoever made this Battenberg. It's to die for." He twitched as he realised his *faux pas*, making his monocle fall out and splash into his wine. "I mean... I didn't mean... ahem. Sorry. Bad turn of phrase."

"Here; take another slice before it passes away." I gave him my most reassuring smile, and he looked a little more at ease. But I was feeling far from easy myself; my eyes kept drifting towards Quicksilver, who was shuffling through the crowd with his stiff syphilitic walk in a direction that drew him ever closer to Jacob.

I forced my attention back to the man in front of me. "If you don't mind my asking, how do you know Quicksilver?"

"Hmm?" He was busy fishing his monocle from his wine with his fingers and wrapping it in a napkin. "Oh, just an acquaintance of mine from the old days."

"An acquaintance?"

My eyes slid across the room to where Quicksilver had, to my deep discomfort, pulled up next to my husband and struck up a conversation. Somehow, he even seemed to have got Jacob to relax a bit. What could they possibly be saying to each other? Surely Quicksilver wouldn't let anything slip... would he? They were laughing now, like old friends sharing some private joke. Were they laughing about me?

"Yes, an acquaintance. Now if you don't mind, I need to go clean this dratted thing. It's forever getting loose from its string."

He hurried away, and I looked back towards Quicksilver and Jacob, but to my relief they'd parted ways as well.

As I made the rounds I found a lot of "acquaintances" of Quicksilver's. In fact, the party seemed to be peopled by nothing but. No family, no friends, no neighbours, no colleagues, just acquaintance after vague acquaintance.

"Quicksilver, who *are* all these people?"

"Really, Caroline? Haven't you worked it out yet?"

"No. Give me a clue."

"OK. I'll give you one. That lady in the green dress?"

"Yes?"

"One of my old clients. And not of my photographic business."

"I had wondered if *she* might be."

"I wrote her a letter explaining that as she was the most special, the most beloved of all my former clients, I'd be honoured if she'd be here with me – discreetly, of course – on my last day. How could she refuse?"

"Wait. *She* was your most beloved?" I crossed my arms stiffly.

"Of course not, my dear. I wrote everyone the same letter."

"But... you mean..."

"*There* it is. I do so love watching you all try to figure it out, but there really is nothing quite like seeing comprehension dawn. Yes. Everyone in this room is a former lover."

"But what about the men?"

"*Everyone* in this room is a former lover. Well, except for him over there. He's the vicar of Leeds. I invited him out of pure mischief."

I wasn't as shocked as you might think I should be. Amongst the secrets I've been entrusted with, I've heard the most seemingly respectable sort of folks admit to every sexual perversion you could imagine, and a few you probably couldn't. Some of these were so bizarre they made a taste for sodomy look no more than a mild eccentricity. So I continued to play the good host to Quicksilver's guests both male and female, but now careful not to embarrass anyone by asking how they knew him. After all, I wouldn't have cared to answer the question myself.

The punch bowl was emptied, and stronger drinks appeared. By this point just about everybody had cottoned on to the secret of the guest list, and the tense uncertainty of earlier had passed through a quiet awkwardness and then on into a genial camaraderie. One man pulled out a fiddle and struck up a lively number which had people jumping up to dance, some with quite inappropriate partners. The party began to spread beyond the tight confines of the parlour. A couple of ladies perched themselves half-way up the stairs to swap notes and giggle. Three of the men joined with Jacob in the kitchen to sing discordant, table-bashing sorts of songs with glasses raised. The man with the monocle and another man in a green jacket slipped outside, and we all pretended not to notice the noises and the rustling in the bushes. When I spotted the bemused vicar moving towards the window to see what was happening I quickly intercepted him. "We'd all be most honoured if you'd share some of your thoughts," I said, steering him firmly back to the safety of the parlour.

As soon as the sermon was over, the dancing resumed. I looked at Quicksilver, sat in the best chair with a drink in each hand, beaming over the congregation like a benevolent god. This was, I realised, in some ways more like a small death than a big one. He was surrounded only by the people he dearly loved. It was just that, for him, that was an unusually large number of people.

I watched him grow quieter as the rest of the party grew louder. Eventually he caught my sleeve as I passed and said, "Caroline, it's time."

"You're sure?"

"I'm sure. Oh, I was planning to keep drinking till I was half blind, then make a stupid speech, and get people to carry me out, but... I don't want to now. I'm just... tired. I'd rather slip out while nobody's watching."

The room I have set aside for this sort of thing is a small one, but a nice one. It has a big reclined chair, where patients can sit in front of the open window and hear the birds, and watch the bees buzzing over Jacob's hyacinths. Quicksilver nodded in approval as I led him in.

"How many times have you lain back and surrendered to my professional skills, dearest Caroline? Now, I finally get to lie back and surrender to yours."

I'd found out only when he'd signed his consent that he had an official, "real" name; when I recorded his death in my black book, that was the name I used. It felt like the single most intimate secret of all those he'd entrusted to me. I suppose I'd finally gotten to know him unprofessionally. I won't repeat the name here. To me he was, and will always be, Quicksilver.

That night, after all the guests had staggered home, or at least crawled under a bush somewhere to sleep, something was bothering me. Something beyond the death of an old and dear friend. It was only when I was climbing into bed alongside my husband that I realised what it was.

"Jacob. *You* were in the room."

"Hmm? What's that, my love?"

Everyone in this room is a former lover. That's what he'd said. He'd said it twice.

"At the party today. *You* were in the room. And you're not the vicar of Leeds."

"I... what?"

"You've been very quiet all day. Quieter than usual. And you were so nervous, at the party. That man Quicksilver... I saw you talking to him, it almost looked like... you didn't *know* him, did you?"

He squirmed in the bed. "Well, I didn't want to trouble you about it, but... yeah. I did know him. A bit. None too well."

"How?"

"It were back in the days before we married, he were just..." there was a long pause as he searched for the right word... "an acquaintance."

"I see." Did I see? Jacob had once admitted, when he came to ask me to end his life, that he'd hired an intimate companion for a while during his darker days. I'd had the tact never to mention it again once we were betrothed, and neither had he. I'd always assumed it had been a *female* companion. But had he ever actually said that? And then there was that strange relationship he'd had with his Captain Henriksen, who'd left him a fortune in his will. Didn't that all make far more sense if... if...

Or was I just adding two and two to get five?

"Caroline?"

"Yes?"

"You've never let a client have a party at our house before. And you've been right off all day. Did *you* know him?"

For a moment I was on the verge of telling him everything, and dragging the truth out of him too. But... no.

"I'd run across him once or twice. He was just... an acquaintance."

I'd had enough of hearing other people's secrets. Let Jacob keep his, if he really had any to keep, and let me keep mine.

Chapter 14

"Oh Lord, Oh Lord, why have you forsaken me?"
So lamented the Saviour as He hung upon
His cross. But God had not forsaken Him. For
He sent one of His lowliest servants, a woman
shrouded in black, to ease His suffering. She was
allowed to approach Him, for His guards thought
her no threat; they had not seen the dagger
beneath her robe. Thus was the blood of Christ
spilled on the earth of Golgotha. The bible gives
this woman no name, yet history has called her
the First Blackshroud.

When Christ returned to the Earth, He
blessed forgiveness on this woman who had
ended His life. Such was the beginning of a new
era, in death as of so many things, in which
"Thou Shalt Not Kill" was replaced by "Thou
Shalt Kill Only In Mercy".

"Here." I closed the *Modern Guide to Practical Blackshroudery*
and slid it across the table to Cordelia. She looked in some
distaste at the yellowed, well-thumbed pages, some of which
had worked quite loose from the binding, with their margins
full of pencilled notes.

"What am I supposed to do with this?"

"Read it. Everything you need to know is in there. Everything
you can learn from a book, at least."

"But I have the *New Manual of Blackshroudery* already. The
second edition, published just last year. All three volumes."
She poked at the *Modern Guide*'s spine, which was half-way
through a divorce with the rest of the book.

"You never know, this one might be in three volumes too if it's read a couple more times."

She slid the book back to me with a single outstretched finger.

Her name was Cordelia Carrcroft, and she was my apprentice. My first surprise, when her letter arrived out of the blue, was that the Carrcroft family wanted anything to do with me whatsoever. After the embarrassing death of Sir Edwin, I'd rather assumed I'd been blacklisted for life. Perhaps they hadn't realised that Blackshroud Summers of that time and Blackshroud Arthington of the present were one and the same person.

There was a negotiation. The Carrcrofts named a monthly sum. I protested that I couldn't possibly afford to pay an apprentice that much. Then it transpired that *they* were offering to pay *me*.

"I don't like her," Jacob told me, after an agreement was hastily reached.

"Whyever not?"

"I don't know. Something about her."

But there seemed very little not to like. Cordelia was clever, unfailingly polite, and startlingly eager to learn. There were only a couple of things I found a little unsettling. One was the way she treated Millicent like a servant, instead of more like a member of the family as did Jacob and I. But then, I told myself, Millicent *was* a servant, after all. The other thing that bothered me was the way she turned her nose up at the spare bedroom of Paradise Cottage as though it were a dusty corner of some rustic shepherd's hut.

"I don't need to know that," she told me when I challenged her to name all the streets that led off Regent Street, from Quarry Hill to Skinner Lane.

"You *do* need to know that. A blackshroud needs to know where to find her clients."

"I certainly won't find any of *my* clients *there*. That area is a slum."

I found myself thinking it was a shame that Esther had recently retired from the business. I might have loaned Cordelia out to her; it would have done her some good to see some real slums. That is, if I'd been on speaking terms with Esther. Which I wasn't.

Instead, I tried to impress on her some of the less glamorous parts of the job.

"You'll have to learn to deal with people at their absolute worst."

"Yes, you've told me before. More than once, in point of fact. The dying are often malodorous and grotesque, and one must endeavour to look as though one hasn't noticed. Or were you going to repeat the warning that the bowels may relax upon death, leading to a mess which one must correct before allowing the family to see the body?"

"Oh, the dying aren't so bad, it's the relatives you want to watch out for. Grief turns some people into absolute monsters."

But Cordelia seemed quite intent on her choice of career, and admirably ready to take the rough parts with the smooth. She threw herself into every task I found for her with industry and conscience, and no-one had the smallest doubt that she'd sail through her examination with the Society when it came, least of all Cordelia herself. "My second cousin plays bridge with the chief examiner," she explained.

I found other benefits of having her around: I had entered the good graces of the influential Carrcroft family. The odd client or two started to come my way from far above my usual lower-middle-class clientele. Cordelia, I realised, could my ticket into the highest and most lucrative echelon of my profession.

Blackshroud Ambrose had announced her retirement not long after Esther had, creating an opening at the very top of the hierarchy as well as at the bottom. Ambrose's only apprentice,

Selina Abbott, had left the trade years ago to teach piano, leaving no obvious successor. Mercy Shepherd was perhaps the most likely candidate to step into her shoes, but with the Carrcrofts singing my praises into influential ears, it was just barely imaginable that it could be me.

Ambrose was moving to the Lake District to enjoy her waning years, leaving behind her home and surgery, a gothic villa in Headingley only a little smaller in scale than the Carrcrofts' own residence. Cordelia encouraged me to take a look round. It had a lavish parlour with two bay windows giving different views over the grounds, and moulded ceilings so tall I couldn't reach them sat on Jacob's shoulders waving my cane in the air (we tried). There were electric lights in every room, and even a telephone.

"Jacob, we *have* to buy it," I said as I climbed out of the dumbwaiter. "Just *look* at it. It even has a *tower!*"

"But you hate high places."

"I don't have to *go* in the tower. I still want to own one."

"I ain't sure we can afford this."

"We can sell Paradise Cottage, and I'm sure I can get a mortgage for the rest. Moving in here will really mark me out as the top blackshroud in the area. I can start charging *serious* money for my services. We'll have it paid off in just a few years."

He peered unenthusiastically out of a window at a neat line of elms. "But I don't want to leave our home. What's wrong with the way we are?"

I went up to him and put an arm around his shoulder. "Don't you have *any* ambition?"

"No. Everything I want, I've got already. And I thought you were happy too, until that Carrcroft girl turned your head."

I took my arm away sharply. "I *do* wish you'd stop badmouthing Cordelia. She's been nothing but a blessing."

"It's not based on nothing. She..." He glanced around the empty dining room to make sure we were really alone, before dropping into a confidential murmur. "I caught her in the morgue last night. She were looking at Mr Meyer."

The morgue, as we called it, was a small cellar where we stored the bodies of those who died at Paradise Cottage until the undertakers could collect them.

"Why shouldn't she look at Mr Meyer?"

"You didn't see the *way* she were looking. She were... I dunno. Hungry, maybe."

"Cordelia is training to be a blackshroud, Jacob. Dead bodies are something she's going to produce in abundance. She needs to get used to them. If that involves staring at Mr Meyer, then that involves staring at Mr Meyer. He's hardly going to object."

"You didn't see it. It weren't respectful, is all."

A few more weeks passed before I saw for myself the look Jacob had so objected to, as I caught Cordelia doing something much less innocent than staring at a corpse. I'd been up late reading, until I'd fallen asleep in my chair with the book in my hands. Cordelia must have thought me in bed. As I crept towards the stairs I caught a flicker of candlelight from the pantry. What I saw in there... well, I liked to think I'd seen everything already and was now unshockable, but this proved me wrong yet again.

Cordelia had caught a mouse. Don't ask me how, but she had one. She'd put it in a cut glass jug filled with water, with a glass bowl placed over it so the water went right up to the top without leaving an air gap. It was a mouse-drowning machine. And Cordelia was watching with hypnotised fascination as the poor creature scratched its paws against the inside of its glass prison, searching frantically for the air that wasn't there. And as she watched its death throes, her fingers reached under her skirts to pleasure herself...

I sneaked away as silently as I'd come. But I couldn't shake the image of that dying mouse from my mind. I got no sleep at all that night.

I didn't tell anyone, not even Jacob. How could I? It was entirely outside my comprehension. How could someone take *pleasure* in killing? And what should I do about it? Should I talk to Cordelia? Dismiss her?

In the end I did neither of those things. By a convenient twist of reasoning I managed to convince myself it was none of my business. That, distasteful as it was, it didn't necessarily mean she'd make a bad blackshroud. But I was deeply uneasy in my heart.

In June, Millicent showed into the parlour a shrunken and withered old man who I quite failed to recognise at first, until I mentally subtracted two dozen years and added a large walrus moustache.

"Mr Battersby."

"Blackshroud."

"Very good to see you again. How fares *The Tenterhook*?"

"Shut."

"Oh, I'm very sorry to hear that."

"It's alright. It was time to retire anyhow."

"What brings you here, Mr Battersby?"

"It's Blackshroud Cartwright. She wants you."

It had been many, many years since I'd last spoken to Esther. This wasn't an occasion to be taken lightly. I felt the need to impress on her that I'd made a real success of myself despite her. I squeezed uncomfortably into my tightest corset, put on my sternest and most expensive dress, and had Millicent put my hair up into intimidating curls. Then I had Gingham pull the carriage out and harness up Adonis and Endymion, after giving both carriage and horses a good scrub and polish until they gleamed.

The carriage drew to a graceful stop on Briggate, and Gingham stepped down to open the door for me. Straightening my hat, I marched forwards into Tenterhook Yard.

It was a sad shadow of a place. This whole labyrinth of twisty old yards and lanes between Briggate and Vicar Lane was scheduled for demolition, to make way for glitzy new streets and arcades more fit for the coming twentieth century. *The Tenterhook* itself stood forlorn and empty with blind, boarded windows. Unexpected daylight spilt in from the end of the yard where the building there had already succumbed to the Estate Company's hammers, leaving nothing but jagged teeth of rubble.

Esther was perhaps the only human being still living in this dying place. Heaven help the official who's job it had been to tell *her* to move out. Her sign still bore the name *E. Cartwright*, although the next word *Blackshroud* was scored out with a neat white line. I knocked. There was no answer. I knocked again. And again, louder.

"Are you going to stand there beating my door to splinters all day," thundered a muffled voice from somewhere within, "or are you going to come in?"

I pushed the door open. "Esther?" No answer. I stepped inside, and cautiously climbed the stairs, avoiding a couple of broken steps. I tried not to notice the wallpaper peeling from the walls, or the mouldering damp patch on the ceiling. I stuck my head in the living room. It was in an atrocious state, but didn't contain Esther.

"Stop mucking about and get in here," she called from the parlour. Alone of all her rooms, it had barely changed at all since the days I'd lived there. It had looked derelict and unloved then, and it looked derelict and unloved now. It even had the same ghastly painting of Jesus on the cross, His expression rendered no less piercingly reproachful by the passage of years. Esther, however, had changed beyond belief. She looked so *old*. She sat slumped in the rag-tag upholstered chair, rolls of fat sagging from her frame in wrinkled folds. Dark shadows hung under her eyes and her fingers were bent into claws.

But one thing hadn't changed. She still had a voice like a foghorn.

"Don't stand there gawping, girl! Didn't I teach you any manners at all? Sit down, for goodness' sake!"

I pulled the stool out from under the desk and sat on it, positioning myself so that Jesus was safely out of sight behind me, although I could still feel Him disapproving of the back of my head. "I wish you'd get rid of that thing, Esther. You know I can't abide it."

"I like looking at it. It keeps me humble."

"It'd take a lot more than that to keep *you* humble."

"Oh! And *you're* one to talk! Little Miss Stick-Up-Her-Arse!"

I stood up, my face flushing. "I do *not* apologise for showing a little decorum!"

"Decorum? Is that what they're calling haughtiness these days? For Heaven's sake sit down, girl."

"And will you *please* stop calling me 'girl'? I'm forty-five!"

"I'll stop calling you girl when you stop acting like one and start acting like a blackshroud!"

"You are *not* my mistress any more!"

"No! I'm not! I'm your patient!"

I froze, my mouth already open to shout a comeback. I shut it. "You're... what?"

"I'm your patient."

I sat down. "But... why?"

"Use your eyes, girl! I'm old. I'm not a blackshroud any more. I'm nothing, just a used-up old husk, no good for anything. I won't even have a home in a few more weeks. Besides, I always said I'd take the draught when I couldn't stand on my own two feet." She gestured disagreeably at a pair of walking sticks leaning against the side of her chair. "And here we are."

"Oh, Esther. Do you really imagine I'd leave you here to rot? Come live with us. We'll find space, somehow. It'd be my pleasure. And I've an apprentice of my own these days I think you could teach a few valuable lessons."

"Bugger that. Do you imagine I want to be living off your charity? Look; I've got the Battersbies to witness consent already. And I've even got a bit of the draught stashed away, in case you came short."

I moved the stool closer. "Esther. It's always been my practice to talk through my patients' decisions carefully and at length, to make sure they're making the right one."

"I'll have none of your jibber-jabber, girl! You know me, and you know I don't say things unless I damn well mean them."

I did try to talk things through anyway, but she was as mulishly entrenched as I'd ever seen her. It was with a heavy heart that I agreed to be her blackshroud.

"Take my hand," I said as I rose to my feet, proffering it alongside a well-practised smile of reassurance. "Everything's going to be alright. There's nothing more to be afraid of."

She scowled. "You're doing it all wrong."

"Am I?"

"You're just like the rest of them. All smiles and sweet words and 'come take my hand' and 'it's just like falling asleep'. Like dying's something nice and friendly, to look forward to. Poppycock! Dying's a terrible thing. I've told you that before. It's dishonest to try and make it into something beautiful."

"It *can* be something beautiful."

"No it bloody well can't. Now help me up, girl, and let's get this damn thing over with."

I slipped an arm under her shoulders and helped her to her feet. We hobbled together slowly to her bedroom, with my one real leg bearing more of our weight than her two. As I lay her down I saw tears trickling down her cheeks.

"I'm sorry, girl," she sobbed. "I don't deserve you."

I knelt down beside her. "Come on now! Don't say things like that. You deserve so much better than me."

"No I don't. I'm sorry. I'm sorry I chucked you out. Last time you came, all them years ago. No wonder you've wanted nothing to do with me since."

"You had pretty good reason." I remembered the cover-up of Nathaniel Bennett's death – and the ensuing fall-out with Esther – with the same sad shiver it always gave me.

"No I didn't. You only did what I might've done. I was just so angry, because… because I never wanted *you* to end up like *me*."

"Oh Esther, that's—"

"You were so much better than me. I could always see that. Right from the start."

"Esther!" I grasped her hand between mine. "I could *never* be better than you. You're a wonderful blackshroud, and a wonderful woman. I feel immensely fortunate to have been your apprentice, and deeply privileged to be here at your side today."

"You're just saying that. You're good enough at your job to lie to a sad old woman."

"And you're more then good enough to tell when I'm not."

She wiped the tears and snot with her sleeve. "Well, let's see how good I made you, then," she said in a stronger voice. "Prepare the draught. And don't you *dare* skimp on me."

I felt like an apprentice again as I fished out her familiar old scales and weighed out forty-five grains. I didn't skimp, but I did bungle. My hands were shaking, spilling white powder everywhere, as though twenty-four years of experience had all fled from me under the scrutiny of Esther's hawkish gaze.

"Not like *that!*" she barked. "When did I ever teach you to hold a spoon like *that?* You got more on the table than you did in the bloody glass, girl! Just look at that mess! Do you expect me to get up and *lick* it off the wood? Shape up!"

Somehow, eventually, the draught came together. I sat back down by the bed and offered her the glass. "There's no rush. Only when you feel ready."

"Just give me the glass already, girl, before I die of old age!" She tried to snatch it from me, but failed. I wrapped her fingers around it.

"Would you like to hold my hand?"

"Hold your hand? What am I, a child?" But she held it anyway as she raised the glass to her lips and emptied it in three big gulps.

"Esther?" I said, gently. "That's it. Just relax now. Everything's going to be alright."

She scowled at me. "Be quiet, girl, I don't have much time. I want a three-inch obituary. You got that? Three inches. *Minimum.* If I don't get it, I'm going to bloody well *haunt* you. And a nice funeral, with something in Latin. Can't make out a word of Latin, but it sounds clever. And the rent on this place, it's—"

"Esther." I squeezed her hand and managed a smile. "It's alright. It's all alright. I'll take care of everything from here."

She seemed about to object, but then just nodded and squeezed my hand back. Her eyes were blinking closed now, her breathing slowing, a look of pale calm drifting over her face. "Caroline," she said, as though about to say something, but nothing else came out. And then quietly, peacefully, she died.

I stayed there for a long time, my head bowed, her limp hand resting in mine. Then I tucked her into her bed, checked the time on my old silver pocket watch, added her name to my black book, and left.

It was late when I got back to Paradise Cottage, and only Cordelia was still up and about.

"You look like you've just lost a favourite puppy," she said.

"A bit more than that. I've just helped my old mistress to die." I sat down heavily at the kitchen table.

"*Really?* Who... who was she?"

"Esther Cartwright."

"*Bloody Esther?*"

"No. *Not* Bloody Esther. Esther Cartwright. The finest blackshroud Leeds has ever seen."

"Hmmm... I'd hardly agree with that assessment. I suppose she perhaps did end more lives than anyone else, but I think one must also consider the quality of those lives, not simply the quantity."

I shot her a look. "Cordelia. The worth of a blackshroud is *not* determined by the number of people she kills, and certainly not by the 'quality', as you would have it. It's in her character. Her bearing. Her compassion."

"Of course, of course." She waved my words away as though they were of no consequence, and moved to sit closer. "What did she look like?" she whispered in my ear.

"What? Um, well, she was rather round and flabby with dark hair and—"

"No. As she died. What did she look like as she died?"

"I'm... not sure what you're asking."

"Did she cry, or was she quiet? Was she scared? Were her eyes open?" I stared at Cordelia. An ugly, ravenous look had deformed her face, the same one she'd had when she watched her mouse drown. Only now it was Esther's death she was salivating over in her mind. "Was there a moment when you looked in her eyes and you saw her... die?"

"*Enough!*" I rose to my feet, pushing my chair back with a loud scrape. "I've had enough of this. I know why you want to be a blackshroud, Cordelia. It's not to help people in pain. It's not even for the respect and the money, which I could at least have understood. It's because you *want to kill*."

"What? I do not!" she protested, but she had the panicked look of a mouse trapped in one of her own inventions.

I pointed a shaking finger at her. "I've seen what you get up to at night. It's sick. And I cannot in good conscience allow someone who fantasises about killing to get the opportunity to do so. Esther would never have stood for it, and neither will I!"

She laughed at me. "You're not going to kick me out."

"I most certainly am. Go to bed, and in the morning I want you to pack your things and leave. I'll write you a shining reference for anything you choose to set your hand to, so long as it's not blackshroudery."

She stood up too, and stepped close to me, her face mere inches from mine. "You're *not* going to kick me out, because you need me. You need my family. My family is going to make you into something. So be a good little girl and apologise. Because if you don't, my family can take away everything you have."

A poisonous silence filled the room for a few seconds. "Are you trying to *threaten* me?"

"What do you think?"

I made my thoughts clear with the palm of my hand, which hit her cheek so hard her head snapped round almost ninety degrees. "I'll tell you what I think. I think you're a leech. A nasty, wriggling, blood-sucking little leech. I don't care how rich and powerful your family are. There's no wealth or power in the world that could persuade me to have you under my roof one more night."

"You'll regret this, you stupid old cripple."

I opened the door to the hall. "Out! Forget about leaving in the morning. Get out of my house, girl, right this minute, and don't ever come back!"

"But—"

"*Now!*"

Jacob and Millicent had appeared on the stairs, woken by the shouting. When Cordelia showed no signs of leaving, I turned to my husband. "Jacob. I don't normally approve of men roughhousing women, but if Miss Carrcroft doesn't vacate our property immediately, you have my permission to remove her by any means you find convenient."

"My pleasure," he said, and advanced on Cordelia. That was quite enough for her, and she shot out the door like a hunted rabbit.

It was a dark and sopping night, and she stood glaring at me from the garden path as I occupied the threshold, her dress already clinging to her body.

"Millicent," I called over my shoulder, "please gather Miss Carrcroft's belongings and throw them out of an upstairs window."

"Yes, ma'am."

Cordelia spat in my direction. "You really are Esther's girl, aren't you?"

"Yes. I bloody well am." And I slammed the door shut.

Esther's will was read just after the funeral. I entertained a vague hope she might turn out to have held some vast and unsuspected fortune, but no such luck. She left only a pittance behind her, which all went – for reasons that no-one was at all clear on – to a dogs' home in Scotland. But I wasn't left entirely empty-handed. "To my former apprentice Caroline Arthington: one painting of the Messiah." I hung the dreadful thing on the inside of the bathroom door, despite Jacob's objections, so that He watched over me during my ablutions. It kept me humble.

One doesn't turf a Carrcroft out into the rain without some consequences, and I didn't have long to wait for them. The prestigious clients stopped arriving. Malicious rumours started to spread about me and my household amongst the middle classes of Leeds. Some of them were even true.

"She used to be the workhouse blackshroud..."

"Pulled that servant of hers out of some brothel..."

"The husband was a criminal, you know..."

My social standing – and therefore my income – started to drop. Economies had to be made. My carriage was swapped out for something more modest, and Jacob stepped in to drive it in place of Gingham. I let Mercy Shepherd buy Ambrose's villa in Headingley. To my surprise, I found that more a relief than a disappointment. In my heart of hearts, I hadn't really wanted to leave Paradise Cottage any more than Jacob had.

But the Carrcrofts' hardest blow didn't land until two months later. It was just after Christmas, and Francis and Blanche were round to share a goose casserole, the last of the pudding, a bottle of port and some very good news.

"Everyone," said Francis, standing up at the table and ringing his glass with a teaspoon, as though he were addressing the Royal Society. He glanced at his wife to ask a wordless permission, and she nodded. "I am pleased to announce, that we are assured – that is, we expect, in due course, if all goes well, which I have no doubt whatsoever that it will – an expansion of our current establishment, beyond the two happy souls currently comprising it." And then he sat down with a nervous smile on his face.

"Eh?" said Jacob.

Francis, apparently of the conviction that he'd made himself abundantly clear, blinked at our uncomprehending faces. "We're having a baby."

It was somewhere amidst all the back-slapping and bottle-opening and fatuous name suggestions that followed this announcement – I suggested Caroline for a girl if she came out pretty, or Cordelia if she came out ugly – that the letter arrived. Millicent handed it to me, and when I saw the seal of the Worshipful Society I put it aside until later. It didn't get opened until morning, after the expectant parents had left, and Jacob and I sat alone amidst the debris of the night before. I slit the envelope open with a butter knife, scanned the first few lines, and felt the foundation of my life slip out from under me.

"Caroline, love? What is it?"

"They're... kicking me out."

"*What?*"

"I'm to return my dove and dagger within the week."

"But... they can't do that! Can they? *Why?*"

I shuffled through the pages, the room starting to spin strangely around me. "It says, 'due to your personal connection to a case that has led the profession into disrepute, and even into doubt as to its continued viability, we feel your continued licence to practise has become an embarrassment.'"

"An *embarrassment?!*"

"That's what it says. An embarrassment."

"Is this on account of that Bogg woman?"

"No." I scrunched the pages up into a tight ball and threw it towards the fireplace, but missed. "This is on account of Cordelia's second cousin playing bridge with their chief examiner."

"But..." Jacob gulped for words, as though struggling to choose between outrage, indictment or sheer disbelief. In the end what came out was a simple, "What do we do now?"

"I don't know." I gazed out through the window, where a grey wind was picking up in the treetops. "I really don't know."

Chapter 15

I started working for Mercy Shepherd on Monday. On Tuesday she discovered I wasn't comfortable with heights, and on Wednesday morning I found she'd set up a new desk for me in the tower room.

"I thought you might like it up here," she told me. "The view is breathtaking. You can see all the gardens you could have owned, but don't."

"*How* am I supposed to answer your door from up here? I'm not exactly nimble on the stairs."

"Don't, then. I thought a back-room position might be more suited to someone of your particular charms."

The room had windows on three sides, so I turned the desk round to face the fourth, the screech of wood sliding across wood masking my own muttered curses.

On Thursday Mercy came up to me with a big bottle of the draught. "Get this sent back to the Society. Throw in a letter alongside it. I want a replacement *and* a grovelling apology, so make it thoroughly impolite and grasping. You know. Your usual."

"What's wrong with it?"

"Nothing, except that those imbeciles forgot to put the flavour in. Try it. It's as tasteless as you are."

On Friday she came with a bundle of crumpled notes in scratchy pencil. "Write these up properly for the coroner. And no slapdash work, this time."

I glanced through. "Wait a minute. I already wrote these up on Wednesday."

"Well try harder today. I didn't like your F's. They looked more like S's. You ought to know how to write an F. F stands for failure."

I told her a few other things it stood for too.

Jacob was sat at the kitchen table when I got home, still dressed up in his undertaker's suit, staring at a congealing fried egg on his plate with a face like a funeral.

"Oh dear," I said. "Who died?"

"Johnny Purvis."

"The chap who landed you in gaol?"

He nodded, without lifting his eyes from his plate.

I sat down beside him and placed a hand on his. "Isn't that... good news? After what he did to you, at least you've outlived the bastard."

"I dunno. I always just thought, maybe, I'd meet him some day. And he'd say he were sorry, and I'd say I forgive him. But when I saw him there on the slab, I knew it'd never happen. It's daft, I know."

"It's not daft. And if he didn't get to meet you again, well, that's his loss." I squeezed his hand.

A hint of a smile twitched behind his bleak countenance. "Thanks."

"Did he at least die nicely friendless and destitute?"

"Nah. His wife ordered the priciest gravestone in the catalogue. The one with the urn and the cherubs."

"Well, there's something to be smug about, at least. If I outlive you, Jacob, I promise not to bury you under something vulgar."

His eyes moved from his plate for the first time to give me a questioning look. "You've got the most backwards way of cheering a man up."

"Although try not to drop dead just at the moment, or I might have to stick you in a pauper's grave."

He straightened his tie. "At least I'd go in well dressed for it."

"No, I'd sell that suit to keep me out of the workhouse and roll you in naked."

His eyebrows lowered half an inch. "New job didn't work out, then?"

"I've resigned. In a fairly irreversible manner, too. Things were thrown. Sorry, Jacob. I *did* try this time."

I bit my lip and waited for him to shout at me. He'd never shouted at me before, but I did feel I deserved it. He'd been holding down his new job for seven steady months, while this was the fourth position I'd walked out of – or been kicked out of – after less than two weeks. And we *needed* the extra money.

But of course he didn't shout, or even raise his voice. He just nodded and said, "It's alright," even though it wasn't.

The next day I sat down to compose yet another letter to the Worshipful Society, asking for my reinstatement. The first couple I'd sent had received replies that said "no" in a few polite but definite words. Since then I hadn't even had as much as that. But it didn't stop my heart from racing a little every time I spied the postman turning into the gate.

On that day I was too absorbed in searching my brain for new ways to say "please" that I quite missed the postman, and was only alerted to the letter when Millicent passed it into my hand. I looked at it with a spasm of hope, which quickly died when I saw the plain white envelope, devoid of the Society's distinctive seal. I opened it anyway. It was from Mrs Bogg.

> *I recently heard that you're no longer killing people for money. Good for you. It is never too late to seek God's forgiveness, even for one with as many sins on her soul as you.*
>
> *If you would be interested in laying aside old enmities, I would be happy to receive you to discuss our past differences.*

* * *

I ripped the paper in half, and then in quarters. How *dare* she talk about "discussing our past differences" as though we'd merely had a falling out over a garden wall? Mrs Bogg had tried to get me locked up for murder. She'd pushed me off a rooftop! She'd nearly killed me, had left me crippled and scarred. She'd picketed my door for two years, calling me all sorts of names to anyone who'd listen. She'd given the Society the excuse they needed to ditch me when the Carrcrofts came crawling. Mrs Bogg was behind everything that had gone wrong in my life for the last twenty years. And all I'd done to her was to respect her son's wishes.

And now she had her sights on the whole profession. The anti-blackshroud faction was gaining political ground. The papers were full of it. It seemed a common consensus now that blackshroudery was, if not under a death sentence, at least about to be severely shackled. And Mrs Bogg was both the figurehead and driving force of all that machination.

An idea came to me then, perhaps the darkest idea ever to cross my mind, so alien to my usual pattern of thought that I at once felt dizzy and a little sick just from thinking it. It was an awful idea, utterly repellent, and yet once thought of, utterly impossible to look away from. I picked up the quartered letter and pieced it back together. Here was something I could do for the eternal benefit of all who wore the dove and dagger, and all who needed their aid.

I could help Mrs Bogg to die. Whether she wanted to or not.

When the day arrived, everything was planned out like a railway timetable. And just like most railway timetables, the plan proved more aspirational than an accurate description of the chaotic sequence of events that unfolded.

First off, Francis and Blanche arrived unexpectedly in the morning.

"What do you mean, why am I here? What excuse could I possibly need to visit my charming little sister? I thought you could use the distraction, since you're not busy filling graves these days."

"Right." My hand moved instinctively to my purse, where I'd already hidden the murder weapon.

"Besides, have you *seen* the size of my wife? I thought that if a nice morning's ride didn't shake the child loose, maybe you could scare it out of her instead."

Blanche was so large and unwieldy by this point that she had to be helped into a chair by her husband. There she sat, looking paler and more uncomfortable than usual, picking at her food, until finally she complained of "feminine troubles" and asked to be taken upstairs to lie down. Millicent, after tending to her in private, explained the nature of the troubles to the rest of us in an excited squeak.

"She's having the baby!"

It was an odd couple of hours, watching the clock tick down towards my fatal appointment with Mrs Bogg while listening to the shouting, screaming and crying from Blanche – and occasionally from Francis too – upstairs.

"I feel we should be helping somehow," I told Jacob.

"Millicent knows what she's doing. She were a nurse."

"*I* was a nurse!"

"She were a better nurse."

I nodded. "I know. It's just... it seems ridiculous, that I know so much about ending lives, and so little about beginning them."

He shrugged. There was a fresh bout of screaming from upstairs, alongside some vocabulary I never would have suspected Blanche of knowing.

I stood up, paced uselessly around the room a couple of times, and glanced at the clock again. "I suppose I must forget about this thing with Mrs Bogg, now this is happening?"

"Don't reckon they'll mind. You should go."

"But—"

"Baby'll come out the same with or without you. And I know today's important to you. Seen you fretting on it. Go."

Mrs Bogg appeared to be alone in the house. That was good. My plan – or at least my plan to get away with it – depended on no other witnesses.

Her parlour was a flower basket. Floral wallpaper lined the walls. A thick scent of lavender fouled the air. Opposite the window, a painting of pink carnations was framed by bouquets of dried dahlias and poppy heads. But the only live flowers in the room were a delicate bunch of blue forget-me-nots, which stood on the mantelpiece next to the familiar photograph of Gabriel.

"It would have been his forty-first birthday today," she said, gesturing to the picture.

"I'm sorry."

"*Are* you, though?"

"I'm sorry for your loss. Not for what I did."

"Hmm. I thought not."

Her red hair had faded to grey, and her scowl lines deepened into wrinkles. Sitting there amidst her frilly cushions she almost managed to look like a harmless little old lady. Almost. There was still a flinty hardness in her features; an unquenched fire behind her eyes.

"I invited you here to tell you that *I'm* sorry," she said.

I'd been braced for an argument, and that rather caught me off guard. "What?"

"I'm sorry for what happened on the tower. I shouldn't have pushed you."

I looked at her for a few long seconds. The thing to say was, "I forgive you." I tried to make the words come to my lips, but they wouldn't. Because I *didn't* forgive her. Instead I just said, eventually, "What's happened has happened."

"I'm glad you survived."

"Um... thank you."

"I'm glad you survived, because if you hadn't, I never would have taken my stand outside your door. And if I hadn't done that, I never would have discovered my God-given purpose in life."

"Which is...?"

"To stop evil-minded murderers such as yourself from being able to kill anyone, ever again."

I sighed. "Mrs Bogg, I'd hoped we could have a civilised discussion, without name-calling."

"When I see a murderer I call her a murderer. I won't turn a blind eye to slaughter, just because the butchers wear a badge and call themselves blackshroud."

There followed a long debate which only descended into obscenities and finger pointing a couple of times. I brought up every argument I had in defence of my former profession. Arguments about liberty, about mercy, about reducing suffering. But she was much more practised at this than I was, and had three well-honed arguments for every fumbling one of my own.

"Everyone, no matter how low they look, has it in them to be the next Wellington, or Dickens, or Nightingale," she said. "Every time you end a life, you kill that potential, and the world will never know what it's lost."

"Most of my patients were dying already. I don't think they had much potential for anything except pain and indignity."

"People recover, though, don't they? Sometimes even when no-one expects them to?"

"Well, very occasionally..."

"Then they have potential. Even just potential for small things. A few more meals with their families A few more prayers. One last little smile. Isn't that potential still too precious a thing to lose?"

"But the meaningless suffering you'd have people go through..."

"We don't need blackshrouds to ease suffering any more. Perhaps in past times we did, but now we have morphine. We have nurses and hospices. We can have dignity and comfort in our end without the draught."

I began to be more afraid of Mrs Bogg. She'd grown into an expert debater. Where once she might have shouted about God and spat cheap insults, now she could weave between ethical, moral and philosophical arguments with dangerous ease. She even had *me* starting to wonder if I might have been in the wrong all along. I fully believed that, left unchecked, this woman could come to act as blackshroud to the whole profession.

She had to die. I'd been uncertain, before, if I was really going to go through with the murder, or if I'd just been planning it to make myself feel better. But now I was resolved.

The opportunity came when she poured us each another cup of tea. I asked if I hadn't just heard a knock at the door, or had I imagined it? And when she went to check I made my move. A little folded paper sachet was withdrawn from my purse; something I'd secreted from Mercy Shepherd's batch of tasteless draught. In a well-practised motion I emptied the lot – enough to kill about a dozen Mrs Boggs – into her cup, gave it a few quick stirs until it all dissolved, and threw the incriminating empty sachet into the fireplace.

"No-one there," said Mrs Bogg, returning to the room just seconds after I was back in my seat, trying my best to look innocent. She sat down herself and poured some milk into her tea. Two lumps of sugar went in after it. The teaspoon swirled in her fingers, ringing against the china. She picked up the cup – white with dainty red flowers – between both hands, ignoring the handle, and nursed it in front of her.

"Let's talk about Gabriel," she said.

"If we must."

"You should have come to me. When he asked for the draught. You shouldn't have given it to him. You should have told me."

"What do you imagine would have happened, if I had?"

"He'd still be here."

I shook my head. "He'd have gone to another blackshroud."

"No. I wouldn't have let him."

"Then he'd have taken matters into his own hands."

"Not with me around. He wouldn't have had the chance."

"Really? You'd have taken his razor, his belt, his bootlaces, and locked him in his room? Because that's what it would have taken."

"That's what I would have done, then. Until I talked some sense into the lad."

"What if he never saw sense?"

"Then I'd have watched over him for as long as it took. My whole life, if it came to that."

"And what do you think gives you the right to make that kind of decision for him?"

She looked at me like I'd asked why water was wet. "I'm his mother."

She raised the cup and let the poisoned tea touch her lips. My breath caught in my throat. But it was still too hot, and she blew on it instead of drinking it.

"I loved him," she said, swirling the tea round in circles to cool it faster. "You've never had children, so you won't know what it's like to lose one. Let alone your only son." She withered into her chair a little. "He was the meaning of me. My perfect little angel. And now all I have is an empty bed and a bad photograph. And I keep thinking, did I do something wrong? Did *I* drive him to you? Why couldn't he talk to me? How could he do that to his old mum?"

Tears shone in her eyes. She didn't look like Mrs Bogg the campaign warrior, the bane of blackshroudery, any more. She just looked like a heartbroken old woman who'd lost her son. As she lifted the cup to her lips, some words came unbidden to my mind.

A blackshroud is a mountain. Fortitude is her bedrock; compassion her lofty summit. Her virtue

255

stands tall and unassailable; unyielding against the winds of compromise.

I wanted to be a mountain. I didn't want to be a murderer. I lumbered to my feet, swiped the drink out of her hands and smashed it to pieces against the wall.

She stared at me, wide-eyed, her hands still held in front of her face as though holding an invisible cup. The clock ticked. Her eyes swung to the brown splash on the wallpaper, down to the pile of floral china shards, and then back to me.

"You poisoned my tea."

"Yes." I didn't know what else to say.

She rose to her feet. Mrs Bogg the vulnerable old lady was gone, replaced by Mrs Bogg the steel-spined old soldier I knew and loathed. "I *knew* you were a murderer. I *always* said so. And now *everyone's* going to know."

"But—"

"*Thomas!*" she shouted at the ceiling. "*Louisa!*"

There was a thump of footsteps from above, and mere seconds later a burly manservant burst into the room, followed by a scrawny serving girl. Mrs Bogg looked at the surprise on my face with satisfaction.

"What? Did you think I'd really be alone in the house while I entertained a murderer? Thomas, seize Mrs Arthington."

"Ma'am." The manservant grabbed both my arms and held them behind my back with a little too much relish.

"Mrs Bogg, please listen to me, I—"

"No. I'm done listening to you. Louisa!" she barked, as the girl moved towards the smashed teacup. "Don't touch that, it's evidence. That's where I threw the cup she tried to poison me with."

I spluttered. "That's not what happened! *I* threw it! I was a mountain!"

"Louisa, I need you to run and fetch a constable. Thomas, don't let her escape."

Louisa hurried into her shoes, threw on a coat and was nearly at the front door when someone knocked on it. She reappeared in the parlour door, looking enquiringly at her mistress, as the knocking grew harder and faster, to an almost rabid intensity.

"Well, answer it then!"

A few seconds later Millicent was show into the parlour. She was sweating and breathing in gasps, as though she'd run all the way there, barely even remembering to curtsey to Mrs Bogg before collapsing into a chair. Her white apron was covered in red smears.

"Ma'am..." she said, then had to stop to recover her breath.

"Millicent, I have never been so glad to see a friendly face. But whatever are you doing here? How is Blanche? And the baby?"

"Baby's fine, ma'am. But Mrs Summers... she... she's dead."

"She's... oh. Oh, no. Oh God."

"I'm sorry ma'am, I did everything I could, ma'am, but it wasn't enough."

"I'm sure it's not your fault."

"But that's not why I came, ma'am."

"What, then?"

"I'm sorry for bursting in here like this, in the middle of..." Millicent gestured round in perplexity, as though noticing for the first time the manservant who was still holding my arms rather uncomfortably behind my back... "of this. But it's Mr Summers, ma'am."

"Oh, poor Francis. How's he holding up?"

"Not well, ma'am. Mr Arthington caught him trying to open the safe."

"The safe? But there's nothing in the safe these days."

"We think maybe he didn't know that."

I groaned. There were only two things I used to keep in the safe, and I didn't think Francis was after my money.

"Ma'am, he went off on his horse, and he was in a state like I've never seen before. We've got to find him, ma'am. We're sure he means to do himself some harm."

"Right." I turned my eyes to Mrs Bogg. "I'm sorry I have to cut our engagement short, but as you've just heard, something rather urgent has just cropped up. If you could please tell this oaf to release me, I would be rather grateful."

"Oh, no, you don't! I've finally got you right where I want you. I couldn't put you in gaol for Gabriel, but I *can* put you there for this." She pointed at the brown stain on the wall.

"Please! My brother's life might depend on me."

"He's nothing to do with me, is he?"

"Mrs Bogg. You once told me, when you first turned up in Somers Street, that you were there because you hoped you might save someone's life. Right now, there's someone's life to save. And it's all up to you. So if you're just a bitter, spiteful old woman out to avenge your son's death, by all means, keep me here, bring the police, and have your satisfaction. But if you really are what you say you are, and you're serious about saving lives, then you need to let me go."

The seconds ticked by, no-one in the room daring to breathe, as Mrs Bogg lifted the picture of Gabriel from the mantelpiece and looked at it as though for guidance.

"Thank you!" I called over my shoulder as Thomas escorted me roughly out of the house, but all I received in way of reply was a slammed door. I caught up with Millicent on the pavement.

"I left the baby with Mrs Richards next door, ma'am. Mr Arthington went to check Mr Summers' club, and the local pubs."

"No, he won't find Francis there. I know my brother. He'll have gone home, to Wetherby."

"Shall we head there, then?"

"I'll go. You should head back to Paradise Cottage, in case he washes up back there. Look after the baby."

"Right, ma'am."

I jumped on a tram to New Station. Francis had a good horse, but even so, he couldn't outpace a train. Even with his head start, with a bit of luck with the timetable I might conceivably get there before him. Unfortunately, the timetable wasn't on my side.

"Wetherby?" The porter pointed over his shoulder to where a train was just chuffing out of a platform. "That was it there, love."

"Damn! When's the next one?"

He let out that low descending whistle that means, in the universal language of railwaymen, a really, astonishingly long time.

Hurrying out to the taxi rank, I was dismayed to find it empty, with a long queue of impatient travellers sitting on their cases. I considered begging and cajoling myself to the front of the queue, but I wasn't sure I saw the point. Even if I'd had the fare on me – which I didn't – it would take so long for the average beaten old taxi nag to cover the thirteen miles to Wetherby that Francis would have had plenty of time to do whatever he was going to do. I also considered heading back to Paradise Cottage to pick up my own horse, but that was an even worse idea. The only one I had left was a flatulent old mare by the name of Embarrassment, notable for her outright refusal to walk any faster than a slow plod.

As I emerged onto Boar Lane, still searching for an answer to my transport dilemma, a showy carriage came rattling down the road, pulled by no less than four athletic-looking beasts. Instinctively I stepped out in front of it and waved my arms for it to stop; the driver pulled hard on the reins and it did so, amid a quartet of indignant neighing and clattering hooves.

"Sir!" I shouted up to the man. "I need to beg of you the enormous favour of a ride. It is the utmost emergency."

"Get off the road, you mad woman, or I'll run you down!"

"Binnings?" called a female voice from within the carriage. "Binnings, what's going on out there?"

The door swung open, revealing – much to my mortification – the Carrcroft family arms emblazoned on it. A woman's face

259

leaned out. I felt an instant jolt of recognition, although it took me a few moments to work out exactly *who* I was recognising.

"Well, well!" she called. "Miss S!"

"*Eliza?!* Thank Heaven, I am *so* glad to see you. I need a lift to Wetherby, and I need to get there *fast.*"

"Whatever for?"

"I think my brother is in mortal danger."

"What, Mr Francis? No! I'll not have that. You'd better hop in."

The driver cleared his throat and leaned down. "*Ahem.* Just to remind you, ma'am, we *are* supposed to be picking up Miss Cordelia, and Wetherby is rather a *long* way out."

"Well Miss Cordelia will just have to wait, won't she?" Eliza opened the door wide while I scrambled in, then slammed it shut and tapped twice on the roof. "To Wetherby, Binnings! As fast as you can!"

I heard the driver grumble, but the carriage lurched forward into motion and started to pick up speed.

"Fast enough for you?" asked Eliza.

"Faster, if you can."

She knocked on the ceiling again. "Stop dallying and get a move on, man! I want to see sparks where those hooves hit the cobbles!"

I couldn't help but stare. The woman sitting beside me seemed a totally different person to the evasive, snarl-lipped girl I used to employ.

"Is that fast enough now, Miss S?"

"It'll have to do. And really, Eliza, it's not Miss S any more, it's Mrs A. And it's *not* Mrs A, it's Blackshr... it's Mrs Arthington."

"Wait, *you're* Blackshroud Arthington?" She let out a cackle. "My God. I've heard the Carrcrofts talking about *you.* They really hate your guts."

"Yes, and just what *is* your connection to the Carrcrofts, Eliza?"

"I'm their housekeeper."

"*Really?* That's quite the prestigious position."

"I know. I'm a marvel, Lady Carrcroft keeps saying."

I braced myself as the carriage put on a burst of speed to overtake an electric tram.

"And what will she say when she finds out you stranded her daughter, in order to race her horses a dozen miles at reckless speed, all on behalf of a woman she despises?"

"Eh, I'll say you were a duchess in distress or something, and she'll probably raise my salary. Binnings'll back me up if I slip him a few coins."

"Ah. Glad to see the Eliza I remember is still in there somewhere."

Binnings did a fine job. He kept the horses to a fast trot on the hills, opening into a full canter on the flat. And he showed an admirable disregard for all other users of the road, making carthorses neigh in alarm as he tore past, and bulling his way through junctions without the slightest apology. We pulled up outside my childhood home barely an hour after we left, all four horses panting and sweating with exertion. In the garden I spied my brother's own mount. He'd been carelessly left untethered out front, where he'd wandered into the neighbours' front garden and was munching contentedly on their asters.

"Eliza," I said as I hopped out. "If you don't mind leaving Miss Cordelia to wait a little longer, could you call in at Paradise Cottage and tell them I've found him?"

"No problem, Mrs A."

"Thank you, Eliza. You really are a marvel."

I nodded to Binnings, who gave me a tip of his hat as he eased the horses off at a more gentle pace. Then I turned to the front door – which had been left wide open – took a deep breath, and stepped in.

I rushed from room to room, calling Francis' name. There was no answer. Then I checked the back garden.

"Francis?"

"Caroline?"

I looked up, and my breath caught in my throat. He was standing perched on the very edge of the treehouse, with a rope around his neck.

The treehouse wasn't really a "house" at all. Francis was no carpenter, and his grand plans had resulted in nothing more than a ramshackle wooden platform before being abandoned. Only two years later and it was already in a sorry state. And Francis was in a sorrier state still, with his thinning hair sticking out in disarray and tears glistening on his cheeks.

"Francis! Aren't you getting a bit too old to be climbing trees?"

"Keep back."

"I mean, look at you. You're a fifty-three year old solicitor, and you're crying in a treehouse with a rope around your neck. Do you know how ridiculous that looks? Do you *really* want this to be the last memory I have of you?"

"Please. Leave. I don't want you to watch this."

"Do you even have that thing tied properly? You could never tie a knot to save your life when you were a boy."

"Please! Stop talking and leave!"

"Do you seriously imagine I'm going to walk away and wait for you to hang yourself?"

"That's what you do, isn't it? Help people die."

"Yes. It is. It was. People who *needed* help. People who'd decided to die after sober thought and discussion. I did *not* let silly old men throw their lives away in a spasm of grief, and I'm most certainly not letting *you* do that. Now come down from that tree this instant, and let's talk about it."

"My wife... is dead!"

"Yes. She is. I'm sorry, Francis. But she wouldn't have wanted you killing yourself over her."

"Blanche... oh, my beautiful Blanche..." He closed his eyes and swayed dangerously.

"Francis. Stop that. Francis? Are you listening to me? *Francis!*"

But he wasn't listening any more. He'd wandered into an inner world of sorrow I couldn't penetrate. He kept crying things like, "Light of my life..." and, "My love, my sweet..." while the tears ran freely.

I needed to get up there. Unfortunately, he looked to have pulled the rope ladder up behind him. But the tree grew close to the garden wall, which was almost as high as the treehouse. "Right," I said, and headed towards the woodpile.

"Blanche! I can't live without you! I can't..." his eyes opened for a second. "Caroline, what... what are you doing?"

"Something you taught me. Remember?" I'd clambered on top of the woodpile. From there, I could sit on the roof of the toolshed that used to be the privy, and ease myself onto the slates. I was already wondering if this idea was more lunacy than brilliance, but if my lunacy had drawn Francis out of his madness a little then it was a lunacy worth pursuing. I clambered up to my feet, finding a wobbly balance on the sloping roof.

"But you can't... for God's sake, you can't go clambering about like that, you've only got one leg!"

"Thanks for the reminder."

The false leg was far more of a hindrance than a help in climbing, so I unstrapped it and threw it down onto the woodpile. "This used to be so much easier when I was little," I said as I pushed myself up onto the garden wall, trying very hard not to look down.

"You're insane!"

"Says the man wearing the noose."

I was on top of the wall. I looked down. It was a mistake. The ground seemed to turn in dizzying spirals beneath me, impossibly far below, and I dropped to my hands and knee, holding onto the coping stones for dear life.

"Gods!" Francis called. "Be careful, won't you?"

"Yes. It would be awful having to watch your sibling plunge to their death, wouldn't it, brother dear?"

He had nothing to say to that.

I inched forwards towards the tree with my eyes firmly closed, trying to keep thoughts of falling out of my head and failing spectacularly. My mind was full of hypothetical gusts of wind that might blow me over, of loose stones that would slide out from under me, of unseen hands and pebbles that might come out of nowhere to push me to my death. My every muscle was trembling, but I wasn't – I just *wasn't* – going to stop.

"That's it," Francis said, very close by. "You're here. Reach out, grab my hand." I reached and grabbed, and squeezed tightly. "Now. I'm going to pull you up into the treehouse. On the count of three. Are you ready?"

I nodded, my eyes still clamped shut.

"One... two... *three!*"

And I was being lifted, and then I was down, with wooden boards creaking under my foot. I fell into my brother's arms, shaking.

"That's it. It's alright. You're safe now."

"Francis..."

I opened my eyes. The dreadful madness was gone from his face, but the noose was still around his neck.

"Let's get rid of this, shall we?" I said, slipping it off over his head. He didn't object. "Thank you. For not jumping."

"I'd... never have jumped in front of you. I wouldn't do that to you, little sister. Not that."

He sat down, his legs dangling over the edge. I sat next to him. The ground still wheeled rather uncomfortably far below me, but I discovered I could cope with it, with him beside me.

"I was standing there a while before you came, trying to find the courage to jump. I'd almost found it."

I put an arm round his shoulders. "Suicide isn't an act of courage. Living is."

"But how can I live? Blanche – my Blanche – is dead. She was everything to me. Everything. My whole world. She was what I existed for."

"I can only tell you what I tell everyone in your position. Give it time. I know it must hurt right now, like a ragged wound in your heart, but it will heal."

"I can't believe that."

"No-one ever does. But it's true. I've seen it countless times. It'll hurt for a time. Probably a long time. But there will come a day when you can remember the years you shared with Blanche with a smile. Then you'll be ready to live again."

"I do understand... I mean, you're probably right, but... but... I just..." fresh tears welled in his eyes.

"I know. Let it all out. It's alright."

I held on to him tight as he sobbed and sobbed in my arms. I didn't say anything more, just let his grief stream out of him until his tears ran dry. Then we sat in silence, watching the clouds drift across the sky and the birds flutter between the trees.

We were still there when the daylight started to wane, and Jacob walked into the garden with Millicent behind. He looked up, and raised a hand in greeting.

"Francis," he said. "Good to see you're still with us."

Francis just nodded, glumly.

Jacob took a blanketed bundle from Millicent's arms and raised it up towards him. "Here's someone you should meet."

Francis shook his head. "No, no... no, I don't want to."

"Francis!" I snapped. "Stop acting like a Goddamned child and take the baby."

He reached down, and Jacob reached up, but we were too high. I dropped down the noose. Jacob secured the loop of rope around the little bundle with a strong seaman's knot. I reeled it up into the treehouse, and Francis took possession. Cradling it awkwardly in his arms, as though it were a sleeping tiger that might wake up and bite him, he peeled back the coverings to look at his child's face.

"It's a girl, Mr Summers," said Millicent.

"A girl." Francis gazed into her eyes. "I have a daughter."

No-one said anything. We just watched the new father with his child. He rocked her back and forth experimentally. Finally he turned to me and said, "Isn't she beautiful?"

"Yes Francis," I said. Privately I thought she looked much like every other baby I'd ever seen. "She looks just like her mother."

He nodded, and held the baby up rather grandly in front of him. "I hereby name this child, Caroline Blanche Summers."

Once Millicent had seen Francis and Caroline Junior off to bed, Jacob came up to join me in the treehouse.

"Thought you hated high places?"

"I'm getting used to this one. You did good today."

"So'd you."

"I didn't. I nearly murdered an old woman, in cold blood." I gestured with an almost-touching finger and thumb. "I came *this* close."

"You didn't do it, though?"

"No."

"That's alright, then."

"Is it?"

"Yeah. I reckon."

He put an arm around me, and I leant in close to him.

"She got me thinking," I said. "I may not have killed Mrs Bogg, but I have killed lots of other people. Hundreds. And I bet, amongst those hundreds, there were at least a few who shouldn't have died. People who would have got over their problems. Who would have done great things, or brought joy to others, or at least been happy for a few more years."

Jacob thought about that for a while. "Probably. But probably there's a lot more who'd just've suffered a while longer. You ought to be proud of what you did."

"I don't feel proud."

"Well, you should! You gave people a choice."

"But sometimes they made the wrong choice."

"Then that's their wrong choice to make, isn't it? The important bit is, they had it. *Their* life, *their* choice. No-one else's. That's why that Bogg woman scares the shit out of me. She'd take that choice away."

He turned to face me, his hands on my shoulders.

"I'm so glad you saved me, Caroline, all them years back. I were drowning, and you pulled me out. But if things had worked out different, and I'd chosen to die after all, then that were my choice to make."

"Don't talk like that."

"I *will* talk like that. Dying's not the worst thing can happen to a man. Not by a long shot. Me, I'm not afraid of dying. Not the soft kind of dying you gave folks, anyhow. And as long as I've always got that option, it means I don't need to be afraid of nothing. You gave people that. Whatever nightmare they might get stuck in, you made sure there were always a door leading out."

"A shortcut from Hell?"

"Yeah. I like that. That's what it's about. Showing folks a shortcut from Hell."

We didn't talk any more as we sat, side by side and arm in arm, watching the sun set in front of us. It lit up the sky in all of life's most breathtaking colours as it went, and it was beautiful.

Epilogue

In 1901, Queen Victoria passed away. The royal blackshroud was summoned to ease her final hours, but she would have none of it. "Blackshrouds took my Albert. They shall *not* take me."

Consequently, amidst the national mourning, a new fashion arose for "natural" deaths amongst the middle classes. Whereas before a family might boast of the quietness and dignity of a death, now the boasting was of how long the departing had lingered, and how miserable their condition, as though their last suffering were some great moral achievement.

Mrs Bogg and her followers were quick to jump on the political moment. An act was passed in Parliament. It didn't go quite so far as to abolish blackshroudery completely. But it did limit its application to such a narrow set of situations that it might as well have done as far as most people were concerned.

Rather perversely, this has presented me with an opportunity. Being a blackshroud has always been about much more than just dispensing the draught. It's about helping people to die. People are still dying, and they still need help. They need someone to talk to, whether about wills and the winding down of their affairs or just about their fears and regrets. They need someone to arrange things with coroners and undertakers. And sometimes they just need someone to be there at the end when there's no-one else, to make them as comfortable as they can be and to hold their hand. None of these things were outlawed by the act, and none of them need me to wear the dove and dagger.

I've heard the rumours about me. Rumours that I'm doing more than just holding the hand of the dying; that my patients have a habit of slipping away a little sooner and a little more peacefully than God intended. Some even say that my wooden leg holds a secret compartment, hiding a bottle of black-market draught. "Bloody Caroline," a few have started calling me.

Naturally, I can't confirm these rumours. But neither do I feel like denying them. Let's just say that my services are very much in demand, and leave it at that.

When I'm not working, I've been busy writing this memoir. Of course, there's no way I can possibly publish it; it constitutes the most appalling breach of professional confidentiality. But I wanted to create a record, all the same. For the people of some future age, when not just the names within these pages but the whole of blackshroudery as I have known it are passed out of all memory. This is what it was like. And I am proud to have been a part of it.

Acknowledgements

First, I want to say thank-you to Kevin and Hetha Duffy of Bluemoose Books, for taking a chance on a new, rather clueless author, for everything they've done in shepherding this book through to publication, and for always being an absolute pleasure to work with. Thanks also to everyone else who's been involved in the process, and especially to Fiachra McCarthy for his dazzling work on the cover.

To everyone who works at Swarthmore Education Centre for making it such a magical place, and to all the brilliant people I've met there in the years since I first signed up to their beginners' creative writing course. To my fellow novel-writers in the Rogues group, for some invaluable feedback on my early chapters and for a reassuring sense of not being alone in my madness. And to Dave Beirne for letting me on the stage at his excellent literary open mic nights.

Thanks are also due to Leeds' Local and Family History Library, the Leeds Museum, Abbey House Museum and Thackray Museum of Medicine for helping me to explore Victorian Leeds. On that front, also thanks to John Atkinson Grimshaw, whose highly atmospheric painting of Boar Lane hangs above my writing desk.

The core idea for Blackshroud came out of some deeply miserable times I went through about six years back. I'm eternally grateful to the support of my family and friends, without whom I might not be in the happy position of being able to refer to those times firmly in the past tense. Particular mention must go to my long-suffering parents, for taking me back into the nest when I couldn't cope on my own, and to Stephen Garvani, for putting up with all my nonsense and for dragging me out on so many life-affirming geocaching adventures.

And finally, I want to say an enormous thank-you to my editor, Leonora Rustamova, for taking my rather sloppy, meandering early draft and pushing me to make it better and better. This book wouldn't be what it is without her. But my thanks go far beyond her role as an editor. Leonora has my heartfelt gratitude for being eternally supportive, for inspiring me to write and keep on writing, and for generally being a wonderful human being. *I* wouldn't be what I am without her.